© Sigred Estrada

Nick Hornby is the author of the bestselling novels *Juliet, Naked*; *Slam*; *A Long Way Down*; *How to Be Good*; *High Fidelity*; and *About a Boy*, and the memoir *Fever Pitch*. He is also the author of *Songbook*, a finalist for a National Book Critics Circle Award, *Shakespeare Wrote for Money*, and *The Polysyllabic Spree*, and editor of the short story collection *Speaking with the* Angel. A recipient of the American Academy of Arts and Letters' E. M. Forster Award, and Oscar-nominated for his screenplay, *An Education*, Hornby lives in North London. Visit his website at www.nicksbooks.com.

continued...

"An endearingly minor-key tale of never-too-lateness told in Hornby's dry, Brit-wit tones . . . Hornby's clear-eyed affection for the gratifyingly human Annie (and her deeply flawed suitors) reads like the work of a man who is finally, happily all grown up." —*Entertainment Weekly*

"Nick Hornby has already had an unerring ear for the rhythm and blues of modern love. In his latest novel, a funny, painfully insightful examination of contemporary romance, he mixes that skill with sardonic humor and a pitch-perfect knowledge of pop culture and music and the ways they influence us. . . . Nobody explores music and the way it makes up a soundtrack to our modern lives quite as hilariously as Nick Hornby does. . . . Refreshingly funny, taking on art, obsessive fans, the frequent idiocy of the Internet and other contemporary quandaries even as it unflinchingly examines our very human tendency to avoid change even when we most need it."
—*The Miami Herald*

"We are . . . deep in Hornby country. . . . His style . . . blends dry humor, a dash of sentimentality and immense readability. . . . Hornby's humorous touch is very much intact. . . . *Juliet, Naked* is a rich and perceptive novel, with a keen sense of the lives led by the trio at its core."
—*The Wall Street Journal*

"Charming . . . Nobody captures the zealous devotion and bizarre intensity of amateur music snobs better. . . . He gently satirizes rockaphiles in a way that only endears him to them, and though this new novel will appeal to a broad audience for romantic comedy, anyone with a fading past of Van Morrison will hum along, too. . . . Hornby's dialogue between exasperated women and clueless men hits all the right comic notes." —*The Washington Post*

"The wonderfully witty author of *High Fidelity* and *About a Boy* delivers another novel of musical obsession." —*Newsday*

"From the hilarious *New York Times* bestselling author, a story about life, love, music, superfandom, and the lies we all rely on to get by." —*Chicago Tribune*

"Nick Hornby's warmhearted *Juliet, Naked* returns him to the subject that animated his 1995 classic, *High Fidelity*: rock music and the obsessiveness of its more enthusiastic fans." —*Vogue*

"Hornby's deep humanity and clever observations are as winning as ever."
—*People*

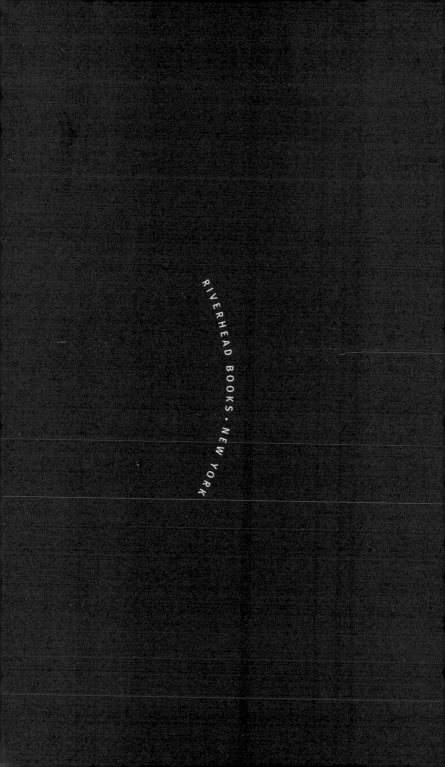

RIVERHEAD BOOKS · NEW YORK

Juliet, Naked

n i c k   h o r n b y

RIVERHEAD BOOKS
Published by the Penguin Group
Penguin Group (USA) Inc.
375 Hudson Street, New York, New York 10014, USA
Penguin Group (Canada), 90 Eglinton Avenue East, Suite 700, Toronto, Ontario M4P 2Y3, Canada
(a division of Pearson Penguin Canada Inc.)
Penguin Books Ltd., 80 Strand, London WC2R 0RL, England
Penguin Group Ireland, 25 St. Stephen's Green, Dublin 2, Ireland (a division of Penguin Books Ltd.)
Penguin Group (Australia), 250 Camberwell Road, Camberwell, Victoria 3124, Australia
(a division of Pearson Australia Group Pty. Ltd.)
Penguin Books India Pvt. Ltd., 11 Community Centre, Panchsheel Park, New Delhi—110 017, India
Penguin Group (NZ), 67 Appolo Drive, Rosedale, North Shore 0632, New Zealand
(a division of Pearson New Zealand Ltd.)
Penguin Books (South Africa) (Pty.) Ltd., 24 Sturdee Avenue, Rosebank, Johannesburgh 2196,
South Africa

Penguin Books Ltd., Registered Offices: 80 Strand, London WC2R 0RL, England

This is a work of fiction. Names, characters, places, and incidents either are the product of the author's imagination or are used fictitiously, and any resemblance to actual persons, living or dead, business establishments, events, or locales is entirely coincidental. The publisher does not have any control over and does not assume any responsibility for author or third-party websites or their content.

First Riverhead hardcover edition: September 2009
First Riverhead trade paperback edition: September 2010
Riverhead trade paperback ISBN: 978-1-59448-477-3

The Library of Congress has catalogued the Riverhead hardcover edition as follows:

Hornby, Nick.
   Juliet, naked / Nick Hornby.
        p.   cm.
   ISBN 978-1-59448-887-0
   1. Rock music fans—Fiction.   2. Man-woman relationships—Fiction.
3. Loneliness—Fiction.   4. Musical fiction.   I. Title.
   PR6058.0689J85   2009   2009023773
   823'.914—dc22

PRINTED IN THE UNITED STATES OF AMERICA

10   9   8   7   6   5   4   3

For Amanda, with love and thanks

one

They had flown from England to Minneapolis to look at a toilet. The simple truth of this only struck Annie when they were actually inside it: apart from the graffiti on the walls, some of which made some kind of reference to the toilet's importance in musical history, it was dank, dark, smelly and entirely unremarkable. Americans were very good at making the most of their heritage, but there wasn't much even they could do here.

"Have you got the camera, Annie?" said Duncan.

"Yes. But what do you want a picture _of_?"

"Just, you know . . ."

"No."

"Well . . . the toilet."

"What, the . . . What do you call those things?"

"The urinals. Yeah."

"Do you want to be in it?"

"Shall I pretend to have a pee?"

"If you want."

So Duncan stood in front of the middle of the three urinals, his hands placed convincingly in front of him, and smiled back over his shoulder at Annie.

"Got it?"

"I'm not sure the flash worked."

"One more. Be silly to come all the way here and not get a good one."

This time Duncan stood just inside one of the stalls, with the door open. The light was better there, for some reason. Annie took as good a picture of a man in a toilet as one could reasonably expect. When Duncan moved, she could see that this toilet, like just about every other one she'd ever seen in a rock club, was blocked.

"Come on," said Annie. "He didn't even want me in here."

This was true. The guy behind the bar had initially suspected that they were looking for a place where they could shoot up, or perhaps have sex. Eventually, and hurtfully, the barman had clearly decided that they were capable of doing neither thing.

Duncan took one last look and shook his head. "If toilets could talk, eh?"

Annie was glad this one couldn't. Duncan would have wanted to chat to it all night.

Most people are unaware of Tucker Crowe's music, let alone some of the darker moments of his career, so the story of what may or may not have happened to him in the restroom of the Pits Club is probably worth repeating here. Crowe was in Minneapolis for a show and had turned up at the Pits to see a local band called the Napoleon Solos which he'd heard good things about. (Some Crowe completists, Duncan being one, own a copy of the local band's one and only album, *The Napoleon Solos Sing Their Songs and Play Their Guitars*.) In the middle of the set, Tucker went to the toilet. Nobody knows what happened in there, but when he came out, he went straight back to his hotel and phoned his manager to cancel the rest of the tour. The next morning he began what we must now think of as his retirement. That was in June 1986. Nothing more has been heard of him since—no new recordings, no gigs, no interviews. If you love Tucker Crowe as much as Duncan and a couple of thousand other people in the world do, that toilet has a lot to answer for. And since, as Duncan had so rightly observed, it can't speak, Crowe fans have to speak on its behalf. Some claim that Tucker saw God, or one of His representatives, in there; others claim he had a near-death experience after an overdose. Another school of thought has it that he caught his girlfriend having sex with his bass player in there, although Annie found this theory a little fanciful. Could the sight of a woman screwing a musician in a toilet really have resulted in twenty-two years of silence? Perhaps it could. Perhaps it was just that Annie had never experienced passion that intense. Anyway. Whatever. All you need to know is that something profound and life-changing took place in the smallest room of a small club.

Annie and Duncan were in the middle of a Tucker Crowe pilgrimage. They had wandered around New York, looking at various clubs and bars that had some kind of Crowe connection, although most of these sites of historic interest were now designer clothes stores, or branches of McDonald's. They had been to his childhood home in Bozeman, Montana, where, thrillingly, an old lady came out of her house to tell them that Tucker used to clean her husband's old Buick when he was a kid. The Crowe family home was small and pleasant and was now owned by the manager of a small printing business, who was surprised that they had traveled all the way from England to see the outside of his house, but who didn't ask them in. From Montana they flew to Memphis, where they visited the site of the old American Sound Studio (the studio itself having been knocked down in 1990), where Tucker, drunk and grieving, recorded *Juliet*, his legendary breakup album, and the one Annie liked the most. Still to come: Berkeley, California, where Juliet—in real life a former model and socialite called Julie Beatty—still lived to this day. They would stand outside her house, just as they had stood outside the printer's house, until Duncan could think of no reason to carry on looking, or until Julie called the police, a fate that had befallen a couple of other Crowe fans that Duncan knew from the message boards.

Annie didn't regret the trip. She'd been to the U.S. a couple of times, to San Francisco and New York, but she liked the way Tucker was taking them to places she'd otherwise never have visited. Bozeman, for example, turned out to be a beautiful little mountain town, surrounded by exotic-sounding ranges she'd never heard of: the Big Belt, the Tobacco Root, the Spanish Peaks. After staring at the small and unremarkable house, they walked into town and sipped iced tea in the sunshine outside an organic café, while in the distance the odd Spanish Peak, or possibly the top of a Tobacco Root, threatened to puncture the cold blue sky. She'd had worse mornings than that on holidays that had promised much more. It was a sort of random, pin-sticking tour of America, as far as she was concerned. She got sick of hearing about Tucker, of course, and talking about him and listening to him and attempting to understand the reasons behind every creative and personal decision he'd ever made. But she got sick of hearing about him at home, too, and she'd rather get sick of him in Montana or Tennessee than in Gooleness, the small seaside town in England where she shared a house with Duncan.

The one place that wasn't on the itinerary was Tyrone, Pennsylvania, where Tucker was believed to live, although, as with all orthodoxies, there were heretics: two or three of the Crowe community subscribed to the theory—interesting but preposterous, according to Duncan—that he'd been living in New Zealand since the early nineties. Tyrone hadn't even been mentioned as a possible destination when they'd been planning the trip, and Annie thought she knew why. A couple of years ago, one of the fans went out to Tyrone, hung around, eventually located what he understood to be Tucker Crowe's farm; he came back with a photograph of an alarmingly grizzled-looking man aiming a shotgun at him. Annie had seen the picture, many times, and she found it distressing. The man's face was disfigured by rage and fear, as if everything he'd worked for and believed in was in the process of being destroyed by a Canon Sure Shot. Duncan wasn't too concerned about the rape of Crowe's privacy: the fan, Neil Ritchie, had achieved a kind of Zapruder level of fame and respect among the faithful that Annie suspected

Duncan rather envied. What had perturbed him was that Tucker Crowe had called Neil Ritchie a "fucking asshole." Duncan couldn't have borne that.

After the visit to the restroom at the Pits, they took advice from the concierge and ate at a Thai restaurant in the Riverfront District a couple of blocks away. Minneapolis, it turned out, was on the Mississippi—who knew, apart from Americans, and just about anyone else who'd paid attention in geography lessons?—so Annie ended up ticking off something else she'd never expected to see, although here at the less romantic end it looked disappointingly like the Thames. Duncan was animated and chatty, still unable quite to believe that he'd been inside a place that had occupied so much of his imaginative energy over the years.

"Do you think it's possible to teach a whole course on the toilet?"

"With you just sitting on it, you mean? You wouldn't get it past Health and Safety."

"I didn't mean that."

Sometimes Annie wished that Duncan had a keener sense of humor—a keener sense that something might be meant humorously, anyway. She knew it was too late to hope for actual jokes.

"I meant, teach a whole course on the toilet in the Pits."

"No."

Duncan looked at her.

"Are you teasing me?"

"No. I'm saying that a whole course about Tucker Crowe's twenty-year-old visit to the toilet wouldn't be very interesting."

"I'd include other things."

"Other toilet visits in history?"

"No. Other career-defining moments."

"Elvis had a good toilet moment. Pretty career-defining, too."

"Dying's different. Too unwilled. John Smithers wrote an essay for the website about that. Creative death versus actual death. It was actually pretty interesting."

Annie nodded enthusiastically, while at the same time hoping that Duncan wouldn't print it off and put it in front of her when they got home.

"I promise that after this holiday I won't be so Tucker-centric," he said.

"That's okay. I don't mind."

"I've wanted to do this for a long time."

"I know."

"I'll have got him out of my system."

"I hope not."

"Really?"

"What would there be left of you, if you did?"

She hadn't meant it cruelly. She'd been with Duncan for nearly fifteen years, and Tucker Crowe had always been part of the package, like a disability. To begin with, the condition hadn't prevented him from living a normal life: yes, he'd written a book, as yet unpublished, about Tucker, lectured on him, contributed to a radio documentary for the BBC and organized conventions, but somehow these activities had always seemed to Annie like isolated episodes, sporadic attacks.

And then the Internet came along and changed everything. When, a little later than everyone else, Duncan discovered how it all worked, he set up a website called "Can Anybody Hear Me?"—the title of a track from an obscure EP recorded after the wounding failure of Crowe's first album. Until then, the nearest fellow fan had lived in Manchester, sixty or seventy miles away, and Duncan met up with him once or twice a year; now the nearest fans lived in Duncan's laptop, and there were hundreds of them, from all around the world, and Duncan spoke to them all the time. There seemed to be a surprising amount to talk about. The website had a "Latest News" section, which never failed to amuse Annie, Tucker no longer being a man who did an awful lot. ("As far as we know," Duncan always said.) There was always something that passed for news among the faithful, though—a Crowe night on an Internet radio station, a new article, a new album from a former band member, an interview with an engineer. The bulk of the content, though, consisted of essays analyzing lyrics, or discussing influences, or conjecturing, apparently inexhaustibly, about the silence. It wasn't as if Duncan didn't have other interests. He had a specialist knowledge of 1970s American independent cinema and the novels of Nathanael West and he was developing a nice new line in HBO television series—he thought he might be ready to teach *The Wire* in the not-too-distant future. But these were all flirtations, by comparison. Tucker Crowe was his life partner. If Crowe were to die—to die in real life, as it were, rather than creatively—Duncan would lead the mourning. (He'd already written the obituary. Every now and again he'd worry out loud about whether he should show it to a reputable newspaper now, or wait until it was needed.)

If Tucker was the husband, then Annie should somehow have become the mistress, but of course that wasn't right—the word was much too exotic and implied a level of sexual activity that would horrify them both nowadays. It would have daunted them even in the early days of their relationship. Sometimes Annie felt less like a girlfriend than a school chum who'd come to visit in the holidays and stayed for the next twenty years. They had both moved to the same English seaside town at around the same time, Duncan to finish his thesis and Annie to teach, and they had been introduced by mutual friends who could see that, if nothing else, they could talk about books and music, go to films, travel to London occasionally to see exhibitions and gigs. Gooleness wasn't a sophisticated town. There was no arts cinema, there was no gay community, there wasn't even a Waterstone's (the nearest one was up the road in Hull), and they fell upon each other with relief. They started drinking together in the evenings and sleeping over at weekends, until eventually the sleepovers turned into something indistinguishable from cohabitation. And they had stayed like that forever, stuck in a perpetual postgraduate world where gigs and books and films mattered more to them than they did to other people of their age.

The decision not to have children had never been made, and nor had there been any discussion resulting in a postponement of the decision. It wasn't that kind of a sleepover. Annie could imagine herself as a mother, but Duncan was nobody's idea of a father, and anyway, neither of them would have felt comfortable applying cement to the relationship in that way. That wasn't what they were for. And now, with an irritating predictability, she was going through what everyone had told her she would go through: she was aching for a child. Her aches were brought on by all the usual mournful-happy life events: Christmas, the pregnancy of a friend, the pregnancy of a complete stranger she saw in the street. And she wanted a child for all the usual reasons, as far as she could tell. She wanted to feel unconditional love, rather than the faint conditional affection she could scrape together for Duncan every now and again; she wanted to be held by someone who would never question the embrace, the why or the who or the how long. There was another reason, too: she needed to know that she could have one, that there was life in her. Duncan had put her to sleep, and in her sleep she'd been desexed.

She'd get over all this, presumably; or at least one day it would become a wistful regret, rather than a sharp hunger. But this holiday hadn't been designed to comfort her. There was an argument that you might as well change nappies as hang out in men's lavatories taking pictures. The amount of time they had for themselves was beginning to feel sort of . . . *decadent*.

At breakfast in their cheap and nasty hotel in downtown San Francisco, Annie read the *Chronicle* and decided she didn't want to see the hedge obscuring the front lawn of Julie Beatty's house in Berkeley. There were plenty of other things to do in the Bay Area. She wanted to see Haight-Ashbury, she wanted to buy a book at City Lights, she wanted to visit Alcatraz, she wanted to walk across the Golden Gate Bridge. There was an exhibition of postwar West Coast art on at the Museum of Modern Art just down the street. She was happy that Tucker had lured them out to California, but she didn't want to spend a morning watching Julie's neighbors decide whether they constituted a security risk.

"You're joking," said Duncan.

She laughed.

"No," she said. "I really can think of better things to do."

"When we've come all this way? Why have you gone like this all of a sudden? Aren't you interested? I mean, supposing she drives out of her garage while we're outside?"

"Then I'd feel even more stupid," she said. "She'd look at me and think, 'I wouldn't expect any different from him. He's one of the creepy guys. But what's a *woman* doing there?'"

"You're having me on."

"I'm really not, Duncan. We're in San Francisco for twenty-four hours and I don't know when I'll be back. Going to some woman's house . . . If you had a day in London, would you spend it outside somebody's house in, I don't know, Gospel Oak?"

"But if you've actually come to see somebody's house in Gospel Oak . . . And it's not just some woman's house, you know that. Things happened there. I'm going to stand where he stood."

No, it wasn't just any house. Everybody, apart from just about everybody, knew that. Julie Beatty had been living there with her first husband, who taught at Berkeley, when she met Tucker at a party thrown by Francis Ford Coppola. She left her husband that night. Very shortly afterward, however, she thought better of it all and went home to patch things up. That was the story, anyway. Annie had never really understood how Duncan and his fellow fans could be quite so certain about tiny private tumults that took place decades ago, but they were. "You and Your Perfect Life," the seven-minute song that ends the album, is supposed to be about the night Tucker stood outside the family home, "Throwing stones at the window / 'Til he came to the door / So where were you, Mrs. Steven Balfour?" The husband wasn't called Steven Balfour, needless to say, and the choice of a fictitious name had inevitably provoked endless speculation on the message boards. Duncan's theory was that he had been named after the British prime minister, the man who was accused by Lloyd George of turning the House of Lords into "Mr. Balfour's poodle"—Juliet, by extension, has become her husband's poodle. This interpretation is now accepted as definitive by the Tucker community, and if you look up "You and Your Perfect Life" on Wikipedia, apparently, you'll see Duncan's name in the footnotes, with a link to his essay. Nobody on the website had ever dared wonder aloud whether the surname had been chosen simply because it rhymed with the word "door."

Annie loved "You and Your Perfect Life." She loved its relentless anger, and the way Tucker moved from auto-biography to social commentary by turning the song into a rant about how smart women got obliterated by their men. She didn't usually like howling guitar solos, but she liked the way that the howling guitar solo in "Perfect Life" seemed just as articulate and as angry as the lyrics. And she loved the irony of it all—the way that Tucker, the man wagging his finger at Steven Balfour, had obliterated Julie more completely than her husband had ever managed. She would be the woman who broke Tucker's heart forever. Annie felt sorry for Julie, who'd had to deal with men like Duncan throwing stones at her windows, metaphorically and probably literally, every now and again, ever since the song was released. But she envied her, too. Who wouldn't want to make a man that passionate, that unhappy, that inspired? If you couldn't write songs yourself, then surely what Julie had done was the next best thing?

She still didn't want to see the house, though. After breakfast she took a cab to the other side of the Golden

Gate Bridge and walked back toward the city, the salt wind somehow sharpening her joy in being alone.

Duncan felt slightly odd, going to Juliet's place without Annie. She tended to arrange their transport to wherever they were going, and she was the one who knew the way back to wherever they had come from. He would rather have devoted his mental energy to Julie, the person, and *Juliet*, the album; he was intending to listen to it straight through twice, the first time in its released form, the second time with the songs placed in the order that Tucker Crowe originally wanted them, according to the sound engineer in charge of the sessions. But that wasn't going to work out now, because he was going to need all his concentration for the BART. As far as he could tell, he had to get on at Powell Street and take the red line up to North Berkeley. It looked easy but, of course, it wasn't, because once he was down on the platform he couldn't find any way of telling what was a red-line train and what wasn't, and he couldn't ask anyone. Asking somebody would make it look as though he wasn't a native, and though this wouldn't matter in Rome or Paris or even in London, it mattered here, where so many things that were important to him had happened. And because he couldn't ask, he ended up on a yellow-line train, only he couldn't tell it was yellow until he got to Rockridge, which meant that he had to go back to the 19th St. Oakland stop and change. What was wrong with her? He knew she wasn't as devoted to Tucker Crowe as he was, but he'd thought that in recent years she'd started to get it, properly. A couple of times he'd come home to find her playing "You and Your Perfect Life," although he'd been unable to interest her in the infamous but superior Bottom Line bootleg version, when Tucker had smashed his guitar to smithereens at the end of the solo. (The sound was a little muddy, admittedly, and an annoying drunk person kept shouting "Rock 'n' roll!" into the bootlegger's microphone during the last verse, but if it was anger and pain she was after, then this was the one.) He'd tried to pretend that her decision not to come was perfectly understandable, but the truth was, he was hurt. Hurt and, temporarily at least, lost.

Getting to North Berkeley station felt like an achievement in itself, and he allowed himself the luxury of asking for directions to Edith Street as a reward. It was fine, not knowing the way to a residential street. Even natives couldn't be expected to know everything. Except of course the moment he opened his mouth, the woman he picked on wanted to tell him that she'd spent a year in Kensington, London, after she'd graduated.

He hadn't expected the streets to be quite so long and hilly, nor the houses quite so far apart, and by the time he found the right house, he was sweaty and thirsty, while at the same time bursting for a pee. There was no doubt he'd have been clearer-headed if he'd stopped somewhere near the BART station for a drink and a visit to the restroom. But he'd been thirsty and in need of a toilet before, and had always resisted the temptation to break into a stranger's house.

When he got to 1131 Edith Street, there was a kid sitting on the pavement outside, his back against a fence that looked as though it might have been erected simply to stop him from getting any further. He was in his late teens, with long, greasy hair and a wispy goatee, and when he realized that Duncan had come to look at the house, he stood up and dusted himself off.

"Yo," he said.

Duncan cleared his throat. He couldn't bring himself to return the greeting, but he offered a "Hi" instead of a "Hello," just to show that he had an informal register.

"They're not home," said the kid. "I think they might have gone to the East Coast. The Hamptons or some shit like that."

"Oh. Right. Oh well."

"You know them?"

"No, no. I just . . . You know, I'm a, well, a Crowologist. I was just in the neighborhood, so I thought, you know . . ."

"You from England?"

Duncan nodded.

"You came all the way from England to see where Tucker Crowe threw his stones?" The kid laughed, so Duncan laughed, too.

"No, no. God no. Ha! I had some business in the city, and I thought, you know . . . What are you doing here, anyway?"

"*Juliet* is my favorite album of all time."

Duncan nodded. The teacher in him wanted to point out the non sequitur; the fan understood completely. How could he not? He didn't get the sidewalk-sitting, though. Duncan's plan had been to look, imagine the trajectory of the stones, maybe take a picture and then leave. The boy, however, seemed to regard the house as if it were a place of spiritual significance, capable of promoting a profound inner peace.

"I've been here, like, six or seven times?" the boy said. "Always blows me away."

"I know what you mean," said Duncan, although he didn't. Perhaps it was his age, or his Englishness, but he wasn't being blown away, and he hadn't expected to be, either. It was, after all, a pleasant detached house they were standing outside, not the Taj Mahal. In any case, the need to pee was preventing any real appreciation of the moment.

"You wouldn't happen to know . . . What's your name?"

"Elliott."

"I'm Duncan."

"Hi, Duncan."

"Elliott, you wouldn't happen to know if there's a Starbucks near here? Or something? I need a restroom."

"Ha!" said the kid.

Duncan stared at him. What kind of answer was that?

"See, I do know one right near here. But I kind of promised myself I wouldn't use it again."

"Right," said Duncan. "But . . . Would it matter if I did?"

"Kind of. Because I'd still be breaking the promise."

"Oh. Well, as I don't really understand what kind of promise you can make with regard to a public lavatory, I'm not sure I can help you with your ethical dilemma."

The boy laughed. "I love the way you English talk. 'Ethical dilemma.' That's great."

Duncan didn't disabuse him, although he did wonder how many of his students back home would even have been able to repeat the phrase accurately, let alone use it themselves.

"But you don't think you can help me."

"Oh. Well. Maybe. How about if I told you how to find it but I didn't come with you?"

"I wasn't really expecting you to come with me, to be honest."

"No. Right. I should explain. The nearest toilet to here is in there." Elliott pointed down the driveway toward Juliet's house.

"Yes, well, I suppose it would be," said Duncan. "But that doesn't really help me."

"Except I know where they keep their spare key."

"You're kidding me."

"No. I've been inside like three times? Once to use the shower. A couple times just to see what I could see. I never steal anything big. Just, you know, paperweights and shit. Souvenirs."

Duncan examined the boy's face for evidence of an elaborate joke, a satirical dig at Crowologists, and decided that Elliott hadn't made a joke since he'd turned seventeen.

"You let yourself into their house when they're out?"

The boy shrugged. "Yeah. I feel bad about it, which is why I wasn't sure about telling you."

Duncan suddenly noticed that on the ground there was a chalk drawing of a pair of feet, and an arrowed line pointing toward the house. Tucker's feet, presumably, and

Tucker's stones. He wished he hadn't seen the drawing. It gave him less to do.

"Well, I can't do that."

"No. Sure. I understand."

"So there's nothing else?"

Edith Street was long and leafy, and the next cross street was long and leafy, too. It was the sort of American suburb where residents had to get into their cars to buy a pint of milk.

"Not for a mile or two."

Duncan puffed out his cheeks, a gesture, he realized even as he was making it, intended to prepare the way for the decision he'd already made. He could have gone behind a hedge; he could have left that second, walked back to the BART station and found a café, walked back again if he needed to. Which he didn't, really, because he'd seen all there was to see. That was the root of the problem. If more had been . . . *laid on* for people like him, he wouldn't have had to create his own excitement. It wouldn't have killed her to mark the significance of the place in some way, would it? With a discreet plaque or something? He hadn't been prepared for the mundanity of Juliet's house, just as he hadn't really been prepared for the malodorous functionality of the men's room in Minneapolis.

"A mile or two? I'm not sure I can wait that long."

"Up to you."

"Where's the key?"

"There's a loose brick in the porch there. Low down."

"And you're sure the key's still there? When did you last look?"

"Honestly? I went in just before you came. I didn't take a single thing. But I can never believe that I'm standing in Juliet's house, you know? Fucking *Juliet*, man!"

Duncan knew that he and Elliott weren't the same. Elliott had surely never written about Crowe—or, if he had, the work would almost certainly have been unpublishable. Duncan also doubted whether Elliott had the emotional maturity to appreciate the breathtaking accomplishment of *Juliet* (which, as far as Duncan was concerned, was a darker, deeper, more fully realized collection of songs than the overrated *Blood on the Tracks*), and nor would he have been able to cite its influences: Dylan and Leonard Cohen, of course, but also Dylan Thomas, Johnny Cash, Gram Parsons, Shelley, the Book of Job, Camus, Pinter, Beckett and early Dolly Parton. But people who didn't understand all this might look at them and decide, erroneously, that they were similar in some way. Both of them had the same need to stand in fucking Juliet's house, for example. Duncan followed Elliott down the short driveway to the house and watched as the boy groped for the key and opened the door.

. . .

The house was dark—all the blinds were down—and smelled of incense, or maybe some kind of exotic potpourri. Duncan couldn't have lived with it, but presumably Julie Beatty and her family weren't sick with nerves all the time when they were in residence, the way Duncan was feeling now. The smell sharpened his fear and made him wonder whether he might throw up.

He'd made an enormous mistake, but there was no undoing it. He was inside, so even if he didn't use the toilet, he'd still committed the crime. Idiot. And idiot boy, too, for persuading him that this was a good idea.

"So there's a small toilet down here, and it's got some cool stuff on the walls. Cartoons and shit. But the bathroom upstairs, you see her makeup and towels and everything. It's spooky. I mean, not spooky to her, probably. But spooky if you only kind of half believe she even existed."

Duncan understood the appeal of seeing Julie Beatty's makeup absolutely, and his understanding added to his sense of self-loathing.

"Yes, well, I haven't got time to mess around," said Duncan, hoping that Elliott wouldn't point out the obvious holes in the assertion. "Just point me toward the downstairs one."

They were in a large hallway with several doors leading

off it. Elliott nodded at one of them, and Duncan marched toward it briskly, an Englishman with pressing West Coast business appointments who'd troweled some time out of his hectic schedule to stand on a sidewalk, and then break into someone's house for the hell of it.

He made the pee as splashy as possible, just to prove to Elliott that the need was genuine. He was disappointed by the promised artwork, however. There were a couple of cartoons, one of Julie and one of a middle-aged man who still looked something like the old photos Duncan had seen of her husband, but they looked like they'd been done by one of those artists who hang out at tourist traps, and in any case they were both post-Tucker, which meant that they could have been pictures of any American middle-class couple. He was washing his hands in the tiny sink when Elliott shouted through the door, "Oh, and there's the drawing. That's still up in their dining room."

"What drawing?"

"The drawing that Tucker did of her, back in the day."

Duncan opened the door and stared at him.

"What do you mean?"

"You know Tucker's an artist, right?"

"No." And then, because this made him sound like an amateur, "Well, yes. Of course. But I didn't know . . ." He didn't know what he didn't know, but Elliott didn't notice.

"Yeah," said Elliott. "In here."

The dining room was at the back of the house, with French windows leading out onto a terrace, presumably, or a lawn—there were curtains drawn over them. The drawing was hung over the fireplace, and it was big, maybe four feet by three, a head-and-shoulders portrait of Julie in profile, half squinting through her cigarette smoke at something in the middle distance. She looked, in fact, as if she were studying another work of art. It was a beautiful portrait, reverential and romantic, but not idealized—it was too sad, for a start. It somehow seemed to suggest the impending end of his relationship with the sitter, although of course Duncan might have been imagining that. He might have been imagining the meaning, he might have been imagining the power and charm. Indeed, he could have been imagining the drawing itself.

Duncan moved in closer. There was a signature in the bottom left-hand corner, and that was thrilling enough to require separate examination and contemplation. In a quarter of a century of fandom, he'd never seen Tucker's handwriting. And while he was staring at the signature, he realized something else: that for the first time since 1986 he hadn't been able to respond to a piece of work by Crowe. So he stopped looking at the signature and stepped back to look at the picture again.

"You should really see it in the daylight," said Elliott. He drew back the curtains on the French windows, and almost immediately they found themselves staring at a gardener mowing the lawn. He saw them and started shouting and gesticulating, and before Duncan knew it, he was out the front door and halfway up the road, running and sweating, his legs shaking with nerves, his heart pounding so hard he thought he might not make it to the end of the street and possible safety.

It wasn't until the doors on the BART closed behind him that he felt safe. He'd lost Elliott almost immediately—he'd run out of that house as fast as he could, but the boy was faster, and almost immediately out of sight. And he never wanted to see him again anyway. It had been pretty much all his fault, there was no doubt about that; he'd provided both the temptation and the means to break in. Duncan had been stupid, yes, but his powers of reasoning had been scrambled by his bladder, and . . . Elliott had corrupted him, was the truth of it. Scholars like him were always going to be vulnerable to the excesses of obsessives, because, yes, they shared a tiny strand of the same DNA. His heart rate began to slow. He was calming himself down with the familiar stories he always told himself when doubt crept in.

When the train stopped at the next station, however, a Latino who looked a little like the gardener in the back garden got into Duncan's car, and his stomach shot toward his knees while his heart leaped halfway up his windpipe, and no amount of self-justification could help him put his internal organs back where they belonged.

What really frightened him was how spectacularly his transgression had paid off. All these years he'd done nothing more than read and listen and think, and though he'd been stimulated by these activities, what had he uncovered, really? And yet by behaving like a teenage hooligan with a screw loose, he had made a major breakthrough. He was the only Crowologist in the world (Elliott was nobody's idea of a Crowologist) who knew about that picture, and he could never tell anyone about it, unless he wished to own up to being mentally unbalanced. Every other year spent on his chosen subject had been barren compared to the last couple of hours. But that couldn't be the way forward, surely? He didn't want to be the kind of man who plunged his arms into trash cans in the hope of finding a letter, or a piece of bacon rind that Crowe might have chewed. By the time he got back to the hotel, he had convinced himself he was finished with Tucker Crowe.

JULIET

FROM WIKIPEDIA,
THE FREE ENCYCLOPEDIA

Juliet, released in April 1986, is singer-songwriter Tucker Crowe's sixth and (at the time of writing) last studio album. Crowe went into retirement later that year and has made no music of any kind since. At the time it received ecstatic reviews, although like the rest of Crowe's work it sold only moderately, reaching number 29 on the Billboard charts. Since then, however, it has been widely recognized by critics as a classic breakup album to rank with Dylan's *Blood on the Tracks* and Springsteen's *Tunnel of Love*. *Juliet* tells the story of Crowe's relationship with Julie Beatty, a noted beauty and L.A. scenester of the early eighties, from its beginnings ("And You Are?") to its bitter conclusion ("You and Your Perfect Life"), when Beatty returned to her husband, Michael Posey. The second side of the album is regarded as one of the most tortured sequences of songs in popular music.

NOTES

Various musicians who played on the album have talked about Crowe's fragile state of mind during the recording of the album. Scotty Phillips has described how Crowe came at him with an oxyacetylene torch before the guitarist's incendiary solo on "You and Your Perfect Life."

In one of his last interviews, Crowe expressed surprise at the enthusiasm for the record. "Yeah, people keep telling me they love it. But I don't really understand them. To me, it's the sound of someone having his fingernails pulled out. Who wants to listen to that?"

Julie Beatty claimed in a 1992 interview that she no longer owned a copy of *Juliet*. "I don't need that in my life. If I want someone yelling at me for forty-five minutes, I'll call my mother."

Various musicians, including the late Jeff Buckley, Michael Stipe and Peter Buck of REM, and Chris Martin of Coldplay, have talked about the influence of *Juliet* on their careers. Buck's side project The Minus Five and Coldplay both recorded songs for the tribute album released in 2002, *Wherefore Art Thou?*

TRACK LISTING

two

Annie scrolled back through the photo library on her computer and started to wonder whether her whole life had been a waste of time. She wasn't, she liked to think, a nostalgic, or a Luddite. She preferred her iPod to Duncan's old vinyl, she enjoyed having hundreds of TV channels to choose from, and she loved her digital camera. It's just that in the old days, when you eventually got your pictures back from the drugstore, you never went backward through time. You shuffled through the twenty-four holiday snapshots, only seven of which were any good, put them in a drawer and forgot about them. You didn't have to compare them to every other holiday you'd had in the last seven or eight years. But now she couldn't resist it. When she uploaded or downloaded or whatever it was you did, the new photos took their place alongside all the others, and the seamlessness was beginning to depress her.

Look at them. There's Duncan. There's Annie. There's Duncan and Annie. There's Annie, Duncan, Duncan, Annie, Duncan standing at a urinal, pretending to have a pee . . . Nobody should have children just because it made the photo library on the computer more interesting. On the other hand, being childless meant that you could, if you were in a negative frame of mind, come to the conclusion that your snapshots were a little on the dull side. Nobody grew up or got bigger; no landmark occasions were commemorated, because there were none. Duncan and Annie just got slowly older, and a little fatter. (She was being loyal here. She hadn't got much fatter at all, she noticed.) Annie had single friends who'd never had kids, but their holiday photos, usually taken in exotic locations, were never boring—or rather, they didn't feature the same two people over and over again, quite often wearing the same T-shirts and sunglasses, quite often sitting by the same swimming pool in the same hotel on the Amalfi coast.

Her single childless friends seemed to meet new people on their travels, people who then became friends. Duncan and Annie had never made friends on holiday: Duncan was always terrified of speaking to anybody, in case they should "get stuck." Once, sitting by the pool at the hotel on the Amalfi coast, Duncan had spotted someone reading the same book as him, a relatively obscure biography of some soul or blues musician. Some people—most people, maybe—would have regarded this as a happy and unlikely coincidence worth a smile or a hello, maybe even a drink and an eventual exchange of e-mail addresses; Duncan marched straight to their bedroom, put the book away and got out another one, just in case the other reader wanted to talk to him. Maybe it wasn't her whole life that had been a waste of time—maybe it was just the fifteen years that she'd spent with Duncan. A chunk of her life, rescued! The chunk that finished in 1993! The photos from the American holiday didn't do much to lift her gloom. Why had she allowed herself to be snapped outside an old-fashioned ladies' underwear shop in Queens, New York, adopting exactly the same pose that Tucker had struck for the album cover of *You and Me Both*?

Duncan's sudden rejection of all things Tucker made it all even more pointless. She kept asking him what had happened at Juliet's house, but he simply claimed that he'd been losing interest for a while, and the morning in Berkeley had underlined the ridiculousness of it all. Annie didn't buy it. He'd been blabbing on about Juliet all through breakfast that morning and he was clearly upset about something that afternoon when she saw him back at the hotel; the evidence suggested a Minneapolis toilet–style incident, destined to provoke wild Internet speculation among Crowologists forever.

She closed her photo library and went down to the hall to pick up all the mail that had been lying on the floor since they got home that morning. Duncan had already picked out all his Amazon parcels, and he wasn't interested in anything else he got, so once she'd finished opening her mail, she started to tear open his, just in case there was anything that shouldn't go straight into the recycling bin. There was an invitation to a symposium for English teachers, two invitations to apply for a credit card and a brown envelope containing a letter and a CD in one of those see-through plastic sleeves.

Dear Duncan (she read),

Haven't spoken to you in a while, but then, there hasn't really been much to talk about, has there? We're releasing this in a couple of months, and I thought you should be one of the first to hear it. Who knew? Not me, and I suspect not even you. Anyway, Tucker has decided that the time is right. These are solo acoustic demos of all the songs on the album.

We're calling it *Juliet, Naked.*

Lemme know what you think, and enjoy!

> Best wishes,
> Paul Hill,
> Press Officer,
> PTO Music

Annie had in her hands a new Tucker Crowe release, and her excitement wasn't even vicarious, just as it wouldn't be vicarious if Duncan were elected prime minister. In the entire fifteen years of their relationship, this had never happened before, and as a consequence she didn't know how to react. She would have called Duncan on his cell, but his cell was right in front of her, plugged into the spare socket by the kettle to recharge; she would have loaded it straight onto his iPod, but he'd taken that with him to work. (Both gadgets had come back from their holiday with drained batteries. One had been taken care of straightaway, the other forgotten about until just before Duncan left the house.) So how was she supposed to mark the occasion?

She took the CD out of its plastic sleeve and put it into the portable player they kept in the kitchen. But instead of pressing the "play" button, her finger hovered above it for a second. Could she really listen to it before he did? It felt like one of those moments in a relationship—and there were enough of them in theirs, God knows—that would look completely innocuous to an outsider, but which were packed with meaning and aggression. Annie could imagine telling Ros at work that Duncan had gone absolutely nuts because she played a new CD when he wasn't at home, and Ros would be suitably appalled and disgusted. But she wouldn't be telling the whole story. She'd be telling a self-serving version, omitting the context. And, of course, it would be legitimate to feel bafflement and outrage if Ros didn't understand, but Annie knew Duncan too well. She understood. She knew that playing the CD was an act of naked hostility, even if anyone peering through the windows wouldn't be able to see the nakedness.

She put the CD back in its sleeve and made herself a cup of coffee. Duncan had only gone to pick up a time-table for the new semester, so he'd be back in less than an hour. Oh, this is ridiculous, she thought. Told herself, anyway, telling oneself being a more self-conscious mode of self-communication, and thus a more efficient way of lying, than thinking. Why couldn't she put on some music she'd almost certainly like while she was pottering around in the kitchen? Why not pretend that Duncan was a normal person, with a healthy relationship to the things that pleased him? She put the disk back in the machine, and this time she pressed "play." And already she was preparing the opening lines of the skirmish to come.

To begin with, she was so stirred up by the act of playing the CD, the drama and the treachery of it, that she forgot to listen to the music—she was too busy composing her retorts. *"It's just a CD, Duncan!" "I don't know if you've ever noticed, but I quite like* Juliet *too."* (That "quite"—so innocent and casual, and yet so wounding. She hoped.) *"It never occurred to me for a moment that I wasn't allowed to listen!" "Oh, don't be such a baby!"* Where had this ill feeling sprung from? It wasn't as if their relationship was any more precarious than it ever had been. But she could see now that a lot of resentment had been locked into her somewhere, and it was busy, restless stuff, roaming around looking for the tiniest open window. The last time she'd felt like this was during a house-share at university, when she'd found herself setting ridiculously complicated and time-consuming traps to catch a housemate whom she suspected of stealing her cookies. It took her a while to understand that the cookies weren't really the point, and that somehow, without her noticing, she'd come to loathe this other girl—her greed, her smugness, her face and voice and bathrobe. Was that happening here? *Juliet,*

Naked was both as blameless and as incendiary as a chocolate chip cookie.

Eventually she managed to stop wondering whether she hated her life partner and to start listening. And what she heard was exactly what she might have guessed she'd hear if she'd read about *Juliet, Naked* in a newspaper: it was *Juliet*, but without all the good bits. That probably wasn't fair. Those lovely melodies were all there, intact, and Crowe had clearly written most of the lyrics, although a couple of the songs were missing choruses. But it was so tentative, so unadorned—it was like listening to one of those people you've never heard of who comes onstage at lunchtime in a folk festival. There wasn't really any music to it yet, no violins, no electric guitars, no rhythm, none of the texture or the detail that still contained surprises, even after all this time. And there was no anger that she could hear, either, no pain. If she were still a teacher, she'd have played the two albums back-to-back to her sixth-formers, so that they could understand that art was pretending. Of course Tucker Crowe was in pain when he made *Juliet*, but he couldn't just march into a recording studio and start howling. He'd have sounded mad and pathetic. He had to calm the rage, tame it and shape it so that it could be contained in the tight-fitting songs. Then he had to dress it up so that it sounded more like itself. *Juliet, Naked* proved how clever Tucker Crowe was, Annie thought, how artful;

but only because of all the things that were missing, not because of anything that you could actually hear.

Annie heard the front door open during "Blood Ties," the second-from-last song. She hadn't really been tidying up the kitchen while she'd been listening, but now she busied herself, and the stab at multitasking was in itself a form of betrayal: *It's just an album I put on! No big deal!*

"How was college?" she asked him when he walked in. "Anything happen while you were away?"

But already he wasn't listening to her. He was standing still, his head pointed toward the speakers like some kind of hunting dog.

"What's . . . Hold on. Don't tell me. That Tokyo radio-show bootleg? The solo acoustic one?" And then, with rising panic, "He didn't play 'Blood Ties' then."

"No, it's . . ."

"Sssshh."

They both listened for a few bars. Annie watched his confusion and began to enjoy it.

"But this . . ." He stopped again. "This is . . . It's *nothing*."

She burst out laughing. But of course! If Duncan had never heard it before, then all he could do was deny its existence.

"I mean, it's something, but . . . I give up."

"*Juliet, Naked*, it's called."

"What's called?" More panic. His world was tilting on its axis, and he was sliding right off.

"This album."

"What album?"

"The one we're listening to."

"This album is called *Juliet, Naked*."

"Yes."

"There is no album called *Juliet, Naked*."

"There is now."

She picked up the note from Paul Hill and handed it to him. He read it, read it again, read it for a third time.

"But this is addressed to me. You opened my post."

"I always open your post," she said. "If I don't open your post, it stays unopened."

"I open the interesting letters."

"You left this one because it looked boring."

"But it isn't boring."

"No. But I had to open it to find that out."

"You had no right," he said. "And then . . . To actually *play* it . . . I don't believe this."

Annie never got a chance to chuck any of her scripted darts at him. He marched over to the CD player, pulled the disk out of the player and marched off.

. . .

The first time Duncan had watched his computer fill in the track names of the CD he'd put into it, he simply didn't believe it. It was as if he were watching a magician who actually possessed magic powers: there was no point in looking for the explanation, for the trick, because there wasn't one—or rather, there wasn't one that he'd ever understand. Shortly after that, people from the message board started sending him songs attached to e-mails, and that was every bit as mysterious, because it meant that recorded music wasn't, as he'd previously always understood, a *thing* at all—a CD, a piece of plastic, a spool of tape. You could reduce it to its essence, and its essence was literally intangible. This made music better, more beautiful, more mysterious, as far as he was concerned. People who knew of his relationship with Tucker expected him to be a vinyl nostalgic, but the new technology had made his passions more romantic, not less.

Over the years, though, he had detected a niggling dissatisfaction with the track-naming part of this new sorcery. He couldn't help imagining, when he inserted a CD into his laptop, that whoever it was in cyberspace monitoring his musical tastes thought them dull, and a little too mainstream. You could never catch him out. Duncan imagined a twenty-first-century Neil Armstrong wearing a helmet with built-in Bang and Olufsen headphones, floating around somewhere a lot like old-fashioned space (except it was even less comprehensible and clearly contained a lot more pornography), thinking, Oh, not another one of these. Give me something harder. Give me something that stumps me for a moment, something that sends me scurrying off to the cyber reference library. Sometimes, when the computer seemed to whir for longer than usual, Duncan got the feeling that he'd set some kind of a challenge; but then one day, when he was stocking up his iPod with back catalog, it had taken nearly three minutes to obtain the track names for *Abbey Road*, and it was clear that any delay was due to a bad connection or something, and not because Neil Headphones was stumped. So recently Duncan had been taking pleasure in those rare occasions when Neil couldn't help him, and he'd had to fill out the titles himself, even though it was boring. It meant that he was off the well-trodden paths and into the musical jungle. Neil Headphones had never heard of *Juliet, Naked*, which was something of a consolation. Duncan couldn't have borne it if the information had popped up without any effort on anyone's part, as if he were the seven-hundredth person to have requested it that day.

He didn't want to listen to *Juliet, Naked* straightaway. He was still too angry, both with Annie and, more obscurely, with the album itself, which seemed to belong to her more than him. So he was grateful for the time it took to name the tracks (he took a gamble on the track listing being the same on *Naked*, as he was already learning to call it, as it was on the original album—the long last song, six minutes even in its demo form, suggested that it would be), and then for his machine to inhale the music into itself. What had she been *thinking* of? He wanted to find a benign interpretation for her behavior, but there just wasn't one. It was malevolence, pure and simple. Why did she hate him so much, all of a sudden? What had he done?

He plugged his iPod in, transferred the album with a still-miraculous click of the finger and flick of the wrist, picked his jacket up from the newel post at the bottom of the stairs and went out.

He went down to the seashore. He'd grown up in the London suburbs, and still couldn't get used to the idea that the sea was five minutes' walk away. It wasn't much of a sea, of course, if what you wanted was a sea that contained even the faintest hint of blue or green; their sea seemed committed to a resourceful range of charcoal gray blacks, with the occasional suggestion of muddy brown. The weather conditions were perfect for his needs, though. The sea was hurling itself at the beach over and over again, like a nasty and particularly stupid pit bull, and the vacationers who still, inexplicably, chose to come here when they could fly to the Mediterranean for thirty quid all looked as though they'd been bereaved that morning. Fallacies really never got more pathetic than this. He got himself a cup of takeout instant coffee from the kebab stand by the pier and sat down on a bench overlooking the ocean. He was ready.

Forty-one minutes later, he was scrabbling around in his pockets for something he could use as a handkerchief when a middle-aged woman came over and touched him on the arm.

"Do you need someone to talk to?" she said gently.

"Oh. Thank you. No, no, I'm fine."

He touched his face—he'd been crying harder than he'd realized.

"You sure? You don't look fine."

"No, really. I've just . . . I've just had a very intense emotional experience." He held out one of his iPod headphones, as if that would explain it. "On here."

"You're crying about music?"

The woman looked at him as if he were some kind of pervert.

"Well," said Duncan, "I'm not crying *about* it. I'm not sure that's the right preposition."

She shook her head and walked off.

. . .

He listened from beginning to end twice more while sitting on the bench, and then started to walk home during the third play. One thing about great art: it made you love people more, forgive them their petty transgressions. It worked in the way that religion was supposed to, if you thought about it. What did it matter that Annie had heard the album before he'd had his chance? Imagine all the people who'd heard the original album before he'd discovered it! Imagine all the people who'd seen *Taxi Driver* before him, come to that! Did that deaden its impact? Did it make it less his? He wanted to go home, hug her and talk about a morning that he would never forget. He wanted to hear what she had to say, too. He valued her insights into Crowe's work—she could be surprisingly shrewd, sometimes, given her unwillingness to immerse herself in the subject, and he wanted to hear whether she'd noticed the same things that he'd picked up: the lack of chorus in "The Twentieth Call of the Day," for example, which gave the song a relentlessness and a self-loathing that you couldn't really detect in its "finished" form. (He'd play this version to anyone who dared to trot out that tired old line about Crowe being the poor man's Dylan. "The Twentieth Call of the Day," in Duncan's opinion, was "Positively Fourth Street," but it had more texture and heft. And Tucker could sing.) And who'd have thought that "And You Are?" could sound so ominous? On *Juliet*, it was a song about two people making a connection straightaway—in other words, it was a simple (but very pretty) love song, a sunny day before the psychic storms started rolling in from the sea. But on *Juliet, Naked*, it was as if the lovers were standing in a little pool of sunlight that was becoming smaller even while they were talking for the first time. They could see the thunder and the rain already, and it made the album more complete, somehow, more coherent. It was a proper tragedy, with the doom about to befall them implied from the very beginning. The flat restraint of "You and Your Perfect Life," meanwhile, gave the song a staggering power that was muffled by the histrionics of the rock 'n' roll version.

Annie was still in the kitchen when he got home, reading the *Guardian* at the kitchen table with a cup of coffee. He went up behind her and hugged her, probably for longer than she was comfortable being hugged.

"What's that for?" she said, with moderate but determined affection. "I thought you were annoyed with me."

"I'm sorry. Stupid. Petty. What does it matter who hears it first?"

"I know. I should have warned you it was a bit on the

dreary side. But I thought that would make you even crosser."

He felt as though he'd been punched in the stomach. He let go of her, took a breath, waited for the impact to fade a little before he spoke again.

"You didn't like it?"

"Well, it was all right. Mildly interesting, if you've heard the other one. I don't suppose I'll play it again. What did you think?"

"I think it's a masterpiece. I think it blows the other one out of the water. And as the other one is my favorite album of all time . . ."

"You're not serious?"

" 'Dreary'! My God! What else is dreary, according to you? *King Lear? The Waste Land?*"

"Don't do that, Duncan. You always lose your powers of reason when you get angry."

"That's anger for you."

"No, but . . . We're not having an argument. We're trying to discuss, you know, a work of art."

"Not according to you. According to you we're trying to discuss a piece of shit."

"There you go. You think it's *King Lear*, I think it's a piece of shit . . . Get a grip, Duncan. I love the other one. I suspect most people will feel the same way."

"Oh, most people. We all know what most people

think about everything. The wisdom of fucking crowds. Jesus. Most people would rather buy an album made by a dancing midget from a reality TV show."

"Duncan Thomson, the great populist."

"I'm just . . . I'm so disappointed in you, Annie. I thought you were better than that."

"Ah, yes. That's the next step. It becomes a moral failing on my part. A character weakness."

"But I'm sorry to say that's how it is. If you can't hear anything in this . . ."

"What? Please. Tell me. I'd love to know what that would say about me."

"The usual stuff."

"Which is what?"

"Which is, I don't know. You're a moron."

"Thanks."

"I didn't say you were a moron. I said you were a moron if you can't hear anything in this."

"I can't."

He left the house again, then, and went back to the bench overlooking the sea with his iPod.

Another hour or so went by before he even thought about the website. He'd be the first to write about the album, if he were quick. Better than that: he'd be the first to alert the Crowe community to its existence, even! He'd listened to *Juliet, Naked* four times, and he had already thought of a great deal he wanted to say about it; in any case, to wait any longer would be to risk his advantage. He didn't think Paul Hill would have contacted anyone else from the message boards yet, but copies would have been pushed through all sorts of mailboxes this morning. He had to go home, however much hostility he felt toward Annie.

He managed to avoid her anyway. She was on the phone in the kitchen, probably to her mother. (And who wanted to speak to a member of the family, immediately on return from holiday? Didn't that prove something? What, he wasn't precisely sure. But it seemed to him that anyone still so connected to family—to *childhood,* essentially— was hardly going to be able to respond to the kind of stark adult truths spread generously through the ten songs on *Juliet, Naked.* She'd get it one day, maybe, but clearly not for a few years yet.)

Their shared office was on the half landing. The real estate agent who sold them the house was inexplicably convinced that they would one day use the tiny room as a nursery, before deciding to move out of town and buy a house with a garden. They would then sell this house to another couple who would, in time, do the same thing. Duncan had wondered whether their childlessness was a direct response to the depressing predictability of it all—

whether the real estate agent had, inadvertently but effectively, made their minds up for them.

It was the opposite of a nursery now. It contained two laptops, placed side by side on a workbench, two chairs, a machine that converted vinyl into MP3s and about two thousand CDs, including bootlegs of every single concert Tucker Crowe had performed between 1982 and 1986, with the exception of the September 1984 show at KB in Malmö, Sweden, which, bizarrely, nobody seems to have taped—a constant thorn in the side of all serious students, given that this, according to a normally reliable Swedish source, was the night Crowe chose to do a never-to-be-repeated cover version of "Love Will Tear Us Apart." He cleared away the bank statements and letters that Annie had opened and placed by his computer for his attention, opened a document and began to type. He produced three thousand words in just under two hours and posted it on the website shortly after five o'clock that afternoon. By ten o'clock that night, there were 163 comments, from fans in eleven different countries.

The next day, he would see that he'd overcooked it a little. "Juliet, Naked *means that everything else Tucker Crowe recorded is suddenly a little paler, a little too slick, a little too digested . . . And if it does that to Crowe's work, imagine what it does to everyone else's.*" He hadn't wanted to get into arguments about the relative merits of James Brown, or the Stones, or Frank Sinatra. He'd meant Crowe's singer-songwriter peers, of course, but the literal-minded hadn't wanted to take it that way. *"This version of 'You and Your Perfect Life' makes the one you're familiar with sound like something off a Westlife album . . ."* If he'd waited, he'd have found that the "Dressed" version (inevitably, *Juliet* came to be known as *Dressed*, for ease of distinction) reasserted its superiority quite comfortably, after its initial shock. And he wished he hadn't mentioned Westlife at all, seeing as some crazed Westlife fan would come across the reference and spend a day posting obscene messages on the message boards.

In his naïveté, he hadn't really expected anger. But then he imagined himself checking the website idly for some tidbit of gossip—news of an interview with the guy who did the cover art for the EP, say—and discovering there was a whole new album out there that he hadn't heard. It would have been like turning on the TV for the local weather forecast, only to find that the sky was falling in. He wouldn't have been happy, and he certainly wouldn't have wanted to read some other bastard's smug review. He would have hated the reviewer, certainly, and he would probably have decided there and then that the album was no good. He began to worry that his ecstatic praise might have done *Naked* a disservice: now nobody—none of the real fans, anyway, and it was difficult to imagine that many other people would bother with it—would be able to listen to it without prejudice. Oh, it was a complicated business, loving art. It involved a lot more ill will than one might have suspected.

The responses that meant the most to him came via e-mail, from the Crowologists he knew well. Ed West's e-mail said, simply, "Fuck me. Gimme. Now." Geoff Old-field's said (with unnecessary cruelty, Duncan thought), "That, my friend, was your moment in the sun. Nothing quite as good will ever happen to you again." John Taylor went for a quote, from "The Better Man": "Luck is a disease / I don't want it near me." He created a mailing list and started sending them all the tracks, one by one. Tomorrow morning, a handful of middle-aged men would be regretting that they had gone to bed much too late.

three

Annie had thought she might be stuck teaching forever, and she'd hated the job so much that, even now, simply arriving at the museum ten or fifteen minutes late made her happy. For a teacher, those fifteen minutes would have represented a humiliating disaster, involving riots, reprimands and disapproving colleagues, but nobody cared whether she arrived three minutes or thirty minutes before a small and infrequently visited museum was due to open. (The truth was that nobody really cared if she arrived three or thirty minutes after it was supposed to have opened, either.) Wandering out for a mid-morning takeout coffee was a frequent and rather pitiful daydream in her old job; now she made sure she did it every day, whether she needed the caffeine or not. Okay, there were some things she missed: that feeling you got when a lesson was going well, when it was all bright eyes and concentration so thick it felt almost humid, something that might cling to your clothes; and sometimes she could do with some of the energy and optimism and life that you could find in any child, no matter how apparently surly and damaged. But most of the time, she was happy still to have made it under the barbed wire that surrounded secondary education and out into the world.

She worked on her own, for great chunks of the day, mostly trying to raise funds, although this was beginning to feel like an increasingly pointless task: nobody, it seemed, had the spare cash for an ailing seaside museum anymore, and possibly never would again. Occasionally, she had to speak to visiting parties of local schoolchildren, which was why she'd been given the chance to escape from the classroom. There was always a volunteer at the front desk, usually Vi or Margaret or Joyce or one of the other old ladies whose aching need to show that they could be useful broke Annie's heart, when she bothered to think about them at all. And when there was a special exhibition being planned, then she worked with Ros, a freelance curator who also taught history at Duncan's college. (Duncan, of course, had never been able to bring himself to talk to her, in case he "got stuck" with her during one of his visits to the staff room.) Ros and Annie were attempting to prepare an exhibition at the moment, a photographic record of the heat-wave summer of 1964, when the old town square was redeveloped, the Stones played the ABC cinema up the road and a twenty-five-foot shark had been washed up on the beach. They had asked for contributions from residents, and they had advertised on all the relevant local- and social-history websites they could think of, but so far they had received only two snapshots—one of the shark itself, which had clearly died of some kind of fungal condition much too gruesome for an exhibition intended to celebrate a golden summer, and one of four friends—coworkers?—having fun on the boardwalk.

This photograph had arrived through the mail a couple of days after they'd posted their Internet ads, and she couldn't believe how perfect it was. The two men were in suspenders and shirtsleeves, and the two women were in floral sundresses; the teeth were bad, the faces were lined, the hair was Brylcreemed, and they looked as if they had never had so much fun in their lives. That's what she said to Ros, when she saw it—"Look at them! It's like this is the best day out they've ever had!" And she laughed, so convinced was she that their enjoyment was due to a happy trick of the camera, or alcohol, or a dirty joke, anything but the day out and the surroundings. And Ros said simply, "Well. That's almost certainly true."

Annie, who was about to have a moderately good time on a three-week tour of the United States—pleasant, but not world-shaking, those mountains in Montana—felt humbled. In 1964, five years before she was born, it was still possible for English people to feel ecstatic about a day off in a northerly seaside town. She looked at them again and wondered what they did, how much money they had in their pockets at that precise second, how long their holidays were, how long their lives were. Annie had never been rich. But she'd been to every European country she wanted to see, to the United States, even to Australia. How, she wondered, had we got to here from there, to this from that? She suddenly saw the point of the exhibition that she'd conceived and planned with no real enthusiasm or sense of purpose. More than that, she suddenly saw the point of the town she lived in, how much it must have meant to people that she and everyone else she knew were losing the capacity to imagine. She always took her job seriously, but she was determined to find a way of making visitors to the museum feel what she felt.

And then, after the dead shark offering, the photos just dried up. She had already given up on 1964, although she hadn't told Ros that yet, and had been trying to think of a way of broadening the hunt without making the exhibition unfocused and sloppy. Being away for three weeks had restored her hope, not least because she had eighteen days' worth of mail to sort through.

There were two more pictures. One had been dropped

off by a man who'd been sorting through his recently deceased mother's things; it was a nice enough snapshot of a little girl standing next to a Punch-and-Judy booth. The other, sent without a cover letter, was of the dead shark. Annie felt that she had the dead shark covered, and she wished she'd never mentioned it. She'd included it in her request only as a nudge to the memory of the aging population of the town. She might as well have sent them a notice saying "Diseased-shark pics wanted." This one seemed to show a hole in the flank where the flesh had simply rotted away.

She went through the rest of the mail, replied to some e-mails and went out for her coffee. It was only on the way back that she remembered Duncan's maniacal activity of the night before. She knew that his review had provoked a reaction, because he kept running up- and downstairs, checking his e-mail, reading the comments on the website, shaking his head and chuckling at the strange and suddenly alive world he inhabited. But he hadn't shown her what he'd written, and she felt she should read it. It wasn't just that, she realized—she actually wanted to read it. She'd heard the music, even before he had, which meant that for the first time ever she'd formed an opinion about it that hadn't been filtered through his own intimidating evangelism . . . She wanted to see for herself just how wrongheaded he could be, how far apart they were.

She logged on to the website (for some reason, she had it bookmarked) and printed the piece so that she could concentrate on it. By the time she'd finished it, she was properly angry with Duncan. She was angered by his smugness, his obvious determination to crow to the fellow fans he was supposed to feel some kind of kinship with; so she was angered by his pettiness, too, his inability to share something that was clearly of value in that shrinking and increasingly beleaguered community. But most of all, she was angered by his perversity. How could those sketches for songs be better than the finished product? How could leaving something half-formed be better than working on it, polishing it, layering and texturing it, shaping it until the music expresses what you want it to express? The more she stared at Duncan's ridiculous piece, the angrier she got, until she got so angry that the anger itself became an object of curiosity to her: it mystified her. Tucker Crowe was Duncan's hobby, and people with hobbies did peculiar things. But listening to music wasn't like collecting stamps, or fly-fishing, or building ships in a bottle. Listening to music was something that she did, too, frequently and with great enjoyment, and Duncan somehow managed to spoil it, partly by making her feel that she was no good at it. Was that it? She read the end of his piece again. "I have been living with Tucker Crowe's remarkable songs for nearly a quarter of a century, and only today, staring at the sea, listening to 'You and Your Perfect Life' as God and Crowe intended it to be heard . . ."

It wasn't that he made her feel incompetent and unsure of herself and her tastes. It was the reverse. He knew nothing about anything, and she'd never really allowed herself to notice it until now. She'd always thought that his passionate interest in music and film and books indicated intelligence, but of course it didn't have to indicate anything of the sort, if he constantly got the wrong end of the stick. Why was he teaching trainee plumbers and future hotel receptionists how to watch American television, if he was so smart? Why did he write thousands of words for obscure websites that nobody ever read? And why was he so convinced that a singer nobody had ever paid much attention to was a genius to rival Dylan and Keats? Oh, it spelled trouble, this anger. Her partner's brain was dwindling away to nothing while she examined it. And *he'd* called *her* a moron! One thing he was right about, though: Tucker Crowe was important, and he revealed harsh truths about people. About Duncan, anyway.

When Ros stopped by to find out whether they'd made any progress with the photographs, Annie still had the website up on her computer.

"Tucker Crowe," said Ros. "Wow. My college boyfriend

used to like him," she said. "I didn't know he was still going."

"He's not, really. You had a college boyfriend?"

"Yes. He was gay, too, it turned out. Can't imagine why we broke up. But I don't understand: Tucker Crowe has his own website?"

"Everyone has their own website."

"Is that true?"

"I think so. Nobody gets forgotten anymore. Seven fans in Australia team up with three Canadians, nine Brits and a couple of dozen Americans, and somebody who hasn't recorded in twenty years gets talked about every day. It's what the Internet's for. That and pornography. Do you want to know which songs he played in Portland, Oregon, in 1985?"

"Not really."

"Then this website isn't for you."

"How come you know so much about it? Are you one of the nine Brits?"

"No. There are no women who bother. My, you know, Duncan is."

What was she supposed to call him? Not being married to him was becoming every bit as irritating as she imagined marriage to him might be. She wasn't going to call him her boyfriend. He was forty-something, for God's sake. Partner? Life partner? Friend? None of these words and phrases seemed adequately to define their relationship, an inadequacy particularly poignant when it came to the word "friend." And she hated it when people just launched in and started talking about Peter or Jane when you had no idea who Peter and Jane were. Perhaps she just wouldn't ever mention him at all.

"And he's just written a million words of gibberish and posted them up for the world to see. If the world were interested, that is."

She invited Ros to inspect Duncan's piece, and Ros read the first few lines.

"Aaah. Sweet."

Annie made a face.

"Don't knock people with passions," said Ros. "Especially passions for the arts. They're always the most interesting people."

Everyone had succumbed to that particular myth, it seemed.

"Right. Next time you're in the West End, go and hang out by the stage door of a theater showing a musical and make friends with one of those sad bastards waiting for an autograph. See how interesting you find them."

"Sounds like I should buy that CD."

"Don't bother. That's what gets me. I played it, and he's completely wrong. And for some reason I'm bursting to say so."

"You should write your own review and stick it up next to his."

"Oh, I'm not an expert. I wouldn't be allowed."

"They need someone like you. Otherwise they all disappear up their own bottoms."

There was a knock on Annie's open office door. An old lady wearing a hoodie was standing there offering them both an envelope. Ros stepped over and took it.

"Shark picture," the old lady said, and waddled off.

Annie rolled her eyes. Ros opened the envelope, laughed and passed the picture over. It featured the same gaping, diseased wound that Annie'd seen in one of the other photos. But someone had had the bright idea of planting a small child on top of the shark. She was sitting there with her bare feet dangling inches from the hole; both toddler and wound were weeping.

"Jesus," said Annie.

"Maybe nobody went to see the Rolling Stones here in 1964," said Ros. "The dead shark was just too much fun."

Annie started writing her review that night. She had no intention of showing it to anyone; it was just a way of working out whether what she thought meant anything to her. It was also a way of sticking a fork into her irritation, which was beginning to swell like a sausage on a barbecue.

If it burst, then she could imagine consequences that she wasn't yet prepared for.

She had to write at work—letters, descriptions of exhibitions, captions, bits and pieces for the museum website—but most of the time, it seemed to her, she had to think up something to say, create an opinion from nothing. This was different; it was all she could do to stop herself from following every single one of the strands of thought she'd been chewing on for the last couple of days. *Juliet, Naked* had somehow given her ideas about art and work, her relationship, Tucker's relationship, the mysterious appeal of the obscure, men and music, the value of the chorus in song, the point of harmony and the necessity of ambition, and every time she finished a paragraph, the next one appeared in front of her, unbidden and annoyingly unconnected to the last. One day, she eventually decided, she would try to write about some of those things, but it couldn't be here and now; she wanted this essay to be about the two albums, the immeasurable and unquestionable superiority of one over the other. And maybe about what people (Duncan, in other words) thought they heard in *Naked* that wasn't actually there, and why these people (he) heard these things, and what it said about them. And maybe . . . No. That was enough. The album had created such mental turbulence that she briefly began to wonder whether it was a work of genius after all, but she dismissed the idea. She knew from her book group that novels none of them had enjoyed could produce stimulating and sometimes even useful conversation; it was the absences in *Naked* (and, therefore, in Duncan) that had made her think, not the presences.

Meanwhile, Duncan's friends on the website had been listening, and several more long reviews had been posted. In Tuckerland, it was something like Christmas; clearly those who believed had stopped work for the festive season, in order to spend time with their extended Internet family and, from the look of some of the pieces of writing, celebrate with a few beers or a spliff. "NOT a masterpiece but masterful nonetheless," was the headline of one review. "WHEN WILL THE POWERS THAT BE RELEASE ALL THE REAL UNRELEASED STUFF?" said another, who went on to say that he knew for a fact that there were seventeen albums of material in the vaults.

"Who's that guy?" she asked Duncan, after trying to read a paragraph of his feverish, occasionally rather affecting prose.

"Oh. Him. Poor old Jerry Warner. He used to teach English at some public school somewhere, but he got caught with a sixth-form boy a couple of years back, and he's been a bit off the rails since. Too much time on his hands. Why do you keep looking at the website, anyway?"

She'd finished her essay now. Somehow *Juliet, Naked*— or her feelings about it, anyway—had woken her from a deep sleep: she wanted things. She'd wanted to write, she wanted Duncan to read what she'd written. She wanted the other message board members to read it, too. She was proud of it, and she had even begun to wonder whether it might not be socially useful in some way. Some of these cranks, she hoped, might read it, blush a deep crimson and return to their lives. There was no end to her wanting.

"I wrote something."

"What about?"

"About *Naked*."

Duncan looked at her.

"You?"

"Yes. Me."

"Gosh. Well. Wow. Ha." He smiled, stood up and started pacing around the room. This was the closest she would ever get to telling him that he was about to become the father of twins. He wasn't thrilled by the news, but he knew he wasn't allowed to be openly discouraging.

"And do you think . . . Well, do you think you're *qualified* to write something?"

"Is it a matter of qualifications?"

"Interesting question. I mean, you're perfectly at liberty to write whatever you want."

"Thanks."

"But for the website . . . People expect a certain level of expertise."

"In the first paragraph of his post, Jerry Warner says that Tucker Crowe lives in a garage in Portugal. How expert is that?"

"I'm not sure you're supposed to take him literally."

"So, what, he lives in a Portuguese garage of the mind?"

"Yes, he's wayward, Jerry. But he can sing every word of every song."

"That qualifies him to busk outside a pub. It doesn't necessarily make him a critic."

"I'll tell you what," said Duncan, as if he had a crazy gut feeling that the receptionist should be offered a place on the board of his company. "Let me see it."

She was holding the piece in her hand. She gave it to him.

"Oh. Right. Thank you."

"I'll leave you to it."

She went upstairs, lay down on the bed and tried to read her book, but she couldn't concentrate. She could hear the sound of his shaking head all the way through the floorboards.

Duncan read the essay twice, just to buy himself some time; the truth was that he knew he was in trouble after the first reading, because it was both very well written and very wrong. Annie had made no factual errors that he could find (although someone on the boards would always point out some glaring and utterly inconsequential mistake, he found, when he wrote something), but her inability to recognize the brilliance of the album was indicative of a failure in taste that appalled him. How had she ever managed to read or see or listen to anything and come to the right conclusion about its merits? Was it all just luck? Or was it just the boring good taste of the Sunday newspaper supplements? So she liked *The Sopranos*—well, who didn't? He'd had a chance this time to watch her have to come to her own conclusions, and she'd messed it up.

He couldn't refuse to put the piece up, though. That wouldn't be fair, and he didn't want to be put in the position of turning her down. And it wasn't as if she didn't get the greatness of Tucker Crowe: this was, after all, a long hymn of praise to the perfection of *Dressed*. No, he'd post it on the site and let the others tell her what they thought of her.

He read it through once more, just to make sure, and this time it depressed him: she was better than him in everything but judgment—the only thing that mattered in the end, but still. She wrote well, with fluency and humor, and she was persuasive, if you hadn't actually heard the music, and she was likable. He tended to be strident and bullying and smart-alecky, even he could see that. This wasn't what she was supposed to be good at. Where did that leave him?

And supposing they didn't shoot her down in flames? Supposing, instead, that they used her as a stick to beat him with? *Naked*, which just about everyone had heard by now, was getting a very mixed reaction, and the negative stuff, he feared, had been provoked by his original, over-enthusiastic review. He was just beginning to change his mind about accepting her into the community when she appeared in front of him.

"Well?" she said. She was nervous.

"Well," he said.

"I feel as though I'm waiting for my exam results."

"I'm sorry. I was just thinking about what you wrote."

"And?"

"You know I don't agree with it. But it's really not bad."

"Oh. Thank you."

"And I'm happy to put it up, if that's what you really want."

"I think so."

"You have to include your e-mail address, you know that."

"Do I?"

"Yes. And you'll get a few nutters contacting you. But you can just delete them, if you don't want to get involved in a debate."

"Can I use a fake name?"

"Why? Nobody knows who you are."

"You've never mentioned me to any of your friends?"

"I don't think so, no."

"Oh."

Annie looked rather taken aback. But was that so weird? None of the other Crowologists lived in the town, and he only ever talked to them about Tucker, or occasionally about related artists.

"Have you ever had a contribution from a woman?"

He pretended to think about it. He'd often wondered why they only ever heard from middle-aged men, but it had never worried him unduly. Now he felt defensive.

"Yes," he said. "But not for a while. And even then they just wanted to talk about how, you know, attractive they found him."

The only women he could invent, it seemed, were clichéd airheads, unable to contribute to serious debate. He'd only had a couple of seconds to imagine them, but even so, he could and should have done better. If he ever did write his novel, he'd have to watch that.

"Do women find him attractive?"

"God, yes."

Now he was beginning to sound weird. Well, not weird, because homosexual attraction wasn't weird, of course it wasn't. But he was certainly sounding more vehement about Tucker's good looks than he had meant to.

"Anyway. Send me the piece as an attachment and I'll put it up tonight."

And, after only a couple of arguments with himself, he did what he'd promised.

At work the next morning, Annie found herself logging on to the website a couple of times an hour. At first, it seemed obvious to her that she'd want some feedback on what she'd written—she'd never done this before, so she was bound to be curious about the process. Later in the day, however, she realized that she wanted to win, to beat Duncan hollow. He'd had his say, and for the most part his say had been greeted by hostility, sarcasm, disbelief and envy; she wanted people to be nicer to her than they had been to him, more appreciative of her eloquence and acuity, and, to her great delight, they were. By five o'clock that afternoon, seven people had posted in the "comments" section, and six of them were friendly—inarticulate, and disappointingly brief, but friendly nonetheless. "Nice work, Annie!" "Welcome to our little online 'community'—good job!" "I completely agree with you. Duncan's so far off-base he's disappeared off of the radar." The only person who wanted to make it clear that he hadn't enjoyed her contribution didn't seem very happy about anything. "Tucker Crowe is FINISHED get over it you people are pathetic just going on and on about a singer who hasn't made an album for twenty years. He was overrated then and he's overrated now and Morrissey is so much better its embarrassing."

She wondered why someone would bother to write that; but then, "Why bother" was never a question you could ask about more or less anything on the Internet, otherwise the whole bunch of them shriveled to a cotton-candy nothing. Why had she bothered? Why does anybody? She was *for* bothering, on the whole; in which case thank you, MrMozza7, for your contribution, and thank you, everybody else, on every other website.

Just before she shut down her computer for the day, she checked her e-mails again. She'd suspected that Duncan had told her she had to provide an address in an attempt to frighten her off; clearly the comments section was the preferred method of providing feedback. Duncan had implied that there would be a host of homicidal cyber-stalkers, spewing bile and promising vengeance, but so far, nothing.

This time, however, there were two e-mails, from someone called Alfred Mantalini. The first was titled "Your Review." It was very short. It said, simply, "Thank you for your kind and perceptive words. I really appreciated them. Best wishes, Tucker Crowe." The title on the second was "P.S.," and the message said, "I don't know if you hang out with anyone on that website, but they seem like pretty weird people, and I'd be really grateful if you didn't pass on this address."

Was it possible? Even asking the question felt stupid, and the sudden breathlessness was simply pathetic. Of course it wasn't possible. It was obviously a joke, even though it was a joke removed of all discernible humor. Why bother? Don't ask. She draped her jacket over the back of her chair and put her bag on the floor. What would be an amusing response? "Fuck off, Duncan"? Or should she just ignore it? But supposing . . . ?

She tried mocking herself again, but the self-mockery only worked, she realized, if she thought with Duncan's head—if she really believed that Tucker Crowe was the most famous man in the world, and that there was more chance of being contacted out of the blue by Russell Crowe. Tucker Crowe, however, was an obscure musician from the 1980s, who probably didn't have much to do at nights except look at websites dedicated to his memory and shake his head in disbelief. And she could certainly understand why he wouldn't want to contact Duncan and the rest of them: the torch they were holding burned way too bright. Why Alfred Mantalini? She Googled the name. Alfred Mantalini was a character in *Nicholas Nickleby*, apparently, an idler and philanderer who ends up bankrupting his wife. Well, that could fit, couldn't it? Especially if Tucker Crowe had a sense of self-irony. Quickly, before she could think twice, she clicked on "Reply" and typed, "It isn't you really, is it?"

This man had been both a presence and an absence in her life for fifteen years, and the idea that she had just sent him a message that might somehow appear somewhere in his house, if he had one, seemed preposterous. She waited at work for an hour or two in the hope that he'd reply, and then she went home.

TUCKER CROWE

FROM WIKIPEDIA,
THE FREE ENCYCLOPEDIA

Tucker Jerome Crowe (b. 1953-09-06) is an American singer-songwriter and guitarist. Crowe came to prominence in the mid- to late seventies, first as the lead singer in the band The Politics of Joy, and then as a solo artist. Influenced both by other North American songwriters such as Bob Dylan, Bruce Springsteen and Leonard Cohen, and by the guitarist Tom Verlaine, he achieved increasing critical success after a difficult start, culminating in what is regarded as his masterwork, *Juliet*, in 1986, an album about his breakup with Julie Beatty that frequently features in "Best of All Time" lists. During the tour to support that album, however, Crowe abruptly withdrew from public life, apparently after some kind of life-changing incident in the men's toilet of a Minneapolis club, and has neither made music, nor spoken in the media about his disappearance, since.

BIOGRAPHY

EARLY LIFE

Crowe was born and raised in Bozeman, Montana. His father, Jerome, owned a dry-cleaning business, and his mother, Cynthia, was a music teacher. Several of the songs on his earlier albums are about his relationship with his parents, for example, "Perc and Tickets" (from *Tucker Crowe*, "perc" being the abbreviation for "perchloroethylene," the chemical used in the dry-cleaning process) and "Her Piano" (from *Infidelity and Other Domestic Investigations*), a tribute to his mother written after her death from breast cancer in 1983. Crowe's older brother, Ed, died in 1972, aged twenty-one, in a car accident. The inquest found that he had "significant" levels of alcohol in his bloodstream.

EARLY CAREER

Crowe formed The Politics of Joy at Montana State and dropped out of school to tour with the band. They split up before they were offered a recording contract, although most of the members of the band played with Crowe on his albums and tours, and his third album was titled *Tucker Crowe and The Politics of Joy*. Crowe's self-titled first album, released in 1977, was a famous music-industry disaster: the record company's confidence in the artist led them to place a series of advertisements in trade magazines and on billboards bearing the hubristic tagline BRUCE PLUS BOB PLUS LEONARD EQUALS TUCKER underneath a photograph of a pouting Crowe wearing eyeliner and a Stetson. A drunken Crowe was arrested for attempting to tear a gigantic poster down on Sunset Boulevard, Hollywood, California, in October 1977.

The rock critics were merciless—Greil Marcus in *Creem* ended his review with the line "Drivel plus feyness plus John Denver equals not much to go on?" Stung, Crowe recorded a savage four-track EP, *Can Anybody Hear Me?* (now the name of a website given over to earnest, sometimes pompous, discussion of his music), which helped to turn his fortunes, and the critical reception, around.

CONCERT TOURS

Crowe toured extensively between 1977 and his retirement, although his live shows are generally regarded as being variable in quality, mostly because of Crowe's alcoholism. Some shows could be as short as forty-five minutes, with long breaks between songs broken only by Crowe's abuse of, and evident scorn for, his audience; other nights, as the justly celebrated "At Ole Miss" bootleg demonstrates, he played for two and a half hours to ecstatic, devoted crowds. Too often, though, a Crowe concert would degenerate into name-calling and violence: in Cologne, Germany, he leaped into the crowd to punch a fan who had repeatedly requested a song he didn't want to play. Most members of The Politics of Joy had quit before the end of Crowe's career, most of them citing abuse from the singer as the reason for departure.

PERSONAL LIFE

Tucker Crowe is presumed to be the father of Julie Beatty's daughter, Ophelia (b. 1987), although her mother has always denied this. He is believed to have achieved sobriety.

RETIREMENT

Crowe is believed to be living on a farm in Pennsylvania, although little is known about how he has spent the last two decades. Rumors of a comeback are frequent, but so far unfounded. Some fans detect his involvement in recent albums by the Conniptions and the Genuine Articles; the album *Yes, Again* (2005) by the re-formed The Politics of Joy is regarded—wrongly, according to the band—to feature two songs by Crowe. *Juliet, Naked*, an album of demo versions of the songs on *Juliet*, was released in 2008.

DISCOGRAPHY

Tucker Crowe—1977

Infidelity and Other Domestic Investigations—1979

Tucker Crowe and The Politics of Joy—1981

You and Me Both—1983

Juliet—1986

Juliet, Naked—2008

AWARDS AND NOMINATIONS

Crowe received an honorary degree from the University of Montana in 1985. *Juliet* was nominated for a Grammy in the "Best Album" category in 1986. Crowe was nominated for a Grammy in the "Best Male Rock Performance" category, for "You and Your Perfect Life," in the same year.

four

While Annie was waiting hopefully in her office for Tucker Crowe's reply, Tucker Crowe was wandering around his local supermarket with his six-year-old son, Jackson, trying to buy comfort food for somebody neither of them knew very well.

"Hot dogs?"

"Yeah."

"I know you like 'em. I was asking you whether you think Lizzie might."

"I dunno."

There was no reason why he would.

"I've forgotten who she is again," said Jackson. "I'm sorry."

"She's your sister."

"Yeah, I know that," said the boy. "But . . . *Why* is she?"

"You know what a sister is," said Tucker.

"Not this kind."

"She's the same as every other kind."

But of course she wasn't. Tucker was being disingenuous. As far as a six-year-old boy was concerned, a sister was someone you saw at the breakfast table, someone who argued with you about what TV shows to watch, someone whose birthday party you tried to avoid because it was so pink, someone whose friends laughed at you a fraction of a second before you left a room. The girl who was coming to stay with them was twenty and had never come to stay with them before. Jackson had never even seen a photograph of her, so he could hardly be expected to know whether or not she was a vegetarian. It wasn't as if this were the first time Jackson had had a mystery sibling thrust upon him, either. A couple of years ago, Tucker had introduced him to twin brothers he'd previously been unaware of, neither of whom had remained a consistent presence in his life.

"I'm sorry, Jackson. She must seem like a different kind of sister to you. She's your sister because you've got the same dad."

"Who's her dad?"

"Who? Who do you think? Who's your dad?"

"So you're her dad, too?"

"That's it."

"Like you're Cooper's dad?"

"Yep."

"And Jesse's?" Cooper and Jesse, the recent twin fraternal inductees.

"You're getting it."

"So who's her mom this time?"

Jackson asked the question with such a pained world-weariness that Tucker couldn't help but laugh.

"This time it's Natalie."

"Natalie from my preschool?"

"Ha! No. Not Natalie from your preschool."

Tucker had a sudden and not unwelcome flash of the Natalie from Jackson's preschool. She was a nineteen-year-old assistant, blonde and sunny. There was a time, as James Brown once sang.

"Who, then?"

"You don't know her. She lives in England now. She lived in New York when I knew her."

"And what about my sister?"

"She's been living in England with her mom. But now she's going to college in the U.S. She's real smart."

All of his children were smart, and their intelligence was a source of pride—possibly misplaced, seeing as he'd only really been around for Jackson's education. Maybe he could at least take credit for choosing to impregnate only smart women? Probably not. God knew he'd slept with some dumb ones.

"Will she read to me? Cooper and Jesse read to me. And Gracie."

Grace was another daughter, his eldest: Tucker couldn't even hear her name without wincing. He had been an inadequate father to Lizzie and Jesse and Cooper, but his inadequacies seemed forgivable, somehow; he could forgive them, anyway, even if the children and mothers concerned were less indulgent. Grace, though . . . Grace was another story. Jackson had met her once, and Tucker had spent the entire visit in a cold sweat, even though his eldest daughter had been as sweet-natured as her mother. That just made it all worse, somehow.

"Why don't you read to her? She'll be impressed."

He put the hot dogs in the shopping cart and then took them out again. What percentage of smart girls were vegetarian? It couldn't be as high as fifty, right? So the chances were that she ate meat. He put them back into the cart. The trouble was that even young female carnivores wouldn't eat red meat. Well, hot dogs were pinky orange. Did pinky orange count as red? He was pretty sure the strange hue was chemical rather than sanguine. Vegetarians could eat chemicals, right? He picked them up again. He wished he'd sired a hard-drinking thirty-year-old mechanic from somewhere in Texas. Then he could just buy steaks and beer and a carton of Marlboros and be done with it. That particular scenario, however, would probably have involved him impregnating some sexy thirty-year-old Texan waitress, and Tucker had misspent his youth on deathly pale English models with cheekbones instead of breasts, and he was now paying the price. Now that he thought about it, he had paid the price then, too. What had he been thinking of?

"What are you doing, Dad?"

"I don't know whether she eats meat or not."

"Why wouldn't she eat meat?"

"Because some people believe that eating meat is wrong. And other people believe it's bad for you. And some people believe both."

"What do we believe?"

"I guess we believe both, but we don't care enough to do anything about it."

"Why do some people believe it's bad for you?"

"They think it's bad for your heart." There was no point in talking to Jackson about the colon.

"So your heart could just stop beating? If you ate meat? But you eat meat, Dad."

There was a tremulous note of panic in Jackson's voice, and Tucker cursed under his breath. He'd walked right into this one, like a sucker. Jackson had recently discovered that his father was going to die at some point in the first half of the twenty-first century, and his premature grief could be unleashed at any time, by anything, including the main tenets of vegetarianism. What made it worse was that Jackson's existential despair had both coincided with and bolstered Tucker's own. His fifty-fifth birthday seemed to have sparked a particularly acute bout of melancholy that he couldn't see being lifted too much by any of the birthdays to come.

"I don't eat so much meat."

"That's a lie, Dad. You eat tons. You had bacon this morning. And you cooked burgers last night."

"I said it's what some people believe, Jack. I didn't say it was true."

"So why do we believe it? If it's not true?"

"We believe that the Phillies are going to win the World Series every year, but that's not true either."

"I never believe that. You just tell me to believe that."

He put the hot dogs back on the shelf one last time and ushered Jackson over to the chicken. Chicken was neither pink nor orange, and he was able to tell Jackson of its health-giving properties without feeling like too much of a liar.

They went home, dumped the shopping and then drove straight over to Newark to pick up Lizzie. Tucker was hoping he'd like her, but the signs weren't promising: they'd e-mailed back and forth for a while, and she seemed angry and difficult. He had to concede, though, that this needn't necessarily mean she was an angry and difficult person: his daughters had found it hard to forgive the parental style he'd adopted for his early kids, which had ended up revolving around his complete absence from their lives. And he was beginning to learn that some of his children always reintroduced themselves to him at some big watershed moment, either in their own lives or in the lives of their mothers, and that tended to weigh the visits down somewhat. He was trying to cut down on introspection, so he really didn't need to import it.

On the way to the airport, Jackson chatted about school, baseball and death until he fell asleep, and Tucker listened to an old R&B mixed tape that he'd found in the trunk. He only had a handful of cassettes left now, and when they were gone, he'd have to find the money for a new truck. He couldn't contemplate a driving life without music. He sung along to the Chi-Lites softly, so as not to wake Jackson, and found himself thinking about the question that woman had asked him in her e-mail: "It isn't you really, is it?" Well, it was him, he was almost positive, but for some reason he'd started fretting about how he could prove it to her: as far as he could see, there was no good way of doing it. There was no detail in his

music too trivial to have remained unnoticed by those people, so telling her who had contributed uncredited back-
ing vocals to a couple of the songs wouldn't help. And just
about every single scrap of the biographical trivia about
him that floated around the Internet like so much space
junk was all untrue, as far as he could tell. Not a single one
of those creeps was aware that he had five kids, by four
different women, for example; but they all knew that he'd
had a secret child with Julie Beatty, pretty much the only
woman he'd avoided knocking up. And when would they
stop going on and on about something that happened in a
restroom in Minneapolis?

He tried very hard not to overinflate his importance
in the cosmos. Most people had forgotten him; very occasionally, he supposed, they'd come across his name in a
music review—some of the older journalists still used him
as a point of reference sometimes—or there'd be an album
in somebody's old vinyl collection, and they'd think, "Oh,
yeah. My college roommate used to listen to him." But the
Internet had changed everything: nobody was forgotten
anymore. He could Google his name and come up with
thousands of hits, and as a consequence he'd started to
think about his career as something that was still current,
somehow, rather than something that had died a long time
ago. If you looked at the right websites, he was Tucker
Crowe, mysterious reclusive genius, rather than Tucker

Crowe, former musician, ex-person. He was flattered, at first, by the people who devoted themselves to online discussions of his music; it helped restore some of the things that had been worn away by everything that had happened to him since he quit. But after a while these people just made him feel ill, especially when they turned their cranky attention to *Juliet*. Still. If he'd kept making albums he'd probably be a tired old joke by now, or at best a cult hero carving out a subsistence living in clubs, or occasionally as the grace-and-favor opening act for a band that he'd apparently helped kick-start, although he could never hear his influence in their music. So stopping had been a very smart career move—provided, that is, you ignored the lack of a career that was the inevitable consequence.

Tucker and Jackson were late, and they found Lizzie wandering up and down the line of limo drivers waving signs, in the vain hope that Tucker might have sent a car for her. He tapped her on the shoulder, and she turned around, scared.

"Hey."

"Oh. Hi. Tucker?"

He nodded, and tried to convey without words that anything she wanted to do was fine by him. She could throw her arms around his neck and cry, she could peck him on the cheek, shake his hand, ignore him altogether and walk to the truck in silence. He was becoming an expert in what he was beginning to think of as Paternal Reintroduction. He could run classes, probably. There were enough people nowadays who could use them.

If Tucker didn't disapprove of national stereotyping, then he'd describe Lizzie's greeting as English. She smiled politely, kissed him on the cheek and still somehow managed to suggest that he was representing all the pond life who'd been unable to get to the airport due to other commitments.

"And I am Jackson," said the boy with an impressive moral gravity. "I am your brother. I am very pleased to meet you." For some reason, Jackson took the view that verb contractions were inappropriate at occasions of this magnitude.

"Half brother," said Lizzie, unnecessarily.

"Correct," said Jackson, and Lizzie laughed. Tucker was glad he'd brought him along.

The conversation during the first part of the drive home was easy enough. They talked about her flight, the movies she'd seen and the couple who'd been reprimanded by a steward for inappropriate behavior ("canoodling," Lizzie called it, after detailed questioning from Jackson); he asked after her mother, and she talked about her studies. In other words, they did as well as they could, seeing as they were two complete strangers sharing a motor vehicle. Sometimes Tucker was mystified by society's obsession with the natural father. All his kids had been raised by competent mothers and loving stepfathers, so why did they need him? They (or their mothers) always talked about wanting to know where they came from and who they were, but the more he heard that, the less he understood it. His impression was that they always knew who they were. He couldn't ever tell them that, otherwise they'd just think he was some kind of brutal asshole.

The tenor of the conversation changed on the last stretch before home, when they'd come off the freeway.

"My boyfriend's a musician," said Lizzie, suddenly.

"Good for him," Tucker said.

"When I told him you were my dad, he couldn't believe it."

"How old is he? Forty-five?"

"No."

"I was just kidding. Most young people don't know my work."

"Oh, I see. No. He knew it. I think he wants to meet you. Maybe next time I come I can bring him."

"Sure." Next time? Surely this visit was some kind of probationary period, if not a job interview.

"Maybe at Christmas?"

"Yes," said Jackson. "Jesse and Cooper are coming at Christmas. So it would be fun if you came, too."

"Who are Jesse and Cooper?"

Oh, shit, Tucker thought. How had that happened? He was almost certain he'd told Natalie about the twins, and he'd kind of assumed that Natalie would pass the news on to Lizzie. Obviously not. This was another example of something he should have done himself, if he were any kind of father. The examples never stopped coming. They were inexhaustible. He would read up on parenting, if he thought it would help, but his errors always seemed too basic for the manuals. "Always tell your kids they have siblings . . ." He couldn't imagine any child-raising guru taking the trouble to write that down. Maybe there was a gap in the market.

"They're my brothers," said Jackson. "Half brothers. Like you. Me."

"Cat had kids from another relationship?" said Lizzie. Even this piece of tangential information was clearly irritating, something she apparently had a right to know. And if she was irritated about Cat having kids she didn't know about, Tucker was guessing that she'd be even more ticked off when she found out they were his. Or was he doing her a disservice? Maybe she'd just be really happy that she had more siblings than she'd suspected. More siblings = more fun, right?

"No," said Tucker.

"So . . ."

Tucker didn't want her to work it out for herself. He wanted to be able to say that he'd told her, even if he'd ended up breaking the news twelve years after the event.

"Jesse and Cooper are mine."

"Yours?"

"Yep. Twin boys."

"When?"

"Oh, a few years ago now. They're twelve."

Lizzie shook her head bitterly.

"I thought you knew," said Tucker.

"No," said Lizzie. "If I knew, I promise you I wouldn't pretend not to know. What would be the point of that?"

"You'd like them," said Jackson, confidently. "I did. But don't play them at any DS game. They will destroy you."

"Jesus Christ," said Lizzie.

"I know, right?" said Jackson.

"And they've been out to stay?"

"Just one time so far," said Tucker.

"So I'm just another one on the conveyor belt?"

"Yeah. You have to be out by tomorrow, otherwise the next one bumps into you and you cause a pileup. I've lost kids like that before."

"You think it's something to joke about?"

"No. I'm sorry, Lizzie."

"I should hope so. You really are unbelievable, Tucker."

Lizzie's mother had somehow been reduced in Tucker's memory to the beautiful picture that Richard Avedon took of her in '82 for some cosmetic ad, a picture that Tucker still had somewhere. He'd somehow mislaid Natalie's obtuseness, her haughtiness, her fragility and her extraordinary humorlessness. How had he forgotten any of that, seeing as those four qualities went half of the way toward explaining why they had split before Lizzie was even born? ("Half" was generous, he thought, but seeing as he'd split with many, many women who possessed none of these faults, logic suggested that he should take some of the blame.) And why hadn't he ever had a thing for warm Texan waitresses? Why had a chilly English girl seemed so compelling? Natalie was supposed to be his Julie Beatty replacement; he'd met her at a time in his life when he was a drunk, drifting from one party to the next simply because he was still being invited to parties. He was beginning to suspect that the invitations would be withdrawn one day, and the models, too, so Natalie had been his last hurrah. Not, of course, that she'd ever have made a noise as coarsely enthusiastic as that.

"Guys, let's not argue. Hey, Lizzie," said Jackson, brightly, "do you eat meat?"

"No," said Lizzie. "I haven't touched it since I was your age. It makes me feel sick, and I find the whole industry morally repugnant."

"But you eat chicken, right?"

Tucker laughed. Lizzie didn't.

. . .

When Cat heard the truck pull into the driveway, she opened the screen door and stood on the porch, restraining Pomus so he didn't jump all over their guest. Tucker looked at her, trying to gauge her mood. She hadn't been a whole lot of use during the twins' visit, but that was mostly to do with their mother: Tucker had told Cat, soon after they'd got together, that his breakup with Carrie had been difficult for him, and he had a vague recollection of implying that the difficulty derived from missing the excellence of the sex. He was surprised that this news pained her. He'd have thought she might be consoled to hear that some relationships were hard to shrug off, that he didn't just plow through them all unharmed.

Tucker carried Lizzie's bag into the house and introduced the girls to each other. For a moment they all stood there, frozen and smiling, although Lizzie's smile was a thin-lipped, functional thing that didn't indicate too much warmth or pleasure. Cat wasn't a girl anymore, Tucker realized now that there was an actual girl in the house: life had got at her around the eyes and the mouth and maybe even the middle. He was no longer an old pervert! Cat was a woman! But on the other hand: he and Jackson had ruined her! She'd misspent her youth on them, and they'd repaid her by making her look worried and old! He suddenly wanted to hold her, and say sorry, but right now, moments after a guest daughter had arrived, probably wasn't the time.

"Go sit in the backyard," said Cat. "I'll bring out drinks."

They walked through the house, Jackson pointing out places of historical and cultural interest—spots where he'd hurt himself, drawings he'd done—along the way. Lizzie appeared underwhelmed.

"I thought you lived on a farm," she said, when they were settled on chairs and benches.

"Why did you think that?" said Tucker.

"I read it on Wikipedia."

"And did you read about yourself there? Or Jackson?"

"No. It said you were rumored to have one child, with Julie Beatty."

"So why would you believe them when they tell you I live on a farm? Anyway, you have my phone number and my e-mail address. Why didn't you just ask me where I lived?"

"It seemed like too weird a question to ask my own father. Maybe you should write your own Wikipedia page. So your children know something about you."

"We have animals," said Jackson defensively. "Chickens. Pomus. One rabbit that died."

The rabbit had been recommended to them as a way to assuage Jackson's fears about the imminent death of his father. Tucker couldn't remember precisely how the idea was supposed to work—maybe that the kid would learn about the natural order of things by looking after a pet over its natural life span, was that it? It made sense at the time, but the rabbit died after two days, and now Jackson talked about his dead rabbit all the time. It was true, however, that he seemed slightly more phlegmatic about the end of Tucker's life, expected any day now.

"The rabbit's buried just over there," Jackson told Lizzie, pointing at the wooden cross on the edge of the lawn. "Dad's going next to him, aren't you, Dad?"

"Yep," said Tucker. "But not yet."

"Soon, though," said Jackson. "Maybe when I'm seven?"

"After that," said Tucker.

"Well. Maybe," said Jackson, doubtfully, as if the point of the conversation was to console Tucker. "Is your mom dead yet, Lizzie?"

"No," said Lizzie.

"Is she well?" Tucker asked.

"She's very well, thank you for asking," said Lizzie. Was there acid in there? Probably. "She was the one who thought I should come to see you."

"Okay," said Tucker.

"It's that thing," said Lizzie.

"Uh-huh." This thing, that thing . . . They all turned out to be the same thing, more or less, so why insist on a definition?

"When you find out you're going to have a kid of your own, you want to understand more about everything else."

"Sure."

"You guessed, didn't you?"

"What?"

"What I just said."

He got the feeling that there had been some information given to him that he hadn't processed properly yet. Maybe he shouldn't treat these getting-to-know-you conversations as a genre.

"Hold on," said Jackson. "That means . . . You're my sister, right?"

"Half sister."

"So . . . I'm going to be . . . What does that mean?"

"You're going to be an uncle."

"Cool."

"And he's going to be a granddad."

Tucker finally understood what he was being told when Jackson burst into tears and went running to find his mother.

Finally, Lizzie thawed a little—at least on the side nearest Jackson, when Tucker led him back a couple of minutes later.

"It doesn't mean your dad's old," she said. "He's not."

"Okay, so how many other kids at my school have dads who are granddads?"

"I'm sure not many."

"None," said Jackson. "Not one."

"Jack, we've been through this," said Tucker. "I'm fifty-five. You're six. I'm gonna live a long time. You'll be a big man before I'm ready to go. Forty, maybe. You'll be sick of me."

Tucker wouldn't want to bet on the life span he was predicting for himself. Thirty years of smoking, ten years of alcohol dependence . . . He'd be amazed if he even got his threescore years and ten.

"You don't know I'll be forty," said Jackson. "You might die tomorrow."

"I'm not going to."

"You might."

Tucker always got sidetracked by the logic in these conversations. Yes, I might die tomorrow, he wanted to say. But that was true even before you found out I was going to be a grandfather. Instead of embarking on paths like these, however, he just had to talk rubbish. Rubbish always worked.

"I can't."

Jackson looked at him, hope renewed.

"Really?"

"Nope. If there's nothing wrong with me today, I can't die tomorrow. There's just not enough time."

"What about a car crash?"

Which anyone of any age could have at any time, you moron.

"Nope."

"Why not?"

"Because we're not going anywhere in the car tomorrow."

"The day after."

"Or the day after."

"How will we get food?"

"We have a ton of food."

Tucker didn't want to be thinking about whether they'd be starved out if they couldn't drive anywhere. He wanted to think about how old he was, and how he was going to die soon, and how his whole life seemed to have slipped away without him noticing.

A while back, Tucker had promised himself that he'd sit down with a piece of paper and try to account for the last couple of decades. He'd write the years down in sequence on the left-hand side, and write down one or two words next to each, words that would at least give some sense of what might have occupied him in those twelve months. The word "booze" and a few ditto marks would do for the end of the eighties; occasionally he'd picked up a guitar or a ballpoint, but mostly he'd just watched TV and poured scotch down his throat until he blacked out. There were other, healthier words he could use later on—"painting," "Cooper and Jesse," "Cat," "Jackson," but actually, even they didn't explain away as many months as he'd be asking them to. How long had he really spent in that tiny apartment he'd rented and used as a studio in the painting years? Six months? And his sons, in the years they were born . . . He'd taken them for walks, sure, but a lot of the time they'd been nursing, or sleeping, and he'd watched them do both. But then, watching was an activity, right? You couldn't do much else, if you were watching.

Occasionally he thought about what his father would have written if faced with a sheet of paper containing a list of all his adult years. He'd had a long, productive life: three kids, a good, strong marriage, his own dry-cleaning business. So what would he write next to, say, '61–'68? "Work"? That one short word would cover seven years of his life perfectly adequately. And Tucker knew for sure what he'd have chosen for 1980: "Europe." Or probably, "EUROPE!" He'd waited a long time to go back, and he'd loved every second of it, and the holiday of a lifetime lasted a month. Four weeks out of the fifty-two! Tucker wasn't trying to flatten out the differences—he knew his dad was the better man. But anyone trying to account for their days in this way was going to wonder where they had all gone, what had been missed.

Jackson was tearful for the rest of the afternoon and early evening. He cried about losing to Lizzie at tic-tac-toe, he cried about having his hair washed, he cried about Tucker dying, he cried about not being allowed to smother his ice cream in chocolate sauce. Tucker and Cat had presumed that he'd stay up and eat with them, but he was so exhausted by his emotional exertion that he ended up going to bed early. Seconds after the boy fell asleep, Tucker realized he'd been using him as a small but effective hostage: nobody could get a clear shot in while Jackson was around. When he went downstairs and rejoined Cat and Lizzie in the garden, he was just in time to hear Cat saying, wryly, "Well, he'll do that to you."

"Who'll do what to who?" he said, cheerfully.

"Lizzie was just telling me about her mom being hospitalized after you dumped her."

"Oh."

"You never told me about that."

"It just never came up when we started dating."

"Funny, huh?"

"Not really," said Lizzie.

And they took on from there. Cat decided that she already felt comfortable enough around her new stepdaughter to give her a candid assessment of the state of her marriage; Lizzie reciprocated with a candid assessment of the damage Tucker had caused through his absence. (She held her stomach protectively all the way through her complaint, Tucker noticed, as if he were about to attack her unborn child with a knife at any moment.) Tucker nodded sagely at various points, and occasionally shook his head sympathetically. Every now and again, when both women simply stared at him, he'd shrug and stare at the ground. There didn't seem an awful lot of point in attempting to defend himself, and anyway he wasn't absolutely sure what line of defense he would have taken. There were a couple of errors of fact embedded in the stories they told each other, but nothing worth correcting. Who really cared that, in her bitterness and rage, Natalie had told Lizzie that he'd slept with another woman *in her apartment*, for example? It was only the location she had wrong, not the act of infidelity itself. The only word that would have explained anything, most of the time, was "drunk." He could have said that, at regular intervals, possibly even after every sentence, but it almost certainly wouldn't have helped.

At the end of the evening, he showed Lizzie to her room and wished her good night.

"Was that all okay?" she said, and she made a face, as if he'd spent the evening dealing with acute heartburn.

"Oh, yeah, fine. You were owed."

"I hope you sort things out with Cat. She's lovely."

"Yeah. Thanks. Good night. Sleep well."

Tucker went back downstairs, but Cat had gone. She had used his absence as an excuse to go to bed without him, and without explanations. They mostly slept in separate rooms now, but they were at a peculiar stage in their relationship where this wasn't accepted as a given: they talked about it every night. Or it got mentioned, at least. "Are you okay in the spare room?" Cat would say, and Tucker would shrug and nod. A couple of times, after a really savage argument that seemed to push them to the point of no return, he'd followed her into their bedroom, and eventually they'd swung things around. There was no talking about it tonight, though. She'd just vanished.

Tucker went to bed, read a little, turned the light out. But he couldn't sleep. *It isn't you really, is it?* that woman had asked, and he started to phrase answers to the question in his head. Eventually he got up and went downstairs to the computer. Annie was going to get more than she'd bargained for.

five

From: Tucker
<alfredmantalini@yonder
horizon.com

Subject: Re: Re: Your Review

Dear Annie,

It really is me, although I can't think of a
good way of proving it to you. How about
this: nothing happened to me in a restroom
in Minneapolis. Or this: I don't have a secret
love child with Julie Beatty. Or this: I stopped
recording altogether after I made the album
Juliet, so I don't have two hundred albums'
worth of material locked away in a shed,
nor do I regularly release material under an

assumed name. Does that help? Probably
not, unless you are sane enough to believe
that the truth about anyone is disappointing,
the truth about me especially so. This is due
to an unfortunate turn of events: the longer I
spent doing nothing at all, aside from watching TV and drinking, the more a small but
impressively imaginative number of people
seemed to be convinced that I was doing
a whole procession of outlandish things—
making hip-hop albums with Lauryn Hill in
Colorado, for example, or making a movie
with Steve Ditko in Los Angeles. I wish I knew
Lauryn Hill and/or Steve Ditko, because I
admire both of them greatly (and because
I'd make myself some money somehow), but
I don't. The fact is, some of these myths are
so colorful that they have deterred me from
re-entering the world; it seems to me that
people were having more fun with me gone
than they could ever have if I was around. Can
you imagine, if I were to give an interview, for
example, to the kind of music magazine still
interested in someone like me? "No, I didn't.
No, I haven't. No, we weren't . . ." It would be

so dull as to be unconvincing. Anyone can say they haven't done anything.

Today I learned that I am going to be a grandfather. As I don't really know the pregnant daughter in question—I don't really know four of my five children, by the way—I was not able to feel joyful. For me, the only real emotional content of the news was the symbolism, what it said about me. I don't feel bad about that, particularly. There's no point in pretending to feel joy when someone you don't know very well tells you she's pregnant, although I suppose I do feel bad that various decisions I've made and avoided have reduced my daughter to the status of a stranger.

Anyway, the symbolism . . . Learning that I was about to become a grandfather felt like reading my own obituary, and what I read made me feel really sad. I haven't done much with whatever talents I was given, whatever your friends on the website think, nor have I been very successful in other areas of my life. The children I never see are products of relationships I messed up, through my indolence and my drinking; the child I do see, my beloved six-year-old son, Jackson, is the product of a relationship that I'm in the process of messing up. His mother has been supporting me for a few years now, so I owe her a lot, but understandably I have begun to irritate her, and her irritation makes me grouchy and defensive.

She thought that our relationship might work because we are different. And though it's true that she is practical and financially astute (she is a wholesaler of organic produce), and can enjoy lengthy business meetings with people who care about money and fruit, these qualities have turned out to be of little use to us when it comes to getting along. I don't value them as much as I should, and in any case my impracticality is no longer allied with my ability to write songs, since I no longer write songs. The artistic temperament is particularly unhelpful if it is just that, with no end product. (I must confess to being as confused as I have ever been, when it comes to the subject of compatibility. I have tried to live with women whose sensibility is similar to mine, with predictably disastrous consequences, but the opposite route seems every bit as hopeless. We get together with people because they're the same or because they're different, and in the end we split with them for exactly the same reasons. I am coming to the conclusion that I need a woman who admires fecklessness and indolence in a man; whether that woman is the CEO of a Wall Street investment firm or a graffiti artist makes no difference to me.)

I had completely forgotten about the existence of those *Juliet* demos until a few months ago, when somebody I used to know found them on a shelf somewhere. He was the one who arranged to release them on CD, but I didn't mind, even though I agree with every word you said about their crudity: I worked and worked on the official versions of those songs, and so did my band, and the idea that a person with ears could listen to those two sets of recordings and decide that the shitty, sketchy one is better than the one we sweated blood over is baffling to me. (To be honest, I would drop every single one of that guy's bootleg collection, all the one hundred and twenty-seven albums he foolishly boasts about owning, on his head, and ban him from listening to music ever again.) But the release of *Naked* was a way of reminding myself that I was once capable of some kind of action; and in any case, I was given a small advance, which I was able to hand straight over to my wife. For an afternoon, I almost felt like a man, bringing home the bacon for his family.

I have given you too much information, I suspect, but I don't see that you can seriously doubt whether I am me. I am very much me, and today I am very much wishing I wasn't.

With best wishes,
Tucker Crowe

Tucker's reply was waiting for Annie when she arrived at work. She could have checked her e-mail on her home computer, before breakfast, and of course she'd been excited enough to have wanted to. But if there had been a reply, there was a chance that Duncan might have seen it, and easily the best thing in her life at the moment was her secret. It had been the best thing even yesterday, when all she'd received were two functional but still amazing messages that gave very little away, but now she had information that Duncan would have regarded as the key to unlocking the mysteries of the universe. She didn't want him to have that key, for all sorts of reasons, most of them ignoble.

She read the e-mail twice, three times, and then went to get her coffee early. She needed to think. Or rather, she needed to stop thinking about the stuff she was thinking about, if she were to have a chance of thinking about anything else today; and what she was thinking about, more than Tucker Crowe and his complicated life, even, was how *Naked* had poisoned the air that she breathed in her home.

The night before, Duncan had come home late and smelling of drink; he was monosyllabic, curt even, when she'd asked him about his day. He'd fallen asleep quickly, but she had lain awake, listening to him snoring and not liking him. Everyone disliked their partners at some time or another, she knew that. But she'd spent her hours in the dark wondering whether she'd ever liked him. Would it really have been so much worse to spend those years alone? Why did there have to be someone else in the room while she was eating, watching TV, sleeping? A partner was supposed to be some mark of success: anyone who shared a bed with someone on a nightly basis had proved herself capable in some way, no? Of something? But her relationship now seemed to her to betoken failure, not success. She and Duncan had ended up together because they were the last two people to be picked for a sports team, and she felt she was better at sports than that.

"Hello, gorgeous," said Franco, the man in the coffee bar.

"Hello," she said. "Usual, please."

Would he have said "Hello, gorgeous" if she were bad at sports, as it were? Or was she reading too much into a cheesy greeting from a man who probably said it twenty times a day?

"How many times a day do you say that?" she said. "As a matter of interest?"

"Honestly?"

"Honestly."

"Only once."

She laughed, and he looked mock hurt.

"You don't see who comes in here," said Franco. "I could say 'Hello, gorgeous' to people who look like my mother or my grandmother. I used to. But it feels wrong. So I keep it for you, my youngest customer."

His youngest customer! Was everything an accident of geography? She could believe it about this town. Franco wouldn't have said what he said if his coffee bar were in London or Manchester; she wouldn't have sleepwalked through fifteen years with Duncan if she lived in Birmingham or Edinburgh. Gooleness was the wind and the sea and the old, the smell of fried food that somehow clung on even when nobody seemed to be frying anything, the ice-cream kiosks that seemed to be boarded up even when there were people around . . . And there was the past. There was 1964, and the Rolling Stones, and the dead shark, and the happy vacationers. Somebody had to live there. It might as well be her.

On the way back to the office she realized that it was Thursday, and Thursday was the day that Moira worked at the front desk. Moira was a Friend of the Museum who was convinced that Annie's childlessness was the result of some lack, a lack that could be cured. She was right, probably, but not in the way she thought. There had been absolutely no conversation prior to Moira's intervention, which had apparently been prompted entirely by Annie's age, rather than by any longing that she had articulated to this woman she didn't actually know. Annie hated Thursdays.

Today it was celery. Moira, a sprightly octogenarian with a fine head of purple-tinged hair, was standing there waiting for her, with a big bunch.

"Hello," said Annie.

"The leaves are what you want. What he wants, anyway."

"Thank you."

"Have you got a blender?"

"I think so."

"Just whizz the leaves up in that and make him drink it."

"Nothing for me? No tea, or seeds, or fruit dipped in milk?"

"Well, we've tried everything for you. So it must be him."

Technically, Moira was right: it was him. He wore a condom.

"I'll try it tonight."

"If you try it tonight, you have to try everything. If you see what I mean. Down in one and upstairs."

"I'll try it Saturday night, then."

Oh, dear God. Why on earth was she giving this woman information about their sexual timetable?

"Oh. He's a Saturday-night man, is he?"

"I should get on with some work."

"Nothing to be ashamed of."

"I'm not ashamed."

But of course she was. She was ashamed of the implied monotony and she was ashamed of her inability to tell the meddling old crone where to get off.

"Oh. Alan. Hello. We don't see you in here very often."

Moira was addressing a man in his seventies who appeared to be wearing both an overcoat and a raincoat, as well as two or maybe even three scarves. He was clutching a jam jar containing what looked like a rotting pickled onion swimming in murky vinegar.

"Someone said you were interested in the shark."

"We are," said Moira, firmly. "Very."

"I've got his eye."

From: Annie Platt
<annie@annienduncan.net

Subject: Beyond Reasonable Doubt . . .

. . . It's you. I read enough fiction to know it's detail that makes a story seem real, and anyone who has gone to all the trouble of making that lot up deserves a reply anyway. And if it's not you, I don't really care, to be honest. I'm having an e-mail conversation with an interesting and thoughtful man who lives a long way away, so where's the harm? (I suppose there's another way of looking at this, which is that you're a lunatic, and all your children and grandchildren are simply the product of a damaged mind. If it turns out that you're a lunatic *I might actually know*, then I swear to God I will kill you. But please ignore that if you're not. And I'm proceeding on the basis that it's you.)

As you have probably worked out, I know people who think a lot of your work, and who think a lot about you. I have thought about you sometimes, but not that often, until relatively recently. Your name cropped up once or twice on a trip I took recently. And your new album, *Juliet, Naked*—or rather, the response to it that a couple of overenthusiastic fans had—got me thinking more about you, and about *Juliet*, than I'd ever done before. I have never written anything like that before, either, but the two albums helped me to see some things that I suspect I've always thought about art and the people who consume it ravenously, but which weren't quite in focus. Of course, there are a lot of things I would like to ask you about your missing two decades, but you probably don't want to be interviewed.

I'm sure that if you put any two random strangers in a room together and got them to talk about their lives, all sorts of patterns and themes and opposites would emerge, to the extent that it would look as though they hadn't been chosen randomly at all. For example: you have too many children who

you don't know, and it's making you unhappy.
I have none, and I don't think I will have any,
and that's making me unhappy, more so than
I would have believed possible, three or four
years ago. So all the time I've spent with
the man that I'm not having children with
is beginning to look like all the time you've
spent drinking and not making albums.
Neither of us will get that time back. And yet,
agonizingly, it's not quite too late either. Do
you ever think that? I hope you do.

I am writing this from my office, which is
in a small seaside museum in a small town in
the northern half of England. I am supposed
to be preparing an exhibition about the
summer of 1964 in this town, but we don't
have very much to exhibit, apart from some
rather unpleasant photos of a dead shark
that got washed up on the beach that year.
And, as of this morning, an eye that apparently belonged to the shark, once upon a
time. A couple of hours ago, a man came into
the museum with something, very possibly
a shark's eye, floating in vinegar in a jam jar.
The man claimed his brother had cut it out of
the shark with a penknife. So far, it's our prize

exhibit. You wouldn't like to write a concept
album about the summer of 1964 in a small
English seaside town, would you? Although it
still wouldn't give me much to show.

She stopped typing. If she'd been using pen and paper,
she would have screwed the paper up in disgust, but
there wasn't a satisfying equivalent with e-mail, seeing as
everything was designed to stop you making a mistake.
She needed a fuck-it key, something that made a satisfying
ka-boom noise when you thumped it. What was she doing?
She'd just received communication from a recluse, a man
who had been hiding from the world for twenty-odd years,
and she was telling him about the shark's eye in a jam jar.
Did he really want to know about that? And what about
her need to have a child? Why not tell someone else? A
friend, say. Or even Duncan, who as far as she knew was
unaware of her unhappiness.

And she was flirting, in her own reserved and complicated way. She wanted him to like her. How else to explain
the circumlocutions about the Tucker Tour of America,
and her relationship with "people who think a lot" of his
work? It would have been much simpler to say that the
man she lived with, the man she wasn't having babies with,
was a Tucker Crowe obsessive, but she didn't want Tucker

to know that. Why not? Did she think he was going to jump on a plane and impregnate her, unless he found out what kind of person she lived with? Even if they embarked on a passionate affair, she could imagine it would be difficult to persuade Tucker not to take precautions, given the unwieldy and unhappy family he already had. Oh, God! Even the self-directed sarcasm was pathetic. It still involved jokes about contraceptive arrangements with a man she had never met.

But if she didn't write about shark's eyes, what was she going to tell him? He'd read everything she had to say about his work, and she couldn't just bombard him with questions—she sensed that would be a good way of never hearing from him again. She was the wrong person to engage in an e-mail correspondence with Tucker Crowe. She didn't know enough, she didn't do enough. She wouldn't reply.

She was supposed to be composing a delicate letter to Terry Jackson, the town councillor who'd had the stupid idea for the 1964 exhibition in the first place, but she couldn't concentrate. She reopened the e-mail to Tucker.

> **Where did *Juliet* come from? Do you know?**
> **Have you read *Chronicles*, Bob Dylan's**
> **autobiography? There's a bit in there where**
> **someone, a producer maybe, tells him that**

they need a song like "Masters of War" (was
it that one?) to finish the album off—this is in
the eighties, when he was recording

But she couldn't remember the name of the album either,
and she couldn't remember what Dylan said when the
producer whose name she couldn't remember asked Dylan
for a song like the song she couldn't remember, to finish
off whatever the album was. She deleted what might have
been an interesting line of inquiry. Duncan would know
it all, of course, and Duncan should be the one writing to
Tucker, except that Tucker wouldn't want to hear from
him. And, of course, she still hadn't told Duncan about
what she'd found in her in-box, and she didn't want to,
either.

She didn't need to know anything about Dylan, she
realized eventually. She was just using a book to make her
point for her, the way academics do.

Where did *Juliet* come from? Do you know?
And what happens to those places? Do they
just get overgrown? Or might you stumble
across them one day? I'm sorry if that seems
too nosy, and I've just promised myself that I
wouldn't bombard you with questions. If you

want to see any photos of my dead shark,
just shout. That seems to be all I have to offer
in return.

By the way, when I got home last night I
started reading *Nicholas Nickleby*, in your
honour.

Was that last line too creepy? Bad luck if it was. It was
true, anyway. This time, she clicked on "send" before she
could change her mind.

six

It was okay, Duncan thought, that he and Annie had never been in love. Theirs had been an arranged marriage, and it had functioned perfectly well: friends had matched up their interests and temperaments carefully, and they'd got it right. He had never once felt itchy, in the way that two connecting pieces of a jigsaw never felt itchy, as far as one could tell. If one were to imagine, for the sake of argument, that jigsaw pieces had thoughts and feelings, then it was possible to imagine them saying to themselves, "I'm going to stay here. Where else would I go?" And if another jigsaw piece came along, offering its tabs and blanks enticingly in an attempt to lure one of the pieces away, it would be easy to resist temptation. "Look," the object of the seducer's admiration would say, "you're a piece of a phone booth, and I'm the face of Mary, Queen of Scots. We just wouldn't look right together." And that would be that.

He was now beginning to wonder whether the jigsaw was the correct metaphor for relationships between men and women after all. It didn't take account of the sheer stubbornness of human beings, their determination to affix themselves to another even if they didn't fit. They didn't care about jutting off at weird angles, and they didn't care about phone booths and Mary, Queen of Scots. They were motivated not by seamless and sensible matching, but by eyes, mouths, smiles, minds, breasts and chests and bottoms, wit, kindness, charm, romantic history and all sorts of other things that made straight edges impossible to achieve.

And jigsaw pieces were not known for their passion, really, either. People could be passionate about jigsaws, but the jigsaws themselves were orderly—passionless, even, you could say. And it seemed to Duncan that passion was a part of being human. He valued it in his music and his books and his TV shows: Tucker Crowe was passionate, Tony Soprano, too. But he had never really valued it in his own life, and maybe now he was paying the price, by falling in love at an inopportune time. Later, he wondered whether *Juliet, Naked* had done something to him—woken him up, shaken some part of him that had gone numb. He'd certainly been more emotional in the days since he first heard it, prone to sudden lurches in the stomach and the occasional, inexplicable prickle of tears.

Gina was a new staff member at the Advanced Performing Arts program, teaching pimply and deluded teenagers that they would never, ever be famous—or, at least, not in their chosen fields, although Duncan harbored the suspicion that some of them were insane enough to stalk and eventually murder somebody they idolized. Gina was a singer, an actor, a dancer, and though she still harbored dreams of doing some of those things professionally, life had worn all of the dreaminess off her. The people who worked in Advanced Performing Arts were freakishly young-looking middle-aged men and women, always waiting for phone calls that never came from touring theater companies and agents; but if Gina still blew on those hopes to keep them glowing gently, she did it outside college hours. And she didn't talk about herself all the time, either, despite having spiky hennaed hair and a lot of chunky jewelry. She sat next to him on a coffee break on her second day, asked him questions, listened to his answers, proved herself to be knowledgeable about some of the things that were important to him. The day after, when she asked whether she could borrow the first season of *The Wire* and told him that she'd taken the job to get away from a terminally ill relationship, he knew he was in trouble. Two days after that, he was wondering what happened when a jigsaw piece told his interlocking friend that he wanted to join a different puzzle altogether. And also, less whimsically, he was wondering what sex with Gina would be like, and whether he'd ever find out.

He'd made very few friends on the staff, mostly because he regarded his colleagues as uncultured bores, even the ones who taught arts courses. And they in turn thought he was a weirdo, forever chasing up some obscure tributary of the mainstream to get to the source of whatever he happened to be interested in that week. They thought he was faddish, but in Duncan's opinion that was because their tastes were set, like concrete, and if the next Dylan came to perform for them in the staff room, they'd roll their eyes and continue to look for new jobs in the *Education Guardian*. Duncan hated them, and that was partly why he'd fallen so hard for Gina, who seemed to recognize that major works of art were being created every day. She was going to be his soul mate, and in a town like this, with its cold, gray sea and its bingo halls and its shivering senior citizens, soul mates came along every couple of hundred years, probably. How was it possible not to think about sex, in those circumstances?

They went out for a drink on the day he took Season One of *The Wire* into work with him, hidden inside a newspaper and then placed in his satchel so that Annie wouldn't see what he was up to. Of course, it was only the secrecy of the act that would have given her any idea, so presumably the smuggling was for his benefit, rather than hers, a way of investing a mundane loan with the faintest scent of adultery. He called Annie to tell her he was going to be late getting home, but she, too, was still at work, and she didn't seem to be troubled by, or even curious about, his whereabouts. She'd been weird, the last few days. He wouldn't be at all surprised if she'd met someone, too. Wouldn't that be perfect? Although he wouldn't want her to leave until he had worked out whether this thing with Gina had potential, and it was early days, as yet, seeing as they hadn't actually been on a date.

They cycled, at Duncan's insistence, to a quiet pub on the other side of town, on the other side of the docks, away from students and staff. She drank cider, a choice Duncan admired, although he was in that frame of mind where anything she ordered—white wine, Baileys and Coke—would have demonstrated her sophistication and exotic singularity. A pint of cider suddenly seemed like the drink he'd been wanting all his life.

"So. Cheers. Welcome aboard."

"Thank you."

They took a big pull of their drinks, and made appreciative lip-smacking sounds indicating (a) that they'd earned this drink and (b) they didn't really know what to say to each other.

"Oh. So." He delved into his bag and produced the boxed set. "Here it is."

"Great. What's it like? I mean, what other programs is it like?"

"Nothing, really. That's what's so great about it. It sort of breaks all the rules. It's a one-off. Unique."

"Like me." She laughed, but Duncan saw the opportunity to inject some early sincerity into the occasion.

"I think that's right," he said. "I mean, obviously there are loads of ways in which, you know, you're different from, well, from an American TV series about Baltimore's underclass. It's actually about lots of other things, too, but all the other things it's about doesn't make it more like you, if you see what I mean, so I won't go into them." This wasn't coming out right, but he was going to plow on anyway. "But in some important ways, you're the same."

"Really? Go on. I'm very curious." She looked amused, rather than appalled. Perhaps he could get away with this.

"Well. I've only just met you. But when you were sitting in the staff room earlier today . . ." He just wanted to pay her a compliment, tell her that he found her attractive, that he was glad she'd come to teach at the college. But now he was stuck with this stupid *Wire* thing. "Well, you stuck out like a sore thumb. In a good way, not a sore-thumb way. Everyone else there is so staid and bitter, and you lit the place up. You're cheerful, and energetic, and pretty, and . . . Okay, *The Wire* isn't cheerful. Or pretty. But when you look at all the other programs around. Well, you just have to look at it. And you."

He thought he'd got away with it, just about.

"Thank you. I hope you won't end up disappointed."

"Oh, I won't."

The terminally ill relationship that Gina had left behind in Manchester was with a choreographer who idolized his mother and hadn't touched her in two years, or said anything kind to her in three. He was almost certainly gay, and hated Gina for failing to cure him of his attraction to other men. What she most wanted in the world was a kind, attentive man who clearly found her attractive. Sometimes you can see car crashes from a long way off, if the road is straight and both vehicles are heading toward each other in the same lane.

Gina vaguely remembered Tucker Crowe, but she was happy to be educated. The day after their drink, Duncan played her *Naked* and *Dressed*, back to back, on her iPod in her small and heartbreakingly under-furnished one-bedroom apartment up the hill at the back of the town, away from the sea and from Annie, and they went to bed together shortly afterward, when she'd said exactly the right things about the rawness and unadorned simplicity of *Naked*. To Duncan anyway, it was sex that felt like sex, too, something needy and alarmingly uncontrollable, rather than something that happened on Saturdays after he and Annie had rented a DVD. Forty-eight excruciating hours after that, in the Indian restaurant around the corner, he was telling Annie that he'd met somebody else.

She was calm when he told her.

"Right," she said. "And by 'met,' I presume we're talking about something more than meeting."

"Yes."

"You've slept with her."

"Yes."

Duncan was sweating, and his heart was racing. He felt sick. Fifteen years! Or more, even! Was it really possible simply to jump from the belly of a fifteen-year relationship into the clear blue sky? Was it allowed? Or would he and Annie be made to attend courses, to see counselors, to go away together for a year or two and explore what had gone wrong? But who would make them? Nobody, that's who. And there was alarmingly little tying him down. He was one of the first people to complain about the increasing encroachment of the state into personal lives, but, actually, shouldn't there be a little more encroachment, when it came to things like this? Where was the protective fence, or the safety net? They made it hard for you to jump off bridges, or to smoke, to own a gun, to become a gynecolo-

gist. So how come they let you walk out on a stable, func-
tioning relationship? They shouldn't. If this didn't work
out, he could see himself become a homeless, jobless alcoholic within a year. And that would be worse for his health
than a packet of Marlboros.

"I should qualify that. Yes, I've, I've, you know, yes, slept
with her, as you say, but it may well have been a mistake.
Can I ask you: do you find this very upsetting? Because I
have to say, I do. I didn't really think it through."

"So why are you telling me about it?"

"Would it have been an option for you? Me not telling you?"

"It's a choice that's rather difficult to offer, though, isn't
it? It was an option for you. But you can't really ask me
whether I want to know whether you've slept with someone else or not. I'd have smelled a rat."

"Unless I'd asked you when I hadn't slept with someone else, I suppose. If I'd asked you right at the beginning,
and then kept asking you . . ."

"Duncan!"

He jumped. She hardly ever shouted.

"Yes. Sorry. I got sidetracked."

"Are you telling me you want out?"

"I don't know. I did know. But now I don't. It suddenly
seems like a big thing to say."

"And it didn't earlier on?"

"Not . . . not as big as it should have done, no."

"Who are you sleeping with?"

"It's not . . . I wouldn't use the present continuous. There's been an, an incident. So 'Who have you slept with?' is probably the question. Or, 'With whom did this possibly one-off incident take place?'"

Annie was looking at him as if she might kill him with her cutlery.

"She's a new colleague at work."

"Right."

She waited, and he began to babble.

"She . . . Well, I was just very attracted to her immediately."

Still nothing.

"It's been a long time, in fact, since I've been as, as drawn to somebody as I am to her."

Silence, but of a deeper and altogether more menacing quality.

"And she loved *Naked*. I played it to her last . . ."

"Oh, for Christ's sake."

"Sorry."

He knew he should apologize, but he wasn't entirely sure what for. It wasn't that he was innocent of all charges, or even that he felt he had any kind of defense. It was just that he was no longer sure how many offenses he'd committed. Annie's irritation at the mention of *Naked* . . . Was that because he'd played it to Gina? Or because she'd liked it, when Annie hadn't?

"I do not want to talk about Tucker fucking Crowe in the middle of this."

So that was probably it: he shouldn't have mentioned Tucker at all. He could see that.

"Sorry. Again."

For the first time in a couple of minutes, Duncan found the courage to look at Annie's eyes. There was an awful lot to be said for familiarity, if you thought about it. It was an extremely underrated virtue, ignorable until the very moment that you were in danger of losing whatever or whoever it was that was familiar—a house, a view, a partner. This was all ridiculous. He would have to extricate himself from the other situation. Surely, with the henna and the clunky jewelry, Gina must be used to one-night stands. Oh, that sounded terrible. He didn't mean that. He just meant that she must have moved in circles where the one-night stand didn't seem particularly shocking. She'd been in touring musicals, for God's sake. He'd just ignore the whole thing, pretend it hadn't happened and avoid her during coffee breaks.

"I'm not moving out of my home," said Annie.

"No. Of course not. Nobody's asking you to."

"Good. As long as that's clear."

"Completely."

"So what's reasonable?"

"What's reasonable? About what?"

"Tomorrow?"

"What's happening tomorrow?"

He hoped that she was talking about a social arrangement he'd forgotten. He hoped that normal life was reasserting itself, and they could put this misfortune behind them.

"You're moving out," said Annie.

"Oh. Wow. Ha. No, no, that's not what I'm talking about," said Duncan.

"It may not be. But it's what I'm talking about. Duncan, I have just wasted half my life with you. What was left of my youth, in fact. I'm not going to waste another day."

She picked up her bag, drew out a ten-pound note, threw it on the table and walked out.

seven

"And how do you feel about that?"

"I feel shitty, Malcolm. How do you think I feel?"

"Define . . . that word."

"Like shit."

"You can do better than that, Annie. You're an articulate young woman. And I'll put ten pence in the swear box for you."

"Please don't."

"I'll let you off the first one, but the second was gratuitous. I don't think it's a good idea to break rules. Whatever the circumstances."

Malcolm fumbled around in his pocket, found a coin and put it in the novelty piggy bank he kept on the bookshelf behind his head. The piggy bank was designed to spin the coin around and around before it came to its final resting place, so for the next minute or so there was silence; neither of them wanted to speak until the spinning had stopped. It seemed to take even longer than usual for the reassuring clink indicating that this ten pence had joined the others, all of them representing oaths uttered by Annie in extremis, none of them anything that would shock a ten-year-old.

A few months before, Annie had told Ros that, out of all her dysfunctional relationships, it was the one with Malcolm that caused her the most anxiety. Until the Friday-night curry, Duncan hadn't been particularly troublesome; she only spoke to her mother for fifteen minutes a week, and saw her rarely since she'd gone to live in Devon. But Malcolm . . . Malcolm she saw every Saturday morning, for a whole hour, and every time she'd raised the subject of not seeing him every Saturday morning, or at any other time, he'd become visibly distressed. Whenever Annie thought about leaving town and her job for Manchester or London or Barcelona, the Malcolmlessness of these places came up embarrassingly early in the fantasy—after the absence of Duncan, probably, but sooner than the attractions of food or weather or culture.

Malcolm was her therapist. She'd seen a business card on the bulletin board in the health center when she first started to become depressed about childlessness, but almost immediately she'd known that Malcolm wasn't right: he was too nervous, too old, too easily shocked, even by Annie, who never did anything to shock anybody. When she'd tried to tell him that he wasn't right for her, however, he had begged her to reconsider, and had dropped his fee from thirty pounds an hour to fifteen, and then, finally, to five. It turned out that Annie was his first and only client. He'd taken early retirement from the Civil Service to train, it had been his ambition for more than a decade, he would learn quickly, he was the only serious therapist in Gooleness anyway, he'd never find anyone as interesting or as sensitive as her . . . Annie simply hadn't had the heart, or the necessary steel, to walk away, and she'd been enduring the spinning coins for two years now. She'd refused to entertain the notion of the swear box, which was why it was always Malcolm's ten-pence pieces that got spun. Why he was so committed to the swear box at all, she had no real idea.

"Why are you so committed to the swear box?"

"We're here to talk about you."

"But don't you ever watch TV? People say . . . that word all the time."

"I watch television. I just don't watch those programs. People don't seem to feel the need to swear on *Antiques Roadshow*."

"You see, Malcolm, that's exactly the sort of remark that makes me think we're not right for each other."

"What? Me saying that people don't swear on the programs I watch?"

"But you have such a prissy way of saying it."

"I'm sorry. I'm trying to learn to be less prissy."

He said it quietly, and humbly, and with a perceptibly self-flagellating tone. Annie felt terrible, as she often did when talking to Malcolm about nothing much. This was why she eventually ended up giving in, telling him the sorts of things she was supposed to share with a therapist, stuff about her parents and her hapless love life: it took them away from the depressing, awkward small talk.

"Humiliated," she said, suddenly.

"Sorry?"

"You were asking me to do better in my description of how I'm feeling. I feel humiliated."

"Of course you do."

"Angry with myself, as well as him."

"Because?"

"Because this was always going to happen. He was going to meet someone, or I was going to meet someone, and that would be it. So I should have got out ages ago. It was just inertia. And now I've been sh . . . dumped on."

Malcolm went quiet. Annie knew that this was a technique analysts were supposed to use: if they waited long enough, then the person undergoing analysis would eventually shout out "I slept with my father!" and everyone could go home. She also knew that, with Malcolm, the reverse was true. If Annie waited for long enough, he would fill his own silences by saying something stupid, and they would argue. Sometimes they spent the entire fifty minutes arguing, which at least made the time go quickly. Malcolm's interjections carried with them no disadvantage that Annie could see, as long as she succeeded in sloughing off the irritation of their inanity.

"It's funny, you know, with your generation." It was all Annie could do to stop herself from licking her lips in anticipation of the fuddy-duddy provocation that was almost bound to follow an introduction like that.

"What is, Malcolm?"

"Well, lots of people I know have an unhappy or frustrating marriage. Or a boring one."

"And?"

"You see, they're quite content, really."

"They're happy in their misery."

"They put up with it, yes."

Never before had Malcolm so neatly summarized the absurd paradox of his ambition, Annie felt. He was an Englishman of a certain age and class, from a certain part of the country, and Englishmen like him believed that there was almost nothing too grim to be endured. To complain was to show weakness, so things got worse and worse, and people became more and more stoical. And yet counseling was nothing without complaint. That was the basis of it, really, airing dissatisfactions and hurts in the hope that something could be done about them. Annie started to laugh.

"What have I said now?" said Malcolm wearily.

Annie could hear her mother's voice in there somewhere. It was the tone she used when Annie had taken her to task for saying that the IRA killed people, or that children needed their fathers—actually, Annie could see now, relatively unobjectionable banalities that in the exotic political climate of the early eighties, had come to sound like incendiary fascist slogans.

"Do you really think you're in the right job?"

"Why wouldn't I be?"

"Well, the reason I come to you at all is because I don't want to be quite content with my unhappy, boring, frustrating marriage. I want more. And you think I'm a bit of a crybaby. You'll probably end up thinking that anyone who sits in this chair is a bit of a crybaby, really."

Malcolm stared hard at the carpet, which was presumably where this conundrum had ended up somehow.

"Well," he said. "I'm not sure that's it."

"So what is it? If it's not that?"

"You said you don't want to be quite content."

"Yes. With. A. Rubbish. Life." She said it as if he were deaf, which of course he might well have been. She became momentarily distracted while she tried to decide whether deafness might have played a part in the unsatisfactory nature of their sessions. When Malcolm didn't seem to hear what she was saying, was it because he wasn't able to?

"The context is important."

"But people who are quite content don't have a rubbish life," he said.

Annie opened her mouth, ready to fire off the dismissive one-liner that always came to her whenever Malcolm offered any kind of observation, but to her surprise, there was nothing there. Her mouth was empty. Could he be right? Did the contentment count more than the life? It was the first time she'd thought about anything Malcolm had ever said to her.

She had never told Duncan that she went to talk about her problems on Saturday mornings. He was under the impression that she went to the gym, or shopping. He wouldn't have been unhappy about it, if he'd found out. He'd have worn it as a badge of honor, even though he hadn't been directly involved in the therapeutic battlefield: for him it would have been yet another example of the kind of thing that separated them from, raised them above, the rest of Gooleness. So that was one reason she kept it a secret. The other was that she didn't really have any problems, apart from Duncan. That he wouldn't have wanted to know, not at first—and then he would have wanted to know everything, and it would have been impossible. So she took her swimming things out with her, or came back with a secondhand book from the thrift shop, or a pair of cheap shoes, or a bagful of groceries, and Malcolm stayed a secret. When she left Malcolm's house up near the elementary school and started to walk back into town, she realized that she didn't need to buy anything to prove to Duncan that she hadn't been telling a complete stranger how much he disappointed her. It felt strange, walking home empty-handed. Strange, a little risky, and, yes, of course, a little sad. It was lies like those that reminded her that she had someone to go home to. But when she got back to her newly empty house, Duncan was sitting in it, waiting for her.

"I've made us some coffee," he said. "In a pot."

The pot was significant, otherwise he wouldn't have mentioned it. Duncan thought that real coffee was a bit of a fuss, what with all the waiting and the plunging, and claimed to be happy with instant. This morning's gesture was presumably intended as some kind of penance for his infidelity.

"Gee, thanks."

"Don't be like that."

"Why would I care what coffee you drink?"

"If I hadn't slept with someone else you'd be pleased."

"If you hadn't slept with someone else you'd be drinking instant."

Duncan conceded the point by saying nothing and taking a sip from his mug.

"You're right, though. It's much nicer."

Annie wondered how many similar concessions Duncan would have to make before they'd have a relationship that might conceivably last them for the rest of their lives. A thousand? And after that, he could begin to work on the things that really bothered her.

"Why are you here?"

"Well. I mean, I still live here, don't I?"

"You tell me."

"I don't think you can just tell someone whether you're living with them or not. It's more a consensual thing," said Duncan.

"Do you want to live here?"

"I don't know. I've got myself into a bit of a mess, haven't I?"

"You have, yes. I should warn, you, Duncan: I'm not going to fight for you. The whole point of you is that you're not the sort of person anyone fights over. You're my easy life option. The moment you stop being that, you're no option at all."

"Right. Well. That's telling me straight. Thank you."

Annie shrugged, an it-was-nothing gesture that capped what she felt had been a flawless couple of minutes.

"Would you say there's any way back for me? If that's what I wanted?"

"Not when you phrase it like that, no."

One thing was clear: the rest of Duncan's Friday night hadn't gone well. Annie was tempted to press him for details, but even in her anger she could recognize that the impulse was not a healthy one. It was easy to imagine, though, that this other woman would have been extremely disconcerted by Duncan's appearance on her doorstep, if that's where he'd gone. He'd never been equipped with a great deal of diplomacy, intuition or charm, even when they'd first started seeing each other, and the little he did possess would have been eroded by fifteen years of underuse. Clearly, this poor woman was lonely—it was almost impossible to arrive in Gooleness from somewhere else without leaving a trail of unhappiness and failure behind—but anyone desperate enough to usher Duncan straight into her life at eleven o'clock on a Friday night would be unemployable, possibly even under medical supervision. Annie's guess was that he'd spent a sleepless night on a couch.

"So what should I do?" It wasn't a rhetorical question. He was looking to Annie for some firm advice.

"You need to find somewhere to stay, preferably this morning. And after that, we'll just have to see."

"But what about my . . ."

"You should have thought about that before."

"I'll just go upstairs and . . ."

"You do what you have to do. I'll go out for a couple of hours."

Later, she wondered how he would have finished the question. What about his what? If she'd been marched down to a bookmaker's at gunpoint and asked to place a bet on what it was Duncan felt he couldn't live without for a couple of days, she'd have put her money on Tucker Crowe bootlegs.

While Duncan was packing, she went to work. She told herself—literally, with words muttered under her breath—that she had loads of e-mail to catch up on, but even Malcolm might have deduced, given all the relevant information, that she wanted to see if she'd heard from Tucker. This was her workplace affair, with a man on another continent that she'd never met, and wasn't ever likely to meet.

The museum didn't open until two on Saturdays, so there was nobody else around; she killed the first few minutes of the promised two-hour absence by wandering around what was officially and grandly known as "the permanent collection." It had been ages since she'd really looked at what they asked people to pay to see, and she wasn't as embarrassed as she thought she might be. Most museums in seaside towns had bathing machines, the peculiar Victorian beach huts on wheels that allowed ladies to go into the sea without exposing themselves to onlookers, but not everybody had a nineteenth-century Punch-and-Judy stall, complete with grotesque puppets. Gooleness, typically, was the last town in the UK to employ dippers and bathers; dippers dunked ladies into the sea, and bathers immersed the gentlemen, and it was a calling that had mostly vanished by the 1850s. Gooleness, however, had been so far behind the times that the museum had late nineteenth-century photographic evidence of both teams. And to her surprise, she could now see that their photograph collection was really pretty good. She stopped before her favorite, a picture of a sand castle competition that must have been held at the turn of the last century. There were very few children visible—one little girl in the foreground, wearing a knee-length dress and a sun hat that might have been made out of newspaper—and the competition seemed to have drawn a crowd of thousands. (Would Ros tell her that this, too, was the best day in some poor coal miner's life, the day he had a front-row view of the Gooleness sand castle competition in 1908?) But Annie's eye was always drawn to a woman over on the right, kneeling on the ground, working on a church steeple, in what looked like a full-length overcoat and a peasant sun hat that made her seem as sad and as destitute as an old peasant in the Vietnam War. You're dead now, Annie always thought when she saw her. Do you wish you hadn't wasted your time doing that? Do you wish you'd thought, Fuck the lot of them, and taken your coat off so you could have felt the sun on your back? We're here for such a short amount of time. Why do we spend any of it building sand castles? She would waste the next two hours, because she had to, and then she would never waste another second of however much time she had left to her. Unless somehow she ended up living with Duncan again, or doing this job for the rest of her working life, or watching *EastEnders* on a wet Sunday, or reading anything that wasn't *King Lear*, or painting her toenails, or taking more than a minute to choose something from a restaurant menu, or . . . It was hopeless, life, really. It was set up all wrong.

Duncan wouldn't have believed it was possible to feel more miserable than he'd felt in the Indian restaurant, telling Annie that he'd been unfaithful and then watching her walk out. But actually, packing his suitcase was, if anything, slightly more uncomfortable. True, the infidelity conversation had involved the most excruciating eye contact he'd ever had to put himself through; it would be a while before he forgot the hurt and the anger he'd had to look at in Annie's eyes, and, if he hadn't known her better, he might have come to the conclusion that there'd been hatred there, too, and possibly some contempt. But now, putting his clothes into a suitcase, he felt physically sick. This was his life, right here, and however many things he put into a bag, he couldn't take it with him. Even if he could take everything he owned, he'd still be leaving it behind.

He'd spent the previous night with Gina, in Gina's bed. She hadn't, as far as he could tell, been surprised to see him; on the contrary, she talked as if she'd been expecting him somehow. Duncan had tried to explain that he would prefer to look on her as a friend with a sofa for the time being, but Gina didn't seem to understand the distinction, possibly because he hadn't explained that he was homeless, nor the circumstances surrounding his homelessness.

"I don't know why you'd want to have sex with me one night and sleep on the sofa the next," she said.

"Well, of course, they weren't consecutive nights," he said, and he could almost hear Annie's eyeballs rolling in their sockets.

"No, but nothing much has happened in between, has it? Unless you've come round here to finish with me. In which case you're not even sleeping on the sofa. You're out." Gina laughed, so Duncan laughed, too.

"No, no. But . . ."

"Good. That settles it."

"It's just that . . ."

Gina put her arms around his neck and kissed him on the lips.

"You smell beery."

"I had . . . I was drinking lager when . . ." He was trying to remember if he'd ever even mentioned Annie. He'd certainly been conscious of saying "We I" a lot in the two or three conversations he'd had with Gina, as in, "We I can never stop after one episode of *The Wire*," or "We I went on a little tour of the U.S. in the summer," although Gina had never shown any curiosity in the derivation of this peculiar new pronoun. And then, when he'd trained himself to exclude the existence of Annie, he'd had to reintroduce her, anonymously, because he felt it was beginning to sound as though he'd spent the previous fifteen years going to the cinema and listening to music on his own. So he'd said things like, "Yes, I saw that. With the woman I was, you know, seeing. At the time."

"I've had a rather difficult evening, actually."

"I'm sorry."

"Yes. I can't remember if I ever mentioned . . . Anyway, I had something to sort out tonight. Because of you."

"Do you mean . . . romantically?"

He was tempted to qualify Gina's adverb, and explain that he wasn't really involved with Annie romantically, that it was more a question of jigsaw pieces. But he could see that might not have been terribly helpful.

"I suppose so, yes."

"A long-term thing?"

Duncan paused. He knew the answer to this question, really. Fifteen years was a long-term thing, unambiguously, so it would be disingenuous to say something like "What do you mean?" or "Define your terms."

"What counts as a long-term thing, for you?"

"A year?"

"Ummm . . ." He made a face that suggested mute calculation. He was more or less counting on his fingers, in his head. "Yes."

"Oh. Oh dear. And was it bloody?"

"It was a bit, yes."

"Is that why you raised the subject of the sofa?"

"I suppose it might have been, yes."

"And are you with her now?"

"No."

"Okay."

And that was all there was to say about his previous relationship, as far as Gina was concerned. Duncan felt homesick the entire night and slept poorly. Gina, however, seemed inappropriately cheerful about everything. Duncan was forced to conclude that she just didn't get the magnitude of his breakup with Annie, possibly because she was shallow and lacking in empathy. Only later did he realize that she was unlikely to get the magnitude of it, because he'd willfully and possibly even deceitfully shrunk it. He'd knocked fourteen years off it and then asked her to acknowledge that she was a home-wrecker. He'd told her it was just a scratch and got cross when she hadn't offered morphine.

Returning home didn't help with his homesickness, inevitably. It simply made it worse. He wanted to linger, maybe even watch a DVD and pretend that it was a normal Saturday morning, but he doubted whether that would help him much. He finished packing his bag—enough for a week or so, no more—and left. Duncan didn't know too much about the vicissitudes of Tucker Crowe's love life—nobody did, really, although there had been much speculation on the web—but he imagined it to have been tumultuous. How did he stand it? How many times had Tucker had to pack his bag like this, say good-bye to a home? Not for the first time, Duncan wished that he knew Tucker personally. He would very much like to ask him what he took with him when he moved out of one life and into another. Was underwear the key? For some reason he imagined Tucker would have a tip for him, something like, "Don't worry about T-shirts," or "Never leave your favorite picture behind." Duncan's favorite picture was an original *Dr. No* poster that he and Annie had found, incredibly, in a junk shop in Gooleness. He was pretty sure he was the one who'd paid for it, so he'd be entitled to remove it. On the other hand, it was quite big, and covered a large damp patch on the bedroom wall. If he left the damp patch exposed, there'd be trouble. He settled for his second-favorite, an eighteen-by-twelve shot of Tucker he'd bought on eBay. It was taken in the late seventies, perhaps at the Bottom Line in New York, and Crowe looked good, young and confident and happy. He'd had it framed, but Annie never wanted it up in the sitting room or the bedroom, so it was propped up against the wall in the office. She wouldn't mind that he'd taken it—indeed, she'd probably mind if he didn't—and it seemed appropriate, seeing as it was Tucker's advice in the first place. Imaginary advice, anyway. It was somewhat embarrassing, perhaps, walking into Gina's flat with a small duffel bag and a large picture, but Gina loved it, or said she did. Gina was enthusiastic about a lot of things.

He spent the weekend almost entirely in Gina's company. They ate good food, watched two movies, went for a walk along the beach, had sex twice, on Saturday night and Sunday night. And everything felt wrong, off, peculiar. Duncan couldn't shake the feeling that he was living somebody else's life, a life that was much more enjoyable than his own had been recently, but which didn't suit him, or fit him, or something. And then, on Monday morning, they cycled into work together, and when it was time for the first classes of the day, Gina kissed him good-bye, on the lips, and squeezed his bottom playfully while colleagues watched, stupefied with excitement. By lunchtime, everybody in the college knew that they were a couple.

eight

What to say? Tucker couldn't think of anything. Or rather, he couldn't think of anything that would help in any way. "Let's give it one more try"? "I'm pretty sure I can change"? "Would you like to go to counseling"? His previous and extensive history of messing up relationships was useful only up to a point: effectively, all it did was make him give in to the inevitable much more quickly. He was like a mechanic who could take one look at an old car and tell its owner, "Well, yes, I could try. But the truth of it is, you'll be back here again in two months, and you'll have spent an awful lot of money in the meantime." He'd attempted to change before; he'd been to marriage counseling, he'd given it another try, and all of this had merely served to attenuate the agony. Experience, then, was something that enabled you to do nothing with a clear conscience. Experience was an overrated quality.

It was news to him that Cat had been "kind of seeing somebody," if only in a "pretty much semi-platonic" way. (He was tempted, in a spirit of devilment, to press for a definition of "semi-platonic," but he was afraid that Cat might actually try to provide one, and neither of them could cope with the ensuing embarrassment.) Try as he might, however, he couldn't see it as front-page news, or even a headline in the sports section. She was a young woman and as a consequence didn't subscribe to the idea that monogamous sexual relationships between men and women were doomed, pointless, miserable, hopeless; she'd get there, he felt, but not for a while yet. Of course she was seeing somebody. Tucker wondered whether he knew the man who was being kind of seen and then wondered whether to ask if he knew him. In the end, he decided against it. He could see what would happen: Cat would tell him that, yes, Tucker had met him before, and Tucker would have to confess that he couldn't bring him to mind. Unless Cat was kind of seeing a friend of his, the name she provided was unlikely to mean much.

Cat was staring at him. He was stirring his coffee and had been for the last few minutes. Had she asked him a question? He rewound until he heard her voice.

"I think we've reached the end of the road," is what she'd said, which wasn't actually a question, although it clearly required an acknowledgment of receipt, at least.

"I'm sorry, sweetheart. But I think you're probably right."

"And that's all you have to say?"

"I think so."

Jackson walked into the room, saw Tucker and Cat sitting there expectantly and ran out again.

"I told you," said Tucker. He tried to keep it to that, but he was actually really angry. Jackson was a smart kid, and it had taken him three seconds to sense the danger in that room: the silence, his parents' obvious nervousness.

"Go get him," said Cat.

"You go get him. This was all your idea." And then, when he could see Cat was going to react, "Telling him was your idea, I mean. Telling him like this. Formally."

Tucker wasn't sure how they should have done it, but he knew they'd got it wrong. Why had Cat decided that the den was the right place? None of them ever used it. It was dark and smelled musty. They might just as well have woken him up in the middle of the night and yelled,

"Something weird and upsetting is going to happen!" at him through a megaphone. And the formation, Cat and Tucker side by side on a sofa, never happened much in real life, either. They were a head-on couple.

"You know I can't," Cat said. "He won't come unless you do it."

And this, of course, was a neat illustration of the trouble she faced. Shortly—not today, not here and now, but sometime soon—Jackson would be forced to choose which parent he was going to live with, and really that was no choice at all. Cat, like your average American dad, hadn't seen much of Jackson since the first six months of his life. She'd been too busy keeping food on the table. Cat knew she wouldn't be eating breakfast with her son much in the near future, which made her determination to end the relationship even more impressive, Tucker thought. And his security, the reassuring knowledge that the apparently unavoidable split couldn't come between him and his son, probably sucked a great deal of the desperation out of his efforts to smooth things over. He and Jackson were the couple, and they didn't need a lawyer.

Jackson was in his room, bashing the hell out of the buttons on a cheap computer game. He didn't look up when Tucker opened the door.

"You want to come back downstairs?"

"No."

"It'll be easier if the three of us talk."

"I know what you want to talk about."

"What?"

" 'Mommy and Daddy are having problems, so we're going to split up from each other. But it doesn't mean we don't love you, blah, blah, blah.' There. Now I don't have to go."

Jesus, thought Tucker. Six years old and already these kids can parody the language of marital failure.

"Where did you get all that from?"

"Like, five hundred TV shows, plus five hundred kids at school. So that's a thousand, right?"

"Right. Five hundred plus five hundred makes a thousand."

Jackson couldn't prevent a tiny flicker of triumph from crossing his face.

"Okay. You don't have to come down. But please be kind to your mother."

"She knows I want to live with you, right?"

"Yeah, she knows, and she's upset about it."

"Dad? Do we have to move to another house?"

"I don't know. Not if you don't want to."

"Really?"

"Sure."

"So it doesn't matter that you don't have any money?"

"No. Not at all."

Tucker was pleased with the dismissive tone. It suggested that only a kid with no knowledge of the way the world worked would even have brought the subject up.

"Cool."

Tucker went back downstairs to explain to his wife that she'd have to give up both her child and her house.

Tucker now accepted, without question, that he couldn't make a marriage, or anything resembling a marriage, work. (He had never been absolutely sure whether he was married to Cat or not. Cat referred to him as her husband, and it always sounded a little off to him, but he'd never been able to ask her directly whether there was any legal basis for her description of his status. She'd be hurt that he couldn't remember. Certainly there'd been no ceremony since sobriety, but anything could have happened before that.) He was one of those people whose flaws remained consistent whoever he was with. He'd had friends who'd had good second marriages, and they always talked about the relief they'd felt when they realized that the first had gone wrong because of the dynamic, rather than any inherent failing in themselves. But as several women, women who didn't really resemble one another in any way, had all complained of the same things, he had to accept that dynamics had nothing to do with anything. It was all him. At the beginning, something—infatuation, hope, whatever—helped disguise his real shape. But then the tide went out, and all was revealed, and it was ugly, dark and jagged and unpleasant.

One of the chief complaints was that he never did anything, which Tucker couldn't help but feel was unfair; not because the complaint was groundless, because it obviously wasn't, but because, in certain circles, Tucker was one of the most famous do-nothings in the United States. All of these women had known that he hadn't done anything since 1986; that, it seemed to him, was his unique selling point, and it was a never-ending source of fascination. But when he'd continued to do nothing, there was outrage. Where was the justice in that? He could see that several of these women, Cat included, had presumed, without ever articulating it or possibly even acknowledging it to themselves, that they'd be able to redeem him, bring him back to life. They'd appointed themselves muses, and he would respond to their love, inspiration and care by making the most beautiful and passionate music of his career. And then, when nothing happened, they were left with an ex-musician who sat around the house drinking, watching game shows and reading Victorian novels in his sweatpants, and they didn't like it much. Who could blame them? There wasn't much to like. With Cat it had been different, because he'd sobered up and taken care of Jackson. But he was still a disappointment to her. He was a disappointment to himself, but that didn't help anyone much.

It wasn't as if he was a happy slacker, either. He'd never been able to shrug away the loss of his talent, for want of a better word to describe whatever the hell it was he once had. Sure, he'd got used to the idea that there wouldn't be a new album, or even a new song, anytime soon, but he'd never learned to look on his inability to write as anything other than a temporary state, which meant that he was permanently unsettled, as if he were in an airport lounge waiting for a plane. In the old days, when he flew a lot, he'd never been able to get absorbed in a book until the plane had taken off, so he'd spent the pre-boarding time flicking through magazines and browsing in gift shops, and that's what the last couple of decades had felt like: one long flick through a magazine. If he'd known how long he was going to spend in the airport lounge of his own life, he'd have made different travel arrangements, but instead he'd sat there, sighing and fidgeting and, more often than was ever really acceptable, snapping at his traveling companions.

"What are you going to *do*?" they asked, all the Cats

and Nats and other wives and lovers and mothers of his children whose names sometimes blurred regrettably together. And he always told them what he thought they should want to hear. "I'm gonna look for a job," he said, or, "I'm retraining as an accountant." And they'd sigh and roll their eyes, which for him merely underlined the impossibility of his situation: how else to answer, other than to say he was going to look for a job, do something else, stop being a former something? A few months back, he'd called Cat on the eye-rolling, asked her for some suggestions. After some deliberation, she announced that she thought he should be a singer-songwriter, but one who actually sang and wrote songs. She hadn't articulated the idea exactly in those terms, of course, but that was pretty much what it amounted to. He'd laughed a lot. She'd gotten angry. One more finger had been prised off the rope they were clinging to.

Up until a couple of years ago, Tucker's best and only friend in the neighborhood had been known as Farmer John, after the old Premiers song, because his name was John and he lived on a farm. Then something strange happened, and one of the eventual consequences was that Farmer John became known affectionately to his nearest and dearest as Fucker. (This select group included, to

Cat's mortification and Tucker's childish delight, Jackson.) The strange thing that happened was this: sometime in 2003, one of the half-crazed fans who refer to themselves as Crowologists drove up the dirt track that led to Farmer John's farm, apparently in the belief that Tucker lived there. While John was walking down to the stranger's car to talk to him, the driver's door opened, the fan emerged and he started frantically taking pictures of John with a fancy-looking camera. Tucker had never really learned how John earned a living; he was no farmer, that was for sure. And every time anyone asked him, he was impressively and sometimes even aggressively evasive. The general presumption was that there was some harmless, low-level illegal activity involved somewhere, which was probably why John went for the photographer, who kept snapping pictures even as he got into the car to make his escape. Within days, the scariest of these photos (and John, a grizzled man with long, matted gray hair, never looked anything less than intimidating anyway) was being passed from website to website. Neil Ritchie, the photographer, became almost famous, the man who'd stolen the first shot of Tucker Crowe in over fifteen years. It was still, even now, the first image you saw if you went to find a picture of Tucker on the Internet.

At first, Tucker was baffled by the easy passage the photo had through cyberspace. Nobody ever asked how a man who looked like *that* in 1986 could look like *this* in 2003. Hair can grow long and get dirty and go gray, sure. But could noses change shape that easily? Could eyes start creeping closer together? Could mouths get wider, lips thinner? But then, the photo was never used anywhere that it was likely to get fact-checked; Tucker had long since drifted away from the mainstream media and into the backwaters where all the screwballs and conspiracy theorists did their fishing. And anyway, to talk about plausibility was to miss the point. The few people who hadn't forgotten him, people who had turned his songs into hymns that contained profoundly helpful guidance on just about everything, *wanted* him to look like Farmer John. Tucker was a genius, according to these people, and he'd gone mad, and that's what mad geniuses looked like. And John's anger was perfect, too. Neil Ritchie almost certainly had other shots of John ambling toward his car, but they just didn't fit with the idea of someone who was clearly so obsessive about his privacy. The moment John went nuts was the moment he turned into Tucker Crowe, damaged recluse. Tucker, meanwhile, the real one, the one who drove Jackson to Little League games, kept his silver hair neatly trimmed, wore moderately fashionable rimless spectacles and shaved every day. He felt like Fucker on the inside, which was why he'd always made sure he looked like somebody you'd be happy to buy insurance from.

Anyway, Farmer John became known to Tucker and Cat (and Jackson) and a few other friends and neighbors as Fake Tucker, and Fake Tucker became, inevitably, Fucker. And when Tucker needed to get out of the house and out into the world, it was Fucker he took with him—not because the confusion was helpful in any way, but because he didn't really know any other men anymore. It was always slightly complicated, though, a night out with The Fuck. Tucker couldn't drink, and Fucker couldn't not drink, and though Tucker could watch someone sipping liquor slowly and in moderation, it didn't do him much good to watch somebody get slammed. So the deal was this: Fucker had to be given an hour's notice, and in that hour he'd work his way through several fingers of Bushmills and get a glow on. By the time Tucker came to pick him up he'd only need a small top-up, and occasionally he'd be ready for a mug of coffee.

Fucker wanted to listen to a band that was playing in a local bar.

"Why?"

"Because it might be fun."

"Oh, man," said Tucker. "Do we have to?"

"You don't drink, you don't listen to music . . . Why do you even ask me to go out at night? How about this? You want to see me, we'll meet for breakfast. Except you probably disapprove of eggs. Or you used to snort them, back in the eighties, so you can't be in the same room as them now."

"I need to talk, I think."

"Why? You screwed it all up with Cat?"

"Yep."

"Wow. Who could have seen that coming?"

Tucker actually valued John's blunt sarcasm. It felt bracing, like one of those sponges Cat liked that were supposed to remove dead skin.

"Maybe you're right. Maybe we should go see a band. That way I don't have to listen to you."

"I've said all I have to say. Apart from you're an idiot. How's Jackson?"

"He's okay. He's not amazed, either, really. He just wanted to make sure that he could be with me and stay in the house."

"And is that possible?"

"Apparently. Cat's going to look for an apartment in town, somewhere Jackson can sleep when he wants to."

"So you stole Cat's house from her?"

"For now."

"What's going to change?"

"Either I start earning some money, or Jackson turns eighteen and goes to college."

"You taking bets on what happens first?"

"Maybe *Juliet, Naked* will make me some money."

"Oh, yeah. I forgot you had a new album out. There

must be a million people who want to hear crappy versions of songs they forgot about years ago."

Tucker laughed. John had never heard his work before he moved into the neighborhood, but one night, drunk, he'd told Tucker that he'd played *Juliet* incessantly when he'd split with his wife. He'd been dismissive of *Naked*, for pretty much the same reasons as that English girl, although he was less eloquent in his expression of them.

It had been a long time since Tucker had been anywhere to hear a band, and he couldn't quite believe how familiar it all felt. Shouldn't something have moved on by now? Did you really still have to lug all your equipment in by yourself, sell your records and T-shirts at the back of the room, talk to the crazy guy with no friends who'd been to see you three times this week already? There wasn't much anyone could do with the live music experience, though. It was what it was. Bars and the bands that played in them didn't have much use for the shiny white Apple world out there; there'd be processed cheese slices for dinner and blocked toilets until the world melted away.

Tucker went to the bar and got their drinks, a Coke for himself and a glass of Jameson for Fucker, and they sat down at a table at the side of the room, away from the tiny, low stage and the lights.

"But you're doing okay," said Fucker.

"Yeah."

"Wondering whether you'll ever have sex again?"

"Not yet."

"You should."

"If you can find someone to sleep with, anyone can." Fucker was seeing a divorced English teacher from the local high school.

"You don't have my charm, though."

"Lisette probably thought you were me anyway."

"You know what? That picture has never done me the smallest bit of good with a woman. Think about that, my friend."

"I have. And the conclusion I've drawn is, it's a picture of you, not me, and it makes you look like a bug-eyed psycho."

The houselights went down, and the band ambled out onto the stage, to the general indifference of the drinkers in the room. They weren't young men, the musicians, and Tucker wondered how often they'd been tempted to quit, and why they hadn't done so. Maybe it was because they hadn't been able to think of anything better to do; maybe it was even because they thought this was fun. They were okay. Their own songs weren't anything special, but they knew that, because they played "Hickory Wind" and "Highway 61" and "Sweet Home Alabama." They knew their audience, anyway. Tucker and John were surrounded by gray ponytails and bald heads. Tucker looked around to see if he could spot anybody under forty and saw a young man who immediately looked away when Tucker caught his eye.

"Uh-oh," said Tucker.

"What's up?"

"That kid over there, by the men's room. I think he's recognized you."

"Cool. That never happens anymore. Shall we have some fun?"

"What do you call fun?"

"I'll think of something."

But then it got too loud to talk much, and Tucker started to get gloomy. He had feared the onset of gloom. It was the real reason he hadn't wanted to come out in the first place. He'd spent a lot of time doing nothing, but the trick to doing nothing, as far as he was concerned, anyway, was not to think while you were doing it. The trouble with going to see bands is that there wasn't much else to do *but* think, if you weren't being swept away on a wave of visceral or intellectual excitement; and Tucker could tell that The Chris Jones Band would never be able to make people forget who they were and how they'd ended up that way, despite their sweaty endeavors. Mediocre loud music penned you into yourself, made you pace up and down your own mind until you were pretty sure you could see how you might end up going out of it. In the seventy-five minutes that he spent with himself, he managed to revisit pretty much every single place he'd have been happy never to see again. He worked back from Cat and Jackson to all the other screwed-up marriages and kids; the professional wasteland of the last twenty years ran alongside them, like a rusted-over railroad running alongside a traffic jam. People underestimated the speed of thought. It was possible to cover just about every major incident of a lifetime during the average bar band's set.

When the band waved to the handful of people applauding them and walked offstage, John disappeared through the door at the side of the stage to find them. A couple of minutes later, he was leading the musicians back for their encore.

"As some of you know, it's a long time since I've done this," said John into the microphone. A couple of people in the bar laughed, either because they knew the story, or because they'd heard him sing before. Tucker watched the kid who'd been staring at them earlier. He was already on his feet and making his way to the foot of the stage. He looked as though he might faint with excitement. John grabbed the mike stand, nodded at the band, and they did their best Crazy Horse impersonation for a ragged but recognizable "Farmer John." Fucker sounded terrible: too loud, off-key and insane, but it clearly didn't matter to his one fan, who was leaping up and down with excitement, while taking as many shots as he could with the camera on his cell phone. John finished with an ungainly leap into the air several seconds after the musicians' last chord and grinned happily at Tucker.

The kid stopped John while he was making his way back to the seat, and John spoke to him for a couple of minutes.

"What did you say?"

"Oh, just a bunch of made-up crap. But it doesn't matter. Tucker Crowe spoke."

When Tucker got home that night, everyone was asleep, so he sat down and wrote to English Annie. She was English Annie because she wasn't the Annie with whom he'd been conducting a chaste but nonetheless morale-boosting flirtation for a while now. American Annie was the mother of Jackson's school friend Toby. She was in her mid-thirties, recently divorced, lonely and pretty. He'd started to think about her within hours—okay, minutes—of Cat telling him that they'd reached the end of the road. Tellingly, however, the thought of Toby's Annie hadn't cheered him much. He'd only been able to see a whole lot of grim consequential inevitabilities: ill-advised sex, his inability to follow through, hurt and the destruction of one of Jackson's most important relationships.

Well, fuck that. Maybe he should concentrate on flirting with someone who lived on another continent, a

woman who only lived in cyberspace and didn't have a son
on Jackson's Little League team, or indeed any kind of son,
which was one of the reasons she'd been so attractively
expansive in the first place. Anyway, English Annie had
been on his mind in the bar. A couple of the questions
she'd asked in her last e-mail were similar to the questions
he'd ended up asking himself during his sonic incarcera-
tion earlier in the evening, and it seemed like it might be
more helpful to think about them as part of a conversation
with someone.

Dear Annie,

Here's another way of proving I am who I
claim to be. Have you ever seen that picture
someone took of a scared crazy person a few
years back? You say you know people who
still like my music—well, they're the kind
of people who are familiar with the photo,
because they are under the impression that
it's me. They think it's a revealing, if unflat-
tering, portrait of a creative genius having
some kind of breakdown, but it's not. It's a fair
likeness of my neighbor John, who is a nice
guy but not a creative genius, as far as I know.
And he wasn't having a breakdown. He was

just flipping out. John went nuts because, not
unreasonably, he didn't like this guy snapping
away at him, possibly because he's got a
whole field of cannabis plants in his backyard.
(I have no idea whether he has or hasn't. I just
know he's touchy about trespassers.)

Tucker stopped, and opened the photo library. He'd
attached a picture to an e-mail a couple of times and he
was pretty sure he could do it again. He found one of
him and Jackson outside Citizens Bank Park earlier on
in the summer and clicked the paper clip icon hopefully.
It seemed to work. But would she think he was hitting
on her? Could sending a photo of himself with his cute
son, no woman in sight, be construed as some kind of
come-on? He removed the attachment, just in case.

Anyway, it's a good story, right? Around here,
John has been christened Fucker (= Fake
Tucker), if you'll pardon my language. And
forgive the yoking together a word alluding
to Our Lord with an obscenity. And tonight,
Fucker sang with a local bar band, thus
overexciting a kid in the audience who clearly
thought he was witnessing my resurrection.

> If anyone tells you I'm making a comeback,
> you can tell them it was Farmer John (which
> is what he sang. You know that song? "I'm in
> love with your daughter, whoa, whoa"?)

No, the photo made sense of the e-mail. How else could he prove that he didn't look like John? And he wasn't trying to prove that he was better-looking than John. He was trying to show that he and John didn't resemble each other, and the whole Wild Man of the Woods thing was a hilarious Internet myth. He reattached the attachment.

> This is me, outside a baseball stadium with
> my youngest son, Jackson. I have always kept
> my hair short since I gave up music, probably
> because I was afraid people might think I'd
> turned into someone like John. Plus, I wear
> glasses, which I didn't use to. I have spent
> a lot of time reading the small print of big
> novels, and

"Big novels?" Why did he feel the need to tell English Annie why he needed to wear glasses? So she didn't think it was because he did too much jerking off? He deleted the last line. It was none of her business. Plus, that "pardon my language" thing sounded prissy. If she couldn't cope with bad language, then fuck her . . . And that phrase begged a few questions. What did he want English Annie to look like? If he knew for sure that she weighed two hundred pounds, would he be pursuing this correspondence? Maybe he should ask her for a reciprocal photo, except then he would really look like some kind of creepy stalker. And anyway, what was he supposed to do with this girl? Invite her to come over? But actually, now that he thought about it . . .

> **I'll probably be coming to England sometime in the next few months to see my grandchild. How far is your museum from London, where my daughter lives? I'd like to see your dead shark pictures. Or do you ever go down south? I don't really know anybody in England, so . . .**

So what? He scrapped the last half sentence, and then the one before it, too. It was okay to tell someone you wanted to see their dead shark pictures, wasn't it? Or did that have a sleazy ring to it, too? And, hold on . . . *"Do you ever go down south?"* Jesus Christ. There was a reason he'd given up talking to people he didn't know.

nine

The extraordinary news that Tucker had made some kind of bizarre public appearance passed Duncan by for a couple of days. There was so much going on in his personal life that he hadn't had time to check the website, an oversight which, he later realized, neatly proved one of Annie's cruel theories about Crowologists.

"I know 'Get a life' is a cliché," she used to say. "But really, if these people actually had anything to do all day, they wouldn't have time to write his lyrics out backward to see if there were any hidden messages in them."

Only one person on the message boards had ever done that, and he did nothing all day because, it was eventually discovered, he was writing from the psychiatric ward of a hospital, but Duncan could see her point. The moment Duncan had found something to do—namely, try to grab the steering wheel back from the maniac who seemed to be driving his life—then Tucker had been forgotten. One evening, when Gina had gone to bed early, Duncan sat down at her computer and rejoined his little community, mostly because he wanted to feel normal for a few minutes, to do something that he used to do. Looking at a picture of Tucker taken a few nights before, onstage with a band Duncan had never heard of, really didn't help with his attempted reorientation. It actually made him feel rather giddy.

It seemed to be genuine. There was no mistaking the man from the infamous Neil Ritchie photo—the same long gray dreadlocks, the same discolored teeth, although this time the teeth were visible because Tucker was smiling, rather than because they were being bared in anger.

It was incredible that anyone who'd ever heard of Tucker was in the crowd to see it: the band were, as far as it was possible to tell, a distinctly ordinary bunch of pub-rockers who played bars all over Pennsylvania but not much farther than that. It turned out that the young man who got the scoop was in the middle of the same sort of Crowe pilgrimage that Duncan and Annie had embarked on in the summer. He, however, had set out to try and find Tucker, and it looked as though he'd struck it astonishingly lucky. But why "Farmer John"? Duncan would have to think about that. A man as deliberate and as thoughtful as Crowe would be trying to say something with the song that broke a twenty-year silence, but what? Duncan certainly had the Neil Young version; he would try to find the original before he went to bed.

There was more, however. The witness, who identified himself only by his initials, ET, had managed to speak to Crowe when he came offstage, and Crowe had spoken back.

> **So I thought well I have to try and I went up to him and I said Tucker I am a big fan and I am so happy to see you singing again. Dumb I know but you try and think of something better. And then I said Will you be singing your own songs onstage anytime soon and he said YES and also he had a new album coming out. And I said yes I know *Naked* and he said no not that piece of shit.**

Duncan smiled to himself. The self-deprecation proved—perhaps, in a strange way, with even more certainty than the photograph—that this was indeed Tucker. It was an old pattern, exemplified in countless interviews from the old days. Tucker knew that *Naked* wasn't a piece of shit, but it was entirely typical of him to describe it as such on its release, to an overeager fan. Duncan decided he wouldn't pass this part of the story on to Annie, though. She'd misunderstand, come to the conclusion that Tucker was validating her opinion of the album, when in fact he was doing the opposite.

I have a new album coming out an album of covers of Dean Martin songs but done kind of roots rock and I kind of went wow and he smiled and then went to sit with his friend and I thought I can't bug him again. So I know the Dean Martin bit sounds weird but that's what he said. I cannot tell you how amazing it all was I am still shaking.

It seemed wrong that he couldn't share any of this with Annie. Gina would be excited when he told her in the morning; but then sometimes he wondered whether her excitement was entirely genuine. Occasionally it felt to him as though it were a little theatrical, although maybe he wouldn't have arrived at that word were it not for her background. But then, she was a performer, and she performed, even when there didn't seem to be very much motivation for her character. She couldn't possibly understand what Tucker's reemergence meant—she hadn't put the time in—but she would jump up and down and shout "Oh my God" anyway. Perhaps it would be better if he didn't tell her, and then he wouldn't end up disliking her for her phoniness. Annie, however, had lived through the entirety of Tucker's disappearance, and she would grasp the emotional impact of the news immediately. Did his relationship with Gina prevent him from sharing things like this with Annie? He thought not. He looked at his watch. She wouldn't be in bed yet, unless her habits had changed profoundly since his departure.

"Annie?"

"Duncan? What's the matter? I was in bed."

"Oh. I'm sorry."

He hoped she wasn't going to bed early on his account, but he feared it might be an indication of depression.

"Listen. Something rather amazing has happened," he said.

"I hope it is something amazing, Duncan. I hope that normal people would share your excitement."

"They would if they knew what it meant."

"It's going to be something to do with Tucker, isn't it?"

"Yes."

She sighed heavily, which he understood as an invitation to continue.

"He sang. Live. In a bar. He joined a, well, an apparently rather mediocre band for an encore of 'Farmer John.' Do you know that song? 'Farmer John, I'm in love with your daughter, whoa-oo-o-ah.' And then he told someone in the audience he was making an album of Dean Martin cover versions."

"Right. Good-o. Can I go to bed yet?"

"Annie, you're cutting off your nose to spite your face."

"I'm sorry?"

"I know you can see how amazing this is. And you're just pretending it's boring because you think you can get back at me. But I'd hoped you'd be above all that."

"I am excited, Duncan, honestly. If we were on video-phone now, you'd see I was beside myself. But it's also late, and I'm tired."

"If you want to be like that."

"I do, really."

"So you don't really see us being able to build some kind of friendship."

"Not tonight, no."

"I suppose . . . Stop me if you feel this analogy is inap-propriate, or, or, *off*. But I do feel that Tucker is our child, in a way. Maybe more mine than yours . . . Maybe, I don't know, he was my son, but he was very young when we met, and you adopted him. And if my son, your stepson, had done something remarkable, I'd want to share that with you even if . . ."

Annie hung up on him. He ended up writing an e-mail to Ed West from the website, but it wasn't the same.

. . .

For the next few days, the message-board regulars shared everything they knew about the song, in the hope that they could decode Crowe's message to the world. They discussed whether the "champagne eyes" of the farmer's daughter were significant—was Tucker acknowledging the role alcohol had played, and maybe was continuing to play, in his life? Even with all the critical ingenuity they had at their disposal, there wasn't much they could make of the rest of the lyrics, which were of the "I love the way she walks/talks/wiggles" variety. Could it be that he was simply announcing his love for a farmer's daughter? There were probably several in his immediate vicinity, so why couldn't he have fallen for one of them? (And of course it was impossible to imagine a farmer's daughter without imagining a pair of apple-rosy cheeks, and perhaps even a becoming heft around the waist and the bottom. Compare and contrast with the pale, size-zero beauty of Julie Beatty and her ilk! If he was truly in love with a farmer's daughter, then the old, unhealthy West Coast days were really over.)

There was much talk of the Neil Young connection, Young being a musician Crowe had always admired, and an artist who had managed to grow old creatively and productively. Was it an expression of regret for all the time wasted? Or was he saying that Young had taught him a way forward? The song's inclusion on Lenny Kaye's influential 1972 *Nuggets* compilation, alongside the likes of the Standells and the 13th Floor Elevators, provoked comment, too, although nobody could make anything really coherent out of the connection. The real point was that, for the second time in a few days, they had been given something to debate. *Naked* and now this . . . It really did feel as though Tucker's hibernation might be drawing to a close.

Annie printed the picture of Tucker and Jackson at work, took it home and stuck it onto the fridge with the Sun Studios fridge magnet that she supposed Duncan would one day reclaim, if he were ever again in a position to think about the smaller details of a home life. It was a lovely picture anyway—Jackson was a beautiful child, and Tucker's pride in him was obvious and touching. But Jackson and Tucker weren't up on her fridge simply because they looked happy, she knew that much, and, whenever they caught her eye, she ended up thinking about what they did for her, and whether it was all terribly unhealthy. There was definitely a sad-sack fantasy element to it, she couldn't deny that: Tucker had mentioned in his e-mail that he was single again, so . . . she didn't need to spell it out. (She wanted to be honest with herself, but honesty didn't mean having to complete every sentence, not when the missing subordinate clause suggested so much emptiness.)

Anyway, there was another, less embarrassing explanation for the cheering effect of the picture: her relationship with Tucker, even as it stood, even excluding the schoolgirl dreams about Tucker coming to London and maybe even to Gooleness and maybe even staying with her and maybe even not staying on the couch, was exciting. How could it not be? She had something that nobody else in the world had, as far as she knew: e-mail conversation with the sort-of-famous Tucker Crowe, an enigmatic, talented, intelligent man who'd disappeared a long time ago. That would brighten anybody's day, surely?

But then there were the darker, Duncan-related pleasures she was discovering in the situation. It had taken her about a minute and a half to work out that, if Duncan ever looked at the fridge, he would have no idea who he was staring at, and the ironies of that were good enough and large enough to eat with a knife and fork, on their own, with no accompanying bitterness. She could tell him anything. And he'd believe her, because he knew for a fact that Tucker Crowe now looked like Rasputin, or maybe Merlin— Annie had checked Duncan's website when Tucker told her about Fucker's unscheduled appearance in the bar, and his picture was there, as Tucker had told her it would be. (And she noticed, with great delight, that Fucker had described *Naked* as a piece of shit. What would Duncan have made of that?) Really, it was all too much. Her real relationship with Tucker would be enough to drive him into a frenzy of jealousy, if he ever found out about it, although she wasn't entirely sure who he'd be jealous of; but even her pretend relationship with the man on the fridge might be enough to provoke a few twinges.

First, though, she needed Duncan to visit, and she needed him to take notice of something that he would never normally spot in a hundred years: a very small change to a domestic environment. Maybe if she blew the picture up so that it covered the entirety of a wall, he might ask her whether she'd done something to the kitchen; but presuming this was beyond her, both financially and technically, she'd have to point it out in some other unsubtle way. She was going to make him look, though, whatever it took. There was no doubt about that.

She left a message for him on his cell when she knew he'd be teaching.

"Hello, it's me. Listen, I'm sorry about the other night. I know you were trying to be friendly, and I can see how you might have needed someone to share the news with. Anyway. If you want to try again, I promise I'll be more receptive."

He called her at work, on his lunch break.

"That was very sweet of you."

"Oh, that's okay."

"Pretty amazing, though, no?"

"Incredible."

"There's a picture up on the website."

"I might have a look, later."

There was a silence. He was so transparent, and she felt an unfamiliar tug of affection. He wanted to keep the conversation going, and he was also looking for an elegant way to turn this tiny spark of interest into something warmer and cozier. It wasn't that he wanted her back, necessarily, she understood that, but she was sure he'd have been hurt and bewildered by her anger. And he'd be homesick, too. He hated not having his things around him, even on holiday.

"Can I come round for a cup of tea sometime?"

Elegance had proved beyond him. He'd settled for desperation, in the hope that she'd respond to his neediness.

"Well . . ."

"At a time convenient to you, of course." As if the inconvenience, rather than the infidelity and the mess it had caused, might be responsible for the hesitation.

"Maybe later in the week? Let the dust settle a bit?"

"Oh. Really? Is there still, you know . . . dust?"

"There is round here. I don't know what it's like at your place."

"I suppose if I say it's not dusty, you'll think, I don't know . . . that everything's all okay for me."

"I'd just think you hadn't noticed, to be honest, Duncan. You never used to notice when you were living here."

"Ah. I thought we were talking about metaphorical dust."

"We were. But there's always room for a joke, surely?"

"Ha, ha. Yes, of course. Whenever you want. I'm sure I deserve a bit of teasing."

She was suddenly overwhelmed by the sheer hopelessness of her relationship with Duncan. It wasn't just hopeless in its current form; it had always been hopeless. It was an unsuitable Internet date with an inadequate, unexciting man that had lasted for years and years and years. And yet something was making her flirt with him, if flirting could ever include bitterness, and exclude fun, joy and the promise of sex. It was the rejection, she decided. And rejection in Gooleness was a special kind of rejection.

"What about Thursday?"

The truth was, she didn't want to wait that long—she wanted him to see the picture as soon as possible. She could see, however, that desperately wanting someone not to recognize a photo of someone else was unattractive, and possibly even indicative of a spiritual crisis.

. . .

Terry Jackson, the town councillor, was unhappy at the lack of progress with the 1964 exhibition and had come to the museum to tell Annie as much.

"So, at the moment, the centerpiece of the exhibition would be what? The pickled shark's eye? Because it's hard to imagine anyone wanting to look at that for long."

"We don't really believe in centerpieces."

"Don't we?"

"No, we . . ."

"Let me put it another way, then. Is the shark's eye the best thing we've got?"

"The idea is that we collect so many great things that we don't talk about the best thing we've got."

Every time Annie met Terry Jackson, she was distracted by his hair, which was gray, but thick and lovingly shaped by Brylcreem. How old had he been in 1964? Twenty? Twenty-one? Ever since he'd outlined his dream exhibition, which she had been naive enough, and arrogant enough, to believe she could turn into a reality, she'd had the feeling that he had left something behind in that year, and that she could help him get it back. The shark's eye clearly wasn't going to do it for him.

"But you haven't got any great things."

"We haven't got enough, certainly."

"I can't say I'm not disappointed, Annie. Because I am."

"I'm sorry. It's a very hard thing to pull off. I think that even if we'd decided to widen it out and try for a 'Gooleness in the 1960s' exhibition, we'd have had difficulties."

"I can't believe that," he said. "This place was bonkers in the 1960s. Loads of stuff going on."

"I can believe it."

"No you can't," he said sharply. "You're just pretending you can believe it to humor me. The truth is, you think this place is a dump and you always have done. You'd love to put a shark's eye in an empty room and tell everybody it summed up Gooleness. You'd think it was funny. I knew we should have got a local girl in to run this place. Someone with a feel for it."

"I know I wasn't brought up here, Terry. But I'd like to think I've developed an affinity with the town."

"Codswallop. You can't wait to leave. Well, now your boyfriend's run off, you can, can't you? Nothing keeping you here."

She studied the wall behind his head hard, in an attempt to retract the one tear that seemed to be forming in her right eye. Why the right? Was it one of those things where the right tear duct was connected to the left side of the brain, and it was the left side of the brain that processed emotional trauma? She had no idea, but trying to work it out helped.

"I'm sorry," said Terry. "I had no right to bring up your personal life. It's a great town, Gooleness, but it is a small town, I'll give you that. My nephew's at the college, and they all seem to know up there."

"Don't worry. And, of course, you're right. There's less to tie me to the town than there was. But I would like to try and get this exhibition on before I leave. If I leave."

"Well. That's very nice of you. And I'm sorry I got a bit hot under the collar about the lack of progress. That year . . . I can't explain it. Everything seemed magical to me, and I thought it might to everyone else, and they'd all come flooding out of their houses with, with . . ."

"That's been part of my problem, you see, Terry. I'm not sure what they'd be donating either."

"Well, I never threw anything away. I kept every newspaper, every cinema ticket, every bloody bus ticket, just about. I've got one of those old-fashioned blue-and-red posters advertising the Rolling Stones, plus Bill Wyman's autograph, because he was the only bugger who'd give me one. I've got photos of my mam standing outside Grant's department store the day before they knocked it down, I've got a boxful of bloody shark photos, I've got pictures of me and my mates down at the old Queen's Head, before they turned it into that cheesy nightclub . . ."

"I wonder if you might think of lending us some of that?"

She was as polite and as understated as she could be, in the circumstances. If she killed him, though, she was pretty sure a jury would understand, provided they'd been briefed on the recent history of small museum funding, and the restrictions that placed on any kind of imaginative exhibiting.

"Nobody wants to look at my old rubbish. I certainly don't. I want to look at somebody else's."

"But would you mind if I looked at it?"

"For ideas, you mean? Get a better picture?"

"Well, that too, yes."

"Oh, if you must."

"Thank you. And I wouldn't rule out lending us some of your memorabilia."

"You'd have to be pretty desperate."

"Yes," she said. "Well." And left it at that.

He was right, of course: she had never taken Gooleness seriously, and neither had Duncan. That, after all, was one of the strongest and richest connections between them: their contempt for the town they lived in, and the people they lived with. That was why they'd been matched up in the first place, and that was why they'd stayed together, huddled against the cold winds of ignorance and Philistinism. So what sort of curator did that make her, if she'd never been persuaded that there was a past or a present worth curating? All she and Duncan had ever been able to see was a lack of culture, and you couldn't put a lack of culture in a museum.

Yes, she could leave, and most of her wanted to leave. Nothing was keeping her in Gooleness, just as Terry had said, apart from some nagging and probably deluded conviction that she was nicer than the sort of person who wouldn't want to stay.

Duncan knew that she got home at six, so he turned up at about three minutes past. Annie had made sure she was back by a quarter to, though, so that she'd have time to do things that turned out not to need doing. It didn't take her as long to hang up her coat as she'd anticipated, and the photo on the fridge didn't actually need moving three inches to the left, then three inches to the right, and then back to where it had been all the time.

And he didn't look at it anyway. He didn't really look at anything.

"I suppose you knew straightaway that I was making a terrible mistake," he said, when she asked him if he wanted a cookie. He was hunched over his tea and staring at the handle on his "bLIAR" mug. (She'd thought about giving him one of the others, in case drinking out of this one made him weepy, but he hadn't noticed it.) "The truth is, I'd have been making a terrible mistake even if I'd been single for all those years. Even if I'd been desperate for, for . . ."

Annie stared at her own mug. She had no intention of asking him questions about Gina.

"You see, the thing is, I think she might be mad."

"You shouldn't be so hard on yourself."

"I know that's supposed to be a joke. But to tell you the truth, that's one of the reasons I've come to that conclusion. She acts as though it's some kind of miracle that we've found each other. That she got a job at the college, and there I was, waiting for her. Well, I know I'm nothing much."

Annie felt the same little pang she'd noticed on the phone the other night, but she was beginning to wonder whether it wasn't just a straightforwardly human pity. She was relieved he'd gone, and he was worried that another woman's interest in him was evidence of her insanity. How could she not feel protective?

"It's all very difficult, isn't it," he said. "This whole business of, of whatever you want to call it."

"I'm not sure what it is. What would you call it?"

"Knowing somebody."

"Ah."

"Well, I knew you. Know you. That seems to me impor-tant. More important than I'd realized. The other night, when I called you . . . I mean, I know it was about Tucker, and I said silly things about how Tucker was sort of our child even though not having a child was a delicate topic. But the impulse . . . You see, I don't really want to tell her anything. Any news I have doesn't belong to her."

"Give it time."

"I'm just not cut out for this sort of change, Annie. I want to live here. With you. And tell you things."

"You can always tell me things."

Annie's heart sank. She couldn't think of a single thing Duncan was ever likely to tell her that she'd actually want to know.

"That's not what I mean."

"Duncan, we've been more friends than lovers for quite a long time. Maybe we should think about making that relationship official."

His face lit up, and for a moment Annie thought she was safely on to the other bank. "Marriage, you mean? Because I'd be happy to . . ."

"No, no. You're not listening. The opposite of marriage. A non-matrimonial, nonsexual, once-a-week-in-the-pub friendship."

"Oh."

Annie was beginning to resent the unfairness of all this. The one good thing about being rejected by Duncan was that she didn't have to end the relationship herself. Now, suddenly, it would appear that she had to both get dumped *and* do the dumping. How had that happened?

"The truth is," she said, acutely conscious that the phrase was being used to introduce an absurd lie, "I've sort of kind of started seeing somebody. I mean, it's very, *very* early days, and we haven't . . ."

If the somebody in question was who she thought it was—and there were no other candidates that came to mind—then "actually met" were the two words missing from the end of that sentence. But Tucker wouldn't mind, she felt. He knew how fiction worked, and what it was for.

"You're seeing somebody? I'm . . . Well, I'm aghast."

If ever Duncan wanted to know the reason why people sometimes found him insufferable, she could point him toward that description of his inner turmoil. Who used the word "aghast" without irony?

"I was pretty aghast myself when you told me about Gina."

"Yes, but . . ."

He was clearly hoping he wouldn't have to expand on the differences between his situation and her own—which were, of course, more profound than he knew. (What if they weren't? What if Gina were as imaginary as Tucker?

This was a more plausible explanation, surely, than the one she had been expected to swallow: that a woman would take one look at Duncan and usher him straight into her bed. Actually, it wasn't Duncan's appearance that was the problem. It was harder to believe that a woman would spend an evening talking to Duncan and still want to sleep with him.)

"But what?"

"Well. Gina was a, was a *given*. She was *known information*. This is something entirely new."

"Gina's quite new. To me, anyway. And anyway, what is she? Some kind of nuclear strike that's supposed to disable the opposition? I'm not allowed a life because you got one first?"

Duncan looked pained.

"There's a lot in there I'd like to take issue with."

"Feel free."

"In order, (a) I don't like to think you're the opposition. That is not how I think of you, and (b) that whole thing of 'getting a life.' I'd like to think you had one already, even before we split up. And, as I have been trying to explain to you, I'm not sure I do have a life. Not in the sense you mean. Anyway. We're getting away from the point. The point being, you've met somebody."

"Yes."

"Do I know him?"

For a moment, Annie was tempted to upbraid him for his presumptuous use of the masculine pronoun, but she couldn't have fun both ways: she couldn't expect much mileage out of the photo on the fridge if she also wanted to convince him that she'd become a lesbian.

Did Duncan know him? Well, yes and no. Mostly no, she decided.

"No."

"That's something, I suppose. Had you . . ."

"I'm not sure I really want to talk about my situation, Duncan. It's private."

"I understand. But it would help me if you could answer one more question."

"Help you how?"

"Had you met him before we . . . before I . . . before recent events?"

"We'd had contact, yes."

"And does he . . ."

"That's it, Duncan. Sorry."

"Fair enough. So where does that leave us?"

"Pretty much where we were, I'd have thought. You're seeing someone—living with someone—and I'm seeing someone. Someone looking at the situation from the outside would say that we've moved on. Especially you."

Annie hoped that this outside observer spent more time looking through Gina's window than her own.

"I know that's what it looks like, but . . . Oh, God. Are you really going to make me go through with this?"

"With what?"

"Gina."

"Duncan, will you listen to yourself?"

"What have I said?"

"I'm not making you do anything. If you don't want to be with Gina, you should tell her. But it's nothing to do with me."

"I can't tell her. Not if there's nothing to tell."

"What are you talking about?"

"Well, if I went back and said, you know, 'Annie and I are getting back together,' or, or, 'Annie's suicidal and I can't leave her,' I'm sure she'd understand. But I couldn't just say, you know, 'You're mad,' could I?"

"Well, no. I'd hope you wouldn't say that to anyone."

"So what should I say?"

"It sounds to me as though you've moved too quickly. You should tell her that . . . Oh, Duncan, this is absurd. A couple of weeks ago you told me you'd met somebody else, and now you want me to script the breakup."

"I'm not asking you to script it. I just need a rough

outline. Anyway, if I do say something to her, where am I going to live?"

"So you'd be prepared to carry on with her forever rather than look for a flat."

"I was hoping to come back here."

"I know, Duncan. But we've split up. It wouldn't be appropriate."

"Half this house is mine."

"I've applied to increase the mortgage and buy you out. I don't know whether they'll let me, but the guy at the building society thought I had half a chance. And if you need to borrow some money before that, I can help. It seems only fair."

The longer this conversation went on, the quicker Annie's ambiguities and confusions cleared up. Duncan's obvious regret helped immensely, in the usual unhealthy way. Now that she wasn't actually being rejected, it was quite clear to her that she didn't want to be with him a moment longer, and her sense of grievance gave her a force and clarity that she wished were always accessible to her.

"I never thought you'd be so . . . *tough.*"

"And I'm tough because I've just offered to lend you money?"

"Well, yes. You'd rather lend me money than have me back."

And another thing: he was stingy, on top of everything else. Duncan would much rather stay in a relationship with a woman he didn't like than lend her a few quid.

"Make me another cup of tea, will you? I'm just nipping upstairs to the loo."

She didn't need to go, and she didn't want another drink, and she didn't want Duncan to stay. But he'd have to go to the fridge for the milk, and if he went to the fridge, he couldn't fail to notice the photo.

By the time she came back he was staring at it.

"That's him, isn't it?"

"I'm sorry. I should have taken it down."

"I don't wish to be rude. But . . . is that his son? Or grandson?"

Annie was momentarily disconcerted: she had got lost in all the layers of irony. Duncan was missing so much crucial information that all he'd been left with was a photo of a bespectacled, silver-haired man with a young boy.

"That is rude, actually."

"I'm sorry. It just wasn't immediately obvious."

"It's his son. He's only your age."

He wasn't, but he could have been. More or less.

"He's probably been around the block a couple of times, then. Any other kids?"

"Duncan, I'm sorry, but I think you should leave. I'm not comfortable with these questions."

It really hadn't been as much fun as she'd hoped.

She still had his e-mail, though, and she'd only read it through once. She'd printed it at work, along with the photograph, and she'd put it in an envelope, to keep it from getting dog-eared and dirtied by all the detritus at the bottom of her workbag. After she'd made herself something to eat, she sat down and unfolded it, but stood up again when she decided she'd like to wear her reading glasses. She hardly ever bothered with them.

She was reminding herself of somebody. The letter (because that's what it was now), the glasses, the armchair . . . How many times had she watched her mother and grandmother sit down to pay proper attention to something that had come in the mail? And who were all those people who wrote to them? Names started to come back, names she hadn't heard in years: Betty in Canada—who was Betty? Why was she in Canada? How come Gran knew her? Auntie Vi in Manchester, who wasn't an auntie . . . When Annie was in her mid-teens, and had thus become surly and superior, she couldn't keep herself from feeling that there was something depressing about the good cheer that invariably accompanied the arrival of those letters. Who cared if Betty's niece was pregnant, or if Auntie Vi's grandson was a trainee vet? If Mum and Gran weren't so isolated and bored, none of this would be regarded as news.

And now here Annie was, allowing her day to become gloriously colored by a communication from a man she'd never even met.

ten

I n the last e-mail Annie had sent Tucker, she'd posed the following question:

What do you do if you think you've wasted fifteen years of your life?

She'd had no reply, as yet, possibly because of the domestic turmoil he'd hinted at the last time he'd written, so she'd had to address the problem on her own. She was currently working on the assumption that time was money. What would she do if she'd just lost fifteen thousand pounds? It seemed to her that there were two alternatives: you could either write it off or try to get it back. And you could try to get it back either from the person who took it from you in the first place or by trying to compensate for the loss in other ways—by selling stuff, or betting on a horse, or doing lots of overtime.

This analogy was only helpful up to a point, obviously. Time wasn't money. Or rather, the time she was talking about couldn't be converted into cash, like the services of a lawyer, or a prostitute. Or rather (one last "or rather," otherwise she'd have to concede that this whole way of thinking about time wasn't working) it could, theoretically, but nobody was going to pay her. She could knock on Duncan's—Gina's!— door and demand compensation for the time she'd wasted on him, but the value would be difficult to calculate, and anyway, Duncan was cheap. She didn't want money, though. She wanted the time back, to spend on something else. She wanted to be twenty-five again.

If she hadn't wasted so much time with Duncan, she might be better equipped to work out where it had gone; she had never been very good at algebra, and algebra was, it seemed to her, what was needed for the kind of thinking she wanted to do. One of the traps she kept falling into—and she couldn't help it, even though she was aware of it—was to equate time with Duncan as time generally. $T = D$, when of course T really equaled $D + W + S + F\&F + C$, where W is work, S is sleep, $F\&F$ is family and friends, C is culture and so on. In other words, she'd wasted only her romantic time on Duncan, whereas life consisted of more than that. In her own defense, though, she would like to point out that D was more than just one element to rack up alongside the others. She saw his F&F, for example, as well as her own, although admittedly he had fewer of both. Who knows whether W would have been different if D hadn't been living in the same town? She was guessing it might have been. They stayed put, doing jobs that satisfied neither of them, because finding new work in the same place at the same time would have been almost impossible. And whose C was it anyway? He was the one who bought the music and the DVDs, he was the one who didn't like going to the theater (or to other towns to see it) . . . She couldn't do equations, really, but she thought it was probably more like

$$T = \frac{W + S + F\&F + C}{D}$$

And there was another part of the equation that she didn't like thinking about: her own stupidity and torpor (OST). She had played a part in all this. She had allowed her life to drift. She would have to multiply the whole bloody lot by OST, thus ending up with a number greater than the one she'd first thought of. And if it turned out she'd wasted twenty or fifty or a hundred years, then whose fault was that?

· · ·

The fifteen years were gone, anyway. And what had gone with them? Children, almost certainly, and if she ever did take Duncan to court, that's what she would sue him for. But what else? What hadn't she done because she'd spent too much time with a boring, faithless nerd, apart from live the kind of life she'd wanted when she was twenty-five? She kept coming back to sex. It was reductive and unimaginative, she knew that, but it was also unarguable: Duncan had kept her from having sex with other people, and quite often with him. (They had never been the most highly sexed couple, but whoever kept score of these things would say he'd turned down her overtures more often than she'd turned down his.) How could she make up for fifteen years of missed opportunity, aged thirty-nine? And how much sex was that anyway? Suppose she'd met somebody she loved passionately fifteen years ago, and the relationship had endured? Then it would be fifteen years of sex with Other Man (OM) minus fifteen years of sex with Duncan. To include quality (Q) in the calculation would require a mathematical sophistication that was beyond her capabilities, even though it was probably necessary to give an accurate final figure.

In other words: she wanted to see if anyone would want to have sex with her. Where to start, in Gooleness?

. . .

She asked Ros, first of all, on the grounds that Ros was younger, and that younger people were closer to sex than she was.

"I can tell you how to meet gay women in London," Ros said.

"Right. Thanks. I'm going to aim at straight men in Gooleness first, but I might get back to you if it doesn't work out."

"What is it you're actually after? A one-night stand?"

"Maybe. If it stretched into a second night, I wouldn't complain. Unless, of course, the first night was horrific. Don't you know any single men?"

"Ummm . . . no. I'm not sure there are any. Not the kind you're looking for."

"What am I looking for?"

"Well, Gooleness has clubs, and lads, and . . . but . . ."

"I know the next four words you're going to say."

"What?"

" 'With all due respect.' "

Ros laughed.

"We could go out," she said. "If you want."

"But you're . . ."

"Gay? Or married?"

"Both."

"Here's the thing: I wouldn't be looking. I'd be helping you to look. We, in the meantime, would be having a night out. And if it looks as though you're in luck, I will make my excuses and leave. Unless you need me for anything."

"Don't be disgusting."

"Don't be prudish. Things have changed since you last slept with somebody for the first time. Unless there's been someone you haven't told me about."

"No. Duncan. In 1993."

"Blimey. You're in for a shock."

"That's what worries me. What sort of shock am I in for?"

"I just imagine a world of pornography and sex toys. And I'm presuming that there is always a minimum of three people involved."

"Oh, God."

"And then five minutes after you've finished doing it with a minimum of two other people, explicit images of your thirty-nine-year-old body will start appearing on your friends' mobile phones. And all over the Internet, of course, but that goes without saying."

"Right. Well. If that's what you have to do."

"Ideally, you'd want someone like you, wouldn't you? I don't mean, you know, a female museum curator. I mean someone who's just come out of a long relationship and is similarly perplexed by what happens now."

"I suppose."

"Let me think. What are you doing Friday night?"

Annie looked at her.

"Yes. Right. Sorry. Let's meet in the Rose and Crown at seven, and I'll bring a plan with me."

"A sex plan?"

"A sex plan."

The Rose and Crown, halfway between the museum and the college, was their usual meeting place. It was an unexceptional downtown pub, usually half-full of shop assistants and office workers too intimidated to drink in some of the seaside bars, all of which seemed to employ DJs, even on Sunday at lunchtime. Annie wondered whether there was, anywhere in the country, a DJ wondering how to break into the business. It seemed unlikely, given the number of establishments that seemed to think they needed one. On the contrary, she suspected demand was such that young people had to be coerced into playing music in bars whether they wanted to or not, like a form of national service. Anyway, the Rose and Crown had a jukebox that offered Vince Hill's version of "Edelweiss," an offer that was only rarely taken up, in Annie's experience. It was hard to imagine many sex plans being drawn up in there. And if any were, they would be safe-sex plans, drawn up slowly, and running to several pages of warnings.

Ros bought two half-pints of pale ale and they sat down at the back of the pub, away from a quiet group of fragrant-looking women who appeared as though they were trying to understand the root cause of a particularly bad day's profits at the Body Shop. Annie realized she was nervous, or excited, or something. Not because she seriously believed that there would be a plan, but because somebody was about to demonstrate interest in how she might spend part of the rest of her life—it had been a very long time since she had provided anyone with anything to talk about. She was somebody's project. She hadn't even been her own project for a while.

"There's a book group," said Ros. "But not in Gooleness, you know, proper. In a village just outside. You could borrow my car."

"And there are single men in it?"

"Well, no. Not at the moment. But a friend who belongs feels that if there were any single arts-graduate males in the area, that's where they'd wash up eventually. There was one a couple of years ago, apparently. Anyway. Just a thought. And the other one I had was that we could go away for the weekend. To Barcelona, maybe. Or Reykjavik, if Iceland still exists."

"So. Let's get this straight. The best way to have sex in

Gooleness is either to join a book club not actually in the town, with no men in it, or to go to another country."

"These are just initial ideas. Others will come. And we haven't even touched on Internet dating. Ah. Look. As if by magic."

Two men in their early forties had come into the pub. While one was at the bar buying two pints of lager, the other was examining the jukebox. Annie studied him and tried to imagine taking off her clothes for him or with him. Would he even want her to? She had absolutely no idea whether she was even passably attractive; she felt as though she hadn't looked in a mirror for years. She was about to ask Ros (and surely having a lesbian friend would be helpful, or was that not how it worked?) when he started shouting at his friend.

"Gav! Gav!"

The music he'd chosen came on, a bright, fast and tinny soul song that sounded like Tamla Motown but wasn't.

"Fucking hell!" said Gav. "Go on, Barnesy. Get yourself warmed up."

"Too much carpet," said Barnesy, who was small, skinny and muscular, and wearing baggy trousers and a Fred Perry sports shirt. If he were sixteen years old, and she was his teacher, Annie would have had him pegged for the kind of kid who would start a fight with the biggest guy in the class, just to show that he wasn't scared.

He put down the duffel bag he was carrying anyway, despite the carpet. It clearly wouldn't take much to push Barnesy over the edge, even though it wasn't entirely clear what lay beneath.

"Don't make excuses," said Gav. "These ladies want to see what you've got. Don't you, ladies?"

"Well," said Ros. "Some of it."

That, Annie thought, was the sort of thing she'd have to come up with if she were ever to start picking up men in pubs. It was the speed that intimidated her. It wasn't as if "Some of it" was a Wildean one-liner, but it did the job, and both men laughed. Annie, meanwhile, was still trying to twist her mouth into a polite smile. It would take her five minutes to complete the smile, and probably another twenty-four hours to produce an accompanying snappy verbal response. Gav and Barnesy would probably have left by then.

What Barnesy had, it turned out, was an extraordinary array of gymnastic dance moves, which he proceeded to demonstrate for the duration of the song. To Annie's untutored eye, Barnesy was a heady mix of break-dancer, martial-arts warrior and Cossack—there were spins and flailing arms and push-ups and kicks—but it was his complete lack of embarrassment, his absolute confidence that what he was doing was something the half dozen people in the pub would want to see, that was really impressive.

"Good God," said Ros, when he'd finished. "What was that?"

"What do you mean, what was that?"

"I've never seen anything like it."

"You don't live in Gooleness then?"

"I do, actually. We both do."

"And you've never seen northern soul dancing?"

"I can't say I have. You, Annie?"

Annie shook her head and blushed. What was the blush for, actually? Why was she embarrassed to say that she hadn't seen northern soul dancing before? She wanted to punch her stupid treacherous cheeks in.

"That's what Gooleness *is*," said Barnesy. "The Gooleness all-nighters. We've been coming here since eighty-one, haven't we, Gav?"

"Where from?"

"Scunny. Scunthorpe."

"You come all the way to Gooleness from Scunthorpe to do northern soul dancing?"

" 'Course we bloody do. Only fifty miles."

Gav came back from the bar with their beers and put them down on the table at which Annie and Ros were sitting.

"What are you doing tonight?"

For a moment, Annie had the absurd notion that Ros was going to tell them precisely what they were doing, and that Gav or Barnesy or both would offer themselves up as the solution to the sex problem. She didn't think she wanted sex with either of them.

"Nothing," said Annie, quickly. The speed of the response, the eagerness it seemed to contain, was the diametric opposite of what she was after. By jumping in to stop Ros from talking about the sex plan, it seemed to her, she was more or less offering sex.

"Well, there we are then," said Gav, who seemed too chubby to be a northern soul dancer, if Barnesy's moves were indicative of the kind of stuff a northern soul dancer needed to strut. "We're laughing, aren't we? Two good-looking men, two good-looking women."

"Ros here is gay," said Annie. And then, helpfully, "A lesbian," as if this might clear up any doubts anyone had about the variety of homosexuality Ros subscribed to. If she had succumbed to the temptation to punch her own cheeks in earlier, the chances are that she wouldn't have been able to say anything quite so mortifyingly crass. Ros, to her credit, merely groaned and rolled her eyes. She would have been entitled to walk out of the pub and never contact Annie again.

"Annie!"

"A lesbian?" said Gav. "A real one? In Gooleness?"

"She's not a lesbo," said Barnesy.

"How can you tell?" said Gav.

"It's just what birds say when they don't like the look of you. Do you remember those two at the Blackpool all-nighter? Told us they weren't into men, and then we saw them with their tongues down the throats of the DJs."

Ros laughed. "I'm sorry if it seems like a brush-off," she said. "But I was gay long before you two walked in."

"Fucking hell," said Barnesy in wonderment. "You just walk around, gay, like."

"Yep."

"I've got to tell you," said Gav, with sudden excitement. "I . . ."

"You don't have to tell me at all," said Ros.

"You don't even know what I was going to say."

"You were going to say that, even though gay men make you sick to your stomach, the idea of gay women you find titillating in the extreme."

"Oh," said Gav. "You've heard that before, have you?"

"How does that work, anyway?" said Barnesy. "If one of you's gay and the other one isn't?"

"How does it work?" said Ros, and then, "Oh. No. We're not together. We're friends."

"Lezby friends," said Gav. "Geddit?"

Barnesy punched him hard on the arm. "That's the second stupid thing you've said. If you count the thing she didn't let you say. How old are you? Fucking idiot. Pardon my language, ladies. Anyway, it don't really matter, does it?"

"In what way?" said Ros.

"If you wanted to come with us. To be honest, I'm too tired for sex after an all-nighter anyway these days, so you being gay isn't as much of a problem as it might have been."

"That's good to hear," said Ros.

"I don't even know what northern soul is," said Annie. She was almost certain that there was nothing offensive in the admission, and, as far as she could tell, she had managed to make it without her face turning scarlet.

"You don't know what it is," said Barnesy, flatly. "How can you not know what it is? You don't like music, is that it?"

"I do. I love music. But . . ."

"What are you into, then?"

"Oh, you know. All sorts."

"Like what?"

This, she thought, was unbearable. Did this question still come up, after all these years? Clearly it did, and clearly it became harder to answer as you got older. In the time before Duncan, it had been easy: she was young, and she liked exactly the same kind of music as the young man asking the question, who, like her, was either on his

way to university, or an undergraduate, or recently graduated. So she could say that she listened to The Smiths and
Dylan and Joni Mitchell, and the young man would nod
and add The Fall to her list. Telling a boy in your class
that you liked Joni Mitchell was really another way of saying, "If the worst comes to the worst and you knock me
up, it'll be okay." But now, apparently, she was expected
to tell people who were not just like her, people who might
not have an arts degree (and she knew she was being presumptuous, but she had decided that Barnesy was not an
English graduate), and she knew that she could not make
herself understood. How could she, when she wasn't able
to use some of the cornerstones of her vocabulary—words
like Atwood and Austen and Ayckbourn? And that was
just the As. It was terrifying, the prospect of having to
engage with another human being without those crutches.
It meant exposing something else, something more than
bookshelves.

"I dunno. I listen a lot to Tucker Crowe?"

Was that true? Or did she just think a lot about Tucker
Crowe? Was it her way of saying "I'm taken. By a man I've
never met, who lives in another country"?

"What's he? Country and bloody western? I hate
that shit."

"No, no. He's more like, I don't know, Bob Dylan, or
Bruce Springsteen. Leonard Cohen."

"I don't mind a bit of the Boss sometimes. That 'Born in the U.S.A.' is all right when you've had a few and you're driving home. Bob Dylan's for students, and I've never heard of the other one. Leonard."

"But I do like soul music, too. Aretha Franklin and Marvin Gaye."

"Yeah, they're all right. But they're not Dobie Gray, are they?"

"Well, no," said Annie. She didn't know who Dobie Gray was, but it was safe to assume that he (he?) was neither Marvin nor Aretha. "What did Dobie Gray do, actually?"

"That was Dobie Gray! 'Out on the Floor'!"

"And you like that one."

"It's, I don't know, the national anthem of northern. It's not a matter of liking it or not. It's a classic."

"I see."

"Yeah. Dobie. And then there's Major Lance, and Barbara Mason, and . . ."

"Right. I've never heard of any of them."

Barnesy shrugged. In that case, the shrug seemed to indicate, there wasn't much he could do for her, and for a moment she could feel herself turning pedagogical, even though she was the one trying to do the learning. "You can do better than that," she wanted to say. "I'm not expecting a Reith Lecture, but you could attempt to describe what the music sounds like." She thought, inevitably, of Duncan—his earnestness, his desire always to make Tucker's music come alive through the words he used to talk about it. Maybe there was more to say about Tucker, what with the Juliet story and the Old Testament influences. But did that make it better, if there was more to unpack? And was Duncan more interesting as a result?

Eventually, through patient probing, Annie and Ros learned that northern soul was so called because people from the north of England, especially people in Wigan, liked it, which struck them both as remarkable and strangely empowering; there were very few areas in life, they felt, where people in Wigan and Blackpool had much influence on the terminology of black American culture. The music had for the most part been made in the 1960s, and as far as they could tell it sounded like Tamla Motown.

"But most Tamla's too famous, see?" said Gav.

"Too famous?"

"Not rare enough. It's got to be rare."

So Duncan would, despite all indications to the contrary, find common ground with Gav and Barnesy after all. There was the same need for obscurity, the same suspicion that if a piece of music had reached a large number of people, it had somehow been drained of its worth.

"Anyway," said Barnesy. "You coming or what?"

Annie looked at Ros, and Ros looked at Annie, and they shrugged and laughed and drained their glasses.

The all-nighter took place in the Gooleness Working Men's Club, a place that Annie must have walked past a thousand times without noticing. She tried to deal herself a feminism card by telling herself that she hadn't noticed because she wasn't welcome, but she knew it wasn't just that: the second word of the club's name was every bit as intimidating as the third.

As they waited behind their new friends to pay (ladies, she noted, were half-price tonight, which meant that she and Ros could get in for a fiver), Annie felt a weird sense of triumph: she was on the verge of discovering the real Gooleness, a town that had effectively evaded her for all these years. Barnesy had told them that what they were about to see—to participate in, even, if she screwed up her courage and danced—was what Gooleness was; he'd been quite emphatic about it. So, as she walked down the stairs into the club, she was looking forward to a seething, teeming, wriggling, wiggling throng of dancers, many of whom she'd recognize: she wanted to see former pupils, local shopkeepers, museum regulars, all of whom would look at her as if to say, "Here we are! What kept you?" This could be it, she thought. This could be the night I feel I belong here.

But when they turned the corner and got their first look at the dance floor beneath them, the triumph shrunk into a little hard knot of embarrassment. There were thirty or forty people spread thinly around the large basement room, only a dozen or so of whom were dancing. Each dancer had acres of space to himself (most of them were men, and most of them were dancing on their own). None of the dancers or the drinkers around the edge was young. It turned out that she'd known all the time what Gooleness was: a place whose best days were behind it, a place that held on grimly to what was left of the good times it used to have, back in the eighties or the seventies or the thirties or the century before last. Gav and Barnesy stopped for a moment on the stairs and looked down wistfully.

"You should have seen it when we first started coming," said Gav. "It was mental." He sighed. "Why does everything have to fucking wither and die? Get the beers in, Barnesy." If Gav or Barnesy had mentioned the withering and the dying, Annie thought, they might not have bothered to come.

Ros and Annie understood that they were not being included in the round, so Ros went off to the bar while Annie watched an elderly man with a mane of gray hair try to decide whether he was going to dance or just tap his feet and snap his fingers. It was Terry Jackson, the councillor with the treasure trove of old bus tickets, and when he noticed Annie, he looked startled, and the finger-snapping stopped.

"Bloody hell," he said. "Annie the museum lady. I wouldn't have thought this was your scene."

"It's old music, isn't it?" she said. She was quite pleased with that. It wasn't downright hilarious, but it was an appropriate and lighthearted response, delivered moderately quickly.

"How d'you mean?"

"Old music. Museums."

"Oh, I see. Very good. Who brought you along?"

She bridled a little. Why did she have to be "brought along"? Why couldn't she have discovered it for herself, come on her own, persuaded others to accompany her? She actually knew the answer to those questions. The bridling was unnecessary.

"A couple of guys we met in the pub." She wanted to laugh at the sheer outlandishness of this most ordinary of explanations. She wasn't someone who met a couple of guys in a pub.

"I probably know them," said Terry. "Who are they?"

"Two chaps from Scunthorpe."

"Not Gav and Barnesy? They're legends."

"Are they?"

"Well, only because they've been coming from Scunny

for twenty-odd years, never miss. And Barnesy can dance, did you know that?"

"He showed us in the pub."

"He's serious. Always got his little tub of talcum powder."

"What does he do with it?"

"Sprinkles it on the floor. For grip, you see? That's what the serious ones do. Talc and a towel, that's what you keep in your sports bag."

"You're not serious then, Terry?"

"I can't dance like I could. But I wouldn't miss one. This is the last thing we've got left here, more or less. It's a sort of long good-bye to the old days, when I had my scooter, and we used to get into . . . *scrapes* on the seafront. The mods up here all became northern soulies. But it's not going to last much longer, is it? Look at us."

Suddenly, Annie saw everything too clearly, and she felt sick. It had all gone, the whole fucking lot; it was all over. Gooleness, Duncan, her childbearing years, Tucker's career, northern soul, all the exhibits in the museum, the long-dead shark, the long-dead shark's cock, and his eye, too, the 1960s, the Working Men's Club, probably working men as well . . . She had come out tonight because she believed there had to be a present tense, somewhere, and she'd followed Gav and Barnesy because she'd hoped they knew where it was. Is. And they'd dragged her to yet another haunted house. Where was the now? In bloody America, probably, apart from the bit that Tucker lived in, or in bloody Tokyo. In any case, it was somewhere else. How could people who didn't live in bloody America or bloody Tokyo stand it, all that swimming around in the past imperfect?

They had children, these people. That was how they stood it. The realization rose slowly through the bitter ale she'd been drinking, and then slightly more quickly through the lager that lay on top of it, and the gin that lay on top of the lager, the increased speed possibly a result of all the bubbles. That was why she wanted children, too. The cliché had it that kids were the future, but that wasn't it: they were the unreflective, active present. They were not themselves nostalgic, because they couldn't be, and they retarded nostalgia in their parents. Even as they were getting sick and being bullied and becoming addicted to heroin and getting pregnant, they were in the moment, and she wanted to be in it with them. She wanted to worry herself sick about schools and bullying and drugs.

An epiphany, then. That seemed to be what it was. But epiphanies were a little like New Year's resolutions, Annie found: they just got ignored, especially if you experienced them during a northern soul night when you'd had a couple of drinks. She'd probably had three or four epiphanies in her entire life, and she'd been either drunk or busy every time. What good was an epiphany then? You really needed one on a mountaintop a couple of hours before you were going to make a life-changing decision, but she couldn't recall ever having had these experiences singly, let alone in tandem. And in any case, what use was an epiphany that revealed to you that everything you did revolved around the dead and the dying? What was she supposed to do with that information?

The consequence of ignoring her epiphany was that she stayed in the club, and drank, and danced a little, with pudgy Gav, mostly, because Barnesy was off doing handstands and kung-fu kicks and dusting the floor with talc, and because Ros left at around midnight, with Annie's permission, and because Terry Jackson stayed at the bar, drinking and getting morose about the good old days, when you could get into a fight without anyone running off whining to the bloody Health and bloody Safety brigade. And when she eventually left, at two in the morning, Barnesy followed her out, and then home, and she found herself inviting a man she had only just met to spend the night on her couch, and then sitting on her sofa watching him attempting to do the splits while declaring his love for her.

"I do."

"No you don't."

"I bloody do. I bloody love you. I've loved you since I saw you in the pub."

"Because my mate turned out to be gay."

"That just made it easier to make my mind up."

Annie laughed and shook her head, and Barnesy looked pained. It was something, anyway. It was an anecdote, an event, a moment that didn't refer back to something earlier in her life, or the life of the country. This was happening now, in her living room. Maybe that was why she'd offered Barnesy the couch in the first place. Maybe she'd hoped he might do the splits while telling her he loved her, and, gratifyingly, that was exactly what was happening.

"I'm not just saying it because I'm, you know, exerting myself acrobatically. It's the other way round. I'm exerting myself because I love you."

"You're very sweet," she said. "But I need to go to bed."

"Can I come with you?"

"No."

"No? Just, like, no?"

"Just no."

"Are you married?"

"Do you mean, is my husband asleep in the marital bed, which is why I'm not letting you in there? No."

"So what's the problem?"

"There's no problem. Well, there is, actually. I'm seeing someone. But he lives in America."

Consistency and repetition were beginning to make the lie feel something like the truth, in the way that a path eventually becomes a path, if enough people walk along it.

"Well, there we are then. America . . ." He turned his palms upward, to enforce the point he felt he'd just made.

"We don't have that kind of relationship."

"Think about it."

"Barnesy, there's nothing to think about."

"I think you're wrong."

"What is there to think about?"

"It's not about thinking, is it?" said Barnesy passionately.

"So I was right. There's nothing to think about."

"I'm getting a divorce. If that makes any difference. I've been thinking I would for a while, but meeting you has made my mind up for me."

"You're married? Bloody hell, Barnesy. You've got a cheek."

"Yes, but hear me out. She hates the all-nighters. She hates northern. She likes bloody . . . I don't know. Girls with big hair who've won them talent shows."

He stopped, and seemed to consider what he'd just said.

"Bloody hell. That's really true. We've got nothing in

common. I've only just realized how unsuited we are. I really am going to get a divorce. I'm not just saying that to you. I'm going to get one anyway."

"Well, see how you feel when you get home."

"My mind's made up."

"I don't think you and I would be much better."

"Why not? You had fun tonight, didn't you?"

"Well. Yes. Some fun. But to be honest I spent much of the evening with Gav. Or Terry Jackson. Or Ros. You were on your own most of the time."

"That's how I dance, though. The way I do it, with the handstands and all that, I have to be on my own on the dance floor. I wouldn't be like that if we were just, you know, inside watching telly."

"Do you mean, you wouldn't be off on your own, with your own telly? Or do you mean that you wouldn't be doing handstands while our favorite program was on?"

"Well. Both. Neither. My fishing I'd do on my own. I mean, I do already. I'm just saying."

"It's good to be straight with each other right from the start."

"You're taking the piss," said Barnesy, mournfully.

"I am a bit."

"Fair enough. I'm talking rubbish, aren't I?" He stood up. "I think I'll be going."

"I'm serious about the sofa."

"That's very kind of you. But I wasn't ever very interested, to be honest. My game plan was always, you know, sex or bust."

"But what's bust?"

"Bust is going back to the all-nighter. I don't usually crap out early. It's a tribute to you that I've wasted any time here at all."

Barnesy offered his hand, and Annie shook it.

"It's been a pleasure, Annie. Not as much of a one as I'd have wanted, but, you know. Can't have everything."

The next morning, she still wasn't entirely sure whether she'd dreamed him, whether his small, muscular body and his talcum powder and his flips and spins were meant to be decoded by a psychoanalyst, who would tell her that she had a peculiar view of male sexuality.

She made the mistake of trying to explain her evening out the following morning, in her session with Malcolm. She was possibly still a little drunk when she went to see him and she decided that Malcolm's stuffiness would provide a satisfyingly easy target for her mood of tipsy recklessness; talking to him about sex plans would be as much fun as squirting him with a water pistol. But she squirted, and he got wet, and then he sat there, looking sad, and she could no longer remember why she ever thought it would be fun.

"A sex plan? You met up with a gay friend to prostitute yourself?"

Where to begin with this?

"Her being gay isn't really relevant." Probably not there.

"I didn't know there was a lesbian in Gooleness." Definitely not there, in fact. Malcolm was not going to find it easy to leave Ros's sexuality unexamined.

"There are at least two. But that's not . . ."

"Where do they go?"

"What do you mean, where do they go?"

"Well, I know I'm out of touch. But I've never heard of any lesbian bars or clubs here."

"Malcolm, they don't need to go to lesbian clubs. In the same way that you don't need to go to heterosexual pubs. Clubs aren't a necessary part of homosexuality."

"Well, I don't think I'd be comfortable in a non-heterosexual pub."

"They go to the cinema. And to restaurants, and pubs, and people's houses."

"Ah," said Malcolm, darkly. "People's houses." The implication was clear: you could get up to almost anything in private homes, behind closed doors.

"Maybe you should talk directly to her," said Annie, "if you're so curious about Gooleness lesbians."

Malcolm blushed.

"I'm not curious. I'm just . . . interested."

"I don't want to come across as egotistical," said Annie, "but can we talk about me?"

"I don't know what you've come here to talk about."

"My problems."

"I've lost track of what they are. There seems to be a different one every week. We don't even mention your long monogamous relationship anymore. All those years seem to count for nothing. You're more interested in picking men up in nightclubs."

"Malcolm, I've told you about this before. If you're going to be judgmental, then perhaps it's better if I stopped coming."

"Well, that sounds to me as if you intend to do a lot of things I'd want to be judgmental about. Which in turn sounds to me as if you should keep coming to see me."

"What would you want to be judgmental about?"

"Well, do you really intend to sleep around?"

She sighed.

"It's as if you don't know me at all."

"I don't know this version of you. The one that suddenly decides she wants to have sex with the first Tom, Dick and/or Harry that comes along."

"Except I didn't, did I?"

"Last night, you mean?"

"I could have slept with Barnesy, but I didn't." She wished she'd taken the trouble to find out his first name. A first name would have helped her preserve some dignity in situations like this.

"And why didn't you?"

"Because, no matter what you think, I'm not a complete slut."

She wasn't any kind of slut at all, of course. She'd slept with one man for fifteen years, sporadically, and mostly without any real enthusiasm. But even saying the words "I'm not a complete slut" had somehow boosted her sexual confidence. She couldn't have imagined saying them twenty-four hours earlier.

"What was wrong with him?"

"Nothing. He was sweet. Odd, but sweet."

"So what were you looking for?"

"I know exactly what I'm looking for."

"Really?"

"Yes. Really. Somebody my age or older. Somebody who reads. Maybe somebody with a, a creative bent of some kind. If he had a child or children of his own, I wouldn't mind. Somebody who's lived a bit."

"I know who you're describing."

Annie doubted it very much, but for a moment she wondered whether Malcolm was going to produce somebody for her—maybe a recently divorced son who wrote poetry and played in the Manchester Philharmonic.

"Really?"

"The opposite."

"The opposite of what?"

"Of Duncan."

It was the second time recently that Malcolm had made an observation that could, presumably wrongly, be described as perceptive. Tucker was the opposite of Duncan. Duncan had no children of his own, no creative bent, and he hadn't lived, not even a little. Or at least, he had never thrown stones at a noted beauty's window, had never been an alcoholic, hadn't toured the United States and Europe, hadn't thrown away a God-given talent. (Even Tucker's way of not living could be described as living, if you had a crush on him.) Was that it? Was she in love with Tucker because he was the opposite of Duncan? Was *Duncan* in love with Tucker because he was the opposite of Duncan? In which case Annie and Duncan had both managed to create an empty space, a complicated one, with all sorts of tricky corners and odd bumps and surprising indents, like a jigsaw piece, and Tucker had filled it precisely.

"That's stupid," she said.

"Oh," said Malcolm. "Oh well. It was just a theory."

Dear Annie,

"What do you do if you think you've wasted
fifteen years of your life?" Are you kidding
me? I don't know if anyone ever told you, but
I'm pretty much the world expert on this particular subject. I mean, obviously I've wasted
more than fifteen years, but I'm hoping you'll
overlook the extra and look upon me as a
kindred spirit anyway. Maybe even your guru.

First of all, you have to get that number
down. Make a list of all the good books you've
read, movies you've seen, conversations
you've had and so on, and give all of these
things a temporal value. With a little bit of creative accounting, you should be able to reduce
it to ten. I've got mine down to about that
now, although I've cheated here and there—
I included the whole of my son Jackson's life,
for example, and he's been at school and
asleep for a lot of the time-wasting years.

I'd like to say that anything that comes in
around a decade you can write off for tax pur-
poses, but that isn't actually the way I feel.
I'm still pretty sick about what I've lost, but
I only admit it to myself late at night, which

is probably why I'm not the best sleeper. What can I tell you? If it really was wasted time—and I'd need to examine your diary pretty carefully before I could confirm that for you—then I have some bad news: it's gone. You can maybe add a little onto the other end by giving up drugs, or cigarettes, or by going to the gym a lot, but my guess is that those years after the age of eighty aren't as much fun as they're cracked up to be.

You know, from my e-mail address, if nothing else, that I have a thing for Dickens— I'm reading his letters at the moment. There are twelve volumes of them, and each volume is several hundred pages long. If he'd only written letters, he'd have had a pretty productive life, but he didn't only write letters. There are four volumes of his journalism, too, big ones. He edited a couple of magazines. He squeezed in an unconventional love life, and a few rewarding friendships. Am I forgetting anything? Oh, yeah: a dozen of the greatest novels in the English language. So I'm beginning to wonder whether my infatuation is caused, in part at least, by him being the opposite of me. He's pretty much the one guy whose life you could look at and think, man, he didn't mess around. That happens, right? People get drawn to opposites?

But there aren't many people like old Charlie. Most humans don't get to do work that's going to last. They sell shower curtain rings, like the John Candy character in that movie. (I mean, the rings might last. But they're probably not what people talk about after you've gone.) So it's not about what you do. It can't be, can it? It has to be about how you are, how you love, how you treat yourself and those around you, and that's where I get eaten up. I used to spend a lot of time drinking and watching TV, not loving anybody, wives or mistresses or kids, and there's no spin I can put on that. Which is why Jackson is such a big deal. He's my last hope, and I'm pouring everything that's left in me through the spout on the top of the little guy's head. That poor kid! Unless he surpasses the combined achievements of Dickens, JFK, James Brown and Michael Jordan, he'll have let me down. And I won't be around to see it anyway.

Tucker

Dear Annie,

I'm sending this e-mail about five minutes
after the last one. My advice, it now occurs
to me, was entirely worthless and borderline
offensive. I suggested that we can redeem
wasted time by cherishing and nurturing our
children, but you don't have any children.
Which is one of the reasons why you feel
you've been wasting time. I'm not quite as
perverse or obtuse as this might seem, but I
can see that my pitch to be your guru could
have gone better.

    I'm coming to London next week, by the
way, in unhappy circumstances. Are we getting
on fine as we are? Or would you like a drink?

It was the part about opposites that did it, of course. She
didn't know who or what she had fallen in love with, but
she was as lost and dreamy and helpless as she'd ever been
in her entire life.

eleven

"How can you just lose a baby?" said Jackson. "It hasn't even been born yet. It can't even go anywhere."

His eyebrows were high above his eyes, suggesting stifled mirth; the boy was pretty sure there was going to be a punch line to this joke, Tucker could tell, but he wasn't going to laugh until he'd been given permission.

"Yeah, well. When people say that someone's lost a baby . . ." He hesitated. Was there an easier, gentler way of doing this? Probably, but fuck it. "When people say that someone's lost a baby, it means the baby died."

The eyebrows fell.

"Died?"

"Yeah. It happens sometimes. Quite a lot, actually. Lizzie was unlucky, because usually it happens really early on, when the baby isn't even really a baby. But hers was a little bit older."

"Is Lizzie going to die, too?"

"No, no. She'll be okay. At the moment she's just very sad."

"So even babies die? Babies that haven't been born? That really, really sucks."

"It really, really does."

"Except," said Jackson, brightening, "except, you're not going to be a granddad."

"Not . . . Not yet, no."

"Not for ages. And if you're not going to be a granddad yet it means you might not die yet." And with that, Jackson started running up and down, whooping.

"Jackson! Stop being such a jerk!"

Tucker only rarely shouted at him, so whenever he did, the effect was dramatic. Jackson stopped dead, covered his ears with his hands and started to cry.

"That hurt my ears. A lot. I wish you'd died instead of that poor little baby."

"You don't mean that."

"This time I really do."

Tucker knew why he'd been so angry: it was guilt. The postponement of grandfatherhood hadn't been the first thing he'd thought of when Lizzie's mother called to tell him the news, but it had certainly been the second, and the space between the two hadn't been as respectful as he would have wished. He'd been reprieved. Someone up there had wanted to extend his—not his youth, of course, nor even, let's face it, his prime, but his pre-grandfatherly state. It wasn't what he'd wanted. He'd wanted Lizzie to be happy, to have a healthy child. But every cloud, and so on.

Meanwhile Jackson's sobs had stopped being angry and bitter. They were now pitiful and remorseful.

"I'm really so, so sorry, Dad. I didn't mean it. I'm glad the baby died and not you."

Somehow kids could never get it quite right.

"Anyway, I suppose we'll have to go to London and see Lizzie, right?"

"Oh, no. I don't think so. That isn't what she'd want."

It hadn't even crossed his mind. Was that bad? Probably. "Probably" was usually the answer to this particular question, in his experience, if the question was self-directed. But Natalie would be around, and Lizzie was close to her stepdad . . . There was no need for him to sit by her bedside not knowing what to say.

"She'd want to see you, Dad. I'd want to see you if I was sick."

"Yeah, but . . . You and me, we're different. I don't know Lizzie as well."

"We'll see," Jackson said.

. . .

Cat came over to take Jackson out for pizza. She'd offered to take Tucker out, too, but he'd declined—the boy needed some time alone with his mother, and anyway, Tucker wasn't ready to play happy modern fractured families yet. He was old-fashioned enough (and simple enough) to believe that if a man and his wife could share a pizza, then they could share a bed. He was, however, somewhat disconcerted to realize when he saw her that he could have done it, sat in the restaurant eating and chatting; this particular wound had taken only a short time to heal. A while back, he might have taken this as an indication of increasing psychic health, but in his experience anything to do with getting older rarely indicated good news. Presumably, then, it was doleful proof that he couldn't bring himself to give much of a shit about anything anymore. She was a good-looking woman, Cat, but he couldn't for the life of him remember what had pulled him toward her. And he could no longer re-create in his mind the circumstances that had led to their marriage, or the production of Jackson, or even the stormy weather of the last year or so.

"I suppose you'll have to go to London," Cat said, when he told her the news about Lizzie.

"Oh, no," he said, although the "Oh" was beginning

to sound superfluous and phony, even to him. This time it had crossed his mind. "I don't think so. That isn't what she'd want." Why not stick with a winning formulation?

"You think?" said Cat.

"It's not as if we're close," said Tucker. "She wouldn't be expecting me to fly across the Atlantic just to be useless."

"Nearly right," said Cat. "She'd be expecting you not to."

"Right," said Tucker. "Which is what I just said."

"No. It wasn't. Your way of putting it suggested that she wouldn't care one way or the other. My way—her way—is to think the worst of you. You don't know much about fathers and daughters, do you?"

"Not a lot, no." Not as much as he should, anyway, seeing as he was the father of a couple of daughters.

"And she flew all the way here to see you when she found out she was pregnant. There's something going on with her."

He finished buttoning up Jackson's coat and kissed him on the top of his head. Of course, the one kid who he hadn't fucked up was the one kid whose offspring he wasn't likely to see.

He phoned Natalie as soon as Cat and Jackson had left.

"When do you think you'll be coming to see her?" said Natalie.

"Oh," said Tucker, and this time the word was airier. "As soon as I can get things organized here."

"But you are coming? Lizzie didn't think you'd make the effort."

"Yeah, I guessed she'd think that. I know her better than she suspects. And she doesn't know me at all."

"She's very angry with you right now."

"Well, I guess this sort of thing stirs up all sorts of inner shit."

"I think you have to get used to it, as your children start to have children. It makes them see how absolutely hopeless you were."

"Great, I'm looking forward to it."

It was only much later, after he'd put Jackson to bed, that he realized he didn't have the money to go to London. He didn't have the money to go to New York City, was the truth of it; Cat was helping him out for the time being. What would come after that was a mystery, although not one he was particularly anxious to solve. Nobody would let Jackson starve, and that was the only thing that mattered. He called Natalie back and told her he'd been unable to make child-care arrangements.

"His mother won't look after him? Gosh."

That "gosh"—so English, so poisonous.

"Of course she would, but . . ."

"But what?"

"But she's away. On business."

"I thought she did things with yogurt."

"Why can't yogurt involve travel?"

"Wouldn't it go off?"

At least he could still feel the open, festering exit wound that Natalie had left, so that was something. That combination of bitchiness and stupidity was as hard to bear now as it had been back then.

"So bring him. I'm sure Lizzie would like to see him. She seemed quite taken with him."

"I don't think that's a good idea."

"Why not?"

"Well, it's the school year, and . . ."

"Lizzie said you and Cat were breaking up."

"That's something that . . . that seems to have happened, yes."

"So you can't afford to fly to London."

"It's not that."

"So you can afford to fly to London."

"If, you know, push came to shove."

"That's exactly where push has come."

"I can't afford to fly to London, no. There is a little cash-flow problem at the moment."

"We'll pay."

"No, I can't . . ."

"Tucker. Please."

"Fine. Thanks."

Having no money wasn't so bad, really, as long as he never did anything other than go for coffee with Fucker once a month or so. Adults, however, especially adults with several children, sometimes found themselves in a position where they needed access to a fund more bountiful than the bedroom change jar that departing ex-spouses had generously left behind. Natalie's husband did something . . . Actually, Tucker had no real idea what he did. He could remember that it was something he disapproved of, or had belittled, anyway, so he probably did something that involved going to meetings, possibly while wearing a suit. Was he an agent of some kind? Movies? It was coming back to him now. Simon (?) headed up the London branch of some unspeakable Hollywood agency. Maybe. He was a no-talent leech, anyway, Tucker was sure about that. It was easy to feel superior to these people while you were the talent. But when you stopped being the talent, then they were just grown-up people with a job, and you were the hopeless case who was going to have to accept charity from them.

"Do you know people in London?" said Natalie. "Is there somewhere you can stay?"

"Yeah," said Tucker. "I mean, she's not right in the center, but we can come in on the train or whatever."

"Where is 'she'?" Tucker was pretty sure there were quote marks around the pronoun. It would be entirely typical of Natalie to put them there.

"It's a place called Gooleness. On the coast."

Natalie shrieked into the phone. "Gooleness! How on earth do you know anyone who lives in Gooleness?"

"Long story."

"It's hundreds of miles outside London. You can't possibly stay there. Mark and I will find you somewhere."

Mark, then, not Simon. And on further reflection, Mark might not, after all, be a no-talent leech. That might well be somebody else's husband.

"Really? I don't want you to go to any trouble."

"Lizzie's flat is empty, for a start. She and Zak are going to stay with us for a little while when she gets out."

Was Zak her boyfriend? Had he heard that name before? The trouble was, there were too many tangential connections. Too many kids, too many stepfathers, too many half brothers and half sisters. He couldn't name half the people related to his children, he realized. Natalie had other kids, for example, but who the hell knew their names? Cat did, that's who.

"And do you still want to bring Jackson with you? Seeing as your child-care problems were completely bogus?"

"I guess not, no."

So he was off to London on his own.

. . .

"When will we get there?"

"Ten minutes. But Jackson, you understand that we're
ten minutes from the airport. And then we have to wait for
the plane. And then we wait for the plane to take off. And
then we fly for seven hours. And then we wait for our bags.
And then we wait for a bus. And then it's maybe another
hour from the airport to Lizzie's apartment. If you don't
think that sounds like much fun, then it's not too late. I
could take you to your mother's, and . . ."

"It sounds like fun."

"All that sitting around waiting sounds like fun."

"Yep."

It hadn't gone well, telling Jackson he was going to see
Lizzie without him, and there had been many, many tears,
followed by total capitulation. There had been times in
his life when he would have paid for tears like these to be
shed on his behalf: every single one of his other children
had cried unstoppably when a mother had attempted to
leave them in his care for a day or an afternoon or even
for twenty minutes while she took a bath, and he'd felt
wretched and useless every time. His own kids had been
afraid of him when they were young. Now he had a child
who needed him and loved him and felt anxious when
he went out (because "out" was all it had ever been with

Jackson, never "away"), and Tucker felt unmanned by it. Fathers weren't supposed to engender this level of dependency. They're supposed to miss bedtimes because of business trips and concert tours.

So he'd had to call Natalie and ask her to fork out money for an extra ticket, which made him feel even more inadequate than he had the first time. It was one thing not being able to afford to pay for himself, but fathers were supposed to be providers, as well as bedtime-missers. This father, however, was forced to depend on the largesse of the ex-wife before last and her leech of a husband.

They checked in, bought a small mountain of candy and a couple of dozen comic books. Tucker was feeling awful, anxious and sweaty; when he took Jackson for a pee he looked in a mirror and was alarmed by the complete absence of color from his face. Unless white could be counted as a color, which it probably could be, when it was this intense. He was almost certainly about to be laid low by flu, or pneumonia, or something, and he cursed his timing: in twenty-four hours' time, he'd be too sick to travel. He could have stayed home without losing face, without being the worst father in the world.

They waited in line to go through security, a process that could have been expressly designed to feed Jackson's morbidity. Tucker told him that they were looking for guns.

"Guns?"

"Sometimes bad guys take guns on planes because they want to rob rich people. But we're not rich, so they won't come near us."

"How will they know we're not rich?"

"Rich people wear stupid watches and smell nice. We're not wearing watches, and we smell bad."

"But why do we have to take our shoes off?"

"You can fit small guns in shoes. You'd have to walk funny, but you could do it."

An old English lady waiting in front of them turned around.

"It's not guns they're looking for, young man. It's bombs. I'm surprised Daddy hasn't heard of the Shoe Bomber. He was English, you know. I mean, Muslim, of course. But English."

Daddy has heard of the Shoe Bomber, thank you very much, you eavesdropping old crone, Tucker wanted to say. Now turn around and shut the fuck up.

"Shoe Bomber?" said Jackson.

Tucker could see right away that, if they ever got as far as London, they wouldn't be coming back. Not by plane, anyway. Mark would be coughing up the dough for a couple of tickets on a cruise ship, unless Jackson knew anything about the *Titanic*. In which case, Mark would be paying for an exclusive English boarding-school education, and Jackson would have to grow up with one of those tony boarding-school accents.

"Yes. He tried to blow up the plane by putting explosives in his shoes. Can you imagine? You wouldn't need very much, I suppose. Just enough to blow a small hole in the plane. And then *fsssssk*! We'd all get sucked out and dropped into the middle of the sea."

Jackson looked up at Tucker. Tucker made a face intended to indicate that the woman was gaga.

"I'm more and more thankful that my life is coming to its end," said the old lady. "I lived through a world war, but I've got a feeling that you're going to be seeing a lot worse than the Blitz when you grow up."

They stepped through the scanner and waved a cheery good-bye to the woman. And then Tucker began to tell the ingenious and preposterous lies that would enable them both to board the aircraft. He'd even had to tell Jackson that the old lady was entirely mistaken about the imminence of her own death, let alone all the other deaths she'd alluded to.

Tucker couldn't remember the last time he'd been on a plane. The day he'd quit music, he had flown, drunk and angry and remorseful and self-loathing, from Minneapolis to New York, and he'd hit on a stewardess, and tried to hit a woman who'd tried to stop him from hitting on the stewardess, so that particular flight tended to be the one that stayed in his mind. He'd been pretty sure at the time that the stewardess was going to be the answer to all his problems. His feeling was that they wouldn't stay together long, but probably there'd be lots of therapeutic fucking. And because she was a stewardess, she'd have to travel a lot, and in her absences he would do some writing, maybe go into a studio near where she lived, rebuild his career. These are all the things she didn't understand when he made his play. She thought he was just grabbing her ass, but there was more to it than that, as he'd tried to explain, tearfully, and at great volume. He loved her.

Jesus. He was lucky she'd been a reasonable human being. He could have found himself in front of a New Jersey judge. Instead he'd met someone else, and then someone else again, had kids . . . Maybe his hunch about the stewardess had been right. He wished he'd managed to convince her of their viability as a couple, although he couldn't wish Jackson away.

He looked down at the seat next to him. The boy was tucked under a blanket with his headphones on and was watching his fifth straight episode of *SpongeBob*. He was happy. Tucker had warned him that he might not like the movie they were showing on the plane, because that was what happened the last time Tucker flew across the Atlantic:

they showed a bad movie you didn't want to watch. Now they showed every bad movie ever made. Jackson had actually giggled when he realized, long before his father had worked out the sheer abundance of the entertainment system, the amount of junk he could consume; he now felt that the flight was a little on the short side. Tucker had given up on the romantic comedy he'd started watching. As far as he could figure out, the problem between the central couple, the thing that was keeping them from being together, was that she had a cat and he had a dog, and the cat and dog fought like cats and dogs, which made the couple, through some mysterious contagion that the film couldn't properly explain, fight like cats and dogs, too. Tucker got the feeling that they'd be able to solve their problems before the two hours were up. He wasn't worried for them. He was now failing to read *Barnaby Rudge*. Dickens seemed wrong among all these little screens and bleeping lights and miniature cans of soda.

He was still feeling wretched, and he couldn't shake off a sense of impending catastrophe, which he seemed to recall was a textbook indicator of something-or-other. Jackson had turned him into a hypochondriac—his son's conviction that just about any cough or unexplained ache was cancer, or old age, anyway, wasn't good for either of them—but he was pretty sure that the sweating, the arrhythmia and the foreboding were a result of his sudden and unexpected emergence from hiding. He knew the people who cared about him out there in the conjectural world of cyberspace described him as a recluse, but he'd never thought of himself that way. He went to shops and bars and Little League games, so it wasn't as if he were Salinger. He just didn't make music or talk to earnest young magazine journalists, and most people didn't do either of those things. But in the airport he'd noticed himself walking around with his eyes and mouth wide open, so maybe he was a little bit more Kaspar Hauser than he'd thought. And planes were unnervingly different, and they were on their way to a big city, to hang out with an ex-wife and daughter who hated him . . . It was a miracle that his heart was able to keep any time at all, so 7/4, if that's what it was, seemed perfectly acceptable. He put his book down and fell into a sickly, clammy doze.

Natalie had sent a car to pick them up. They were taken to Lizzie's apartment somewhere in Notting Hill, and the driver waited for them while they dumped their bags and changed into clean underwear. Tucker was feeling dizzy and nauseous by now, as well as spooked, and though he wanted to rest, he definitely didn't want to puke all over Lizzie's white rugs. Lizzie had been transferred to a regular hospital—a regular swanky hospital, anyway—because of complications, so if he had to puke, he'd try and wait until he got there.

He remembered what it was that a feeling of impending catastrophe typically foreshadowed just as he was in the middle of pushing open the stupidly heavy glass door of the swanky hospital. Somebody, possibly a robot King Kong, put a pair of giant steel arms around his chest and started squeezing. Savage electric pain shot down his arm and up his neck, and he tried not to look at Jackson's pale and frightened face. He wanted to apologize—not for feeling sick, but for all the lies he'd told. "I'm sorry, son," he wanted to say. "That stuff about nobody dying ever . . . It wasn't true. People die all the time. Get over it."

He walked as steadily and as coolly as he could to the reception desk.

"Can I help you?" said the woman. He could see his reflection in her glasses. He tried to look beyond the lenses into her eyes.

"I hope so. I'm pretty sure I'm having a heart attack."

There are all sorts of causes of ripples of movement across continents: floods and famine, revolution, large international sports events. In this case, however, the trigger was the sudden illness of one middle-aged man. Telephones rang in houses and apartments across the U.S. and Europe, and they were answered by attractive, still-slender women in their thirties and forties and early fifties. Hands were clapped to mouths, more phone calls were made, reassurances were given by careful soft voices. Flights were booked, passports were found, arrangements were canceled. The wives and children of Tucker Crowe were on their way to see him.

It was all Lizzie's idea. In real life, she was a sentimental young woman, frequently moved to tears by pets and children and romantic comedies; but life with Tucker wasn't real life, not least because there was so little of it, and the time she had with him always became overwhelmed by the time she had never had. How could it not? It wasn't a fair fight. Just the sight and sound of him made her shrill and resentful: she hated the way her voice rose by an octave when they talked. But when she went to see him in his hospital room, he was asleep, sedated and helpless, and she didn't feel angry anymore. She could be a dutiful and loving daughter, as long as he just lay there. When he awoke, she was determined to talk to him in the same voice she used for the people she loved.

She'd been told that he wouldn't die, but that wasn't the point: they had to seize the moment. If she felt more goodwill toward Tucker than she had ever managed to muster before, then surely everyone else was feeling it, too? And she couldn't help believing that some kind of gathering, some attempt to connect a previously incoherent family, is what he would want. It wasn't her fault that she didn't know him at all.

June 12, 1986, Minneapolis

In the early days of his career, Tucker had collected stories of musicians' bad behavior as if they were baseball cards. They fascinated him not because he wanted to emulate the musicians concerned, but because he was a moralist, and the stories were so unambiguously appalling that they served as a useful piloting guide: in his line of work, it didn't take much to gain a reputation as a decent human being. As long as you didn't hurl a girl out of a window when you'd finished with her, people thought you were Gandhi. He'd even got into fights a couple of times, in a pompous attempt to protect somebody's honor—a girl, a roadie, a motel receptionist. Once, when he'd punched the obnoxious bassist of an indie-rock band that ended up filling stadiums, he was asked who'd died and made him fucking king. The question was rhetorical, of course, but he'd ended up thinking about it. Why couldn't he let these young men behave like young men? Musicians had been assholes since the day the lute was invented, so what did he think he was going to achieve by pushing a couple around when they'd had a drink? For a while, he blamed the kind of novels he read, and he blamed the decency of his parents, and he blamed his brother, who had managed to kill himself by driving into a wall when he was drunk. Books and parents and a tragic fuckup brother, he felt, had given him a solid ethical grounding. He could see now that he'd always been heading for a fall. It turned out that he was the kind of moralist who abhorred the behavior of others because he was so scared of his own weakness; the more he whipped himself into a frenzy of disapproval, the harder it would be to cave in without losing face. He was certainly right to be afraid. When he met Julie Beatty, he discovered that there wasn't very much to him aside from weakness.

When he woke up that morning, Tucker Crowe had no idea that he would end the day by walking out on his own life, but, if he'd known, he wouldn't have minded much, because he was sick of it. If you'd asked him what the problem was . . . Well, if *you* had asked him, he wouldn't have said anything, because he liked to remain laconic, cryptic and gently satirical at all times, because it was cooler that way. Who are you, to be asking Tucker Crowe questions? Some fucking rock journalist? Or, even worse, a fan? But if he'd asked himself—which he did, sometimes, when he wasn't drunk or asleep—he'd tell himself (exclusively) that what made him unhappiest on a daily basis was this: he had come to the inescapable and unhappy conclusion that

Juliet, the album he was currently promoting every night onstage, was utterly inauthentic, completely phony, full of melodrama and bullshit and he hated it.

This wasn't necessarily a problem. Bands were always promoting product that they didn't like very much, and presumably actors and writers did the same: something had to be your worst piece of work. But *Juliet* was different, because it was the only record Tucker had ever made that people seemed to like. It hadn't sold many copies, but over the last few months credulous college kids who'd never read or heard anything containing real pain, let alone experienced it firsthand, were turning up at shows in the hundreds and singing along to every word of every song. They swallowed Tucker's portentous, self-righteous, whiny rage whole, as if it meant something to them, and the only way he could deal with them was to close his eyes and aim his voice somewhere just over their heads. (This coping mechanism, inevitably, had led a reviewer to describe him as "still lost in his pain.") It wasn't as though he thought the songs were entirely without merit. Musically, they were pretty good, and he and the band had got better at playing them, too; most nights they built up a pretty ferocious head of steam. "You and Your Perfect Life," which closed the show every night, was a real tour de force now, and in the midsection of the song, right before the guitar solo, Tucker had taken to incorporating fragments of other famous love songs from an earlier time: "When Something Is Wrong with My Baby" one night; "I'd Rather Go Blind" the next. Sometimes he dropped down on one knee to sing them, and sometimes audiences rose to their feet, and sometimes he felt as though he were a proper entertainer, someone whose job it was to make extravagant emotional gestures to help people feel. And the lyrics for "You and Your Perfect Life" weren't too shabby either, even if they were his. He'd dressed up his rejection by Julie Beatty in some pretty fancy clothes, he thought.

No, the trouble was with Julie Beatty herself. She was an idiot, an airhead, a shallow, vain and uninteresting model who happened to be awfully pretty, and Tucker had discovered this shortly after a collection of hymns to her mystery and power had been presented to an apparently awestruck public. When she first heard the album, she was so moved by Tucker's misery that she promptly left her husband for a second time—the poor guy must have had a crick in his neck by then, from watching his wife running up and down their stairs with a suitcase—and offered herself up to Tucker like a gaudily wrapped present; after three days holed up with her in a hotel room, it became apparent to him that he'd have more in common with a sixteen-year-old Nebraskan cheerleader. She didn't read, didn't talk, didn't think, and she was the vainest human being he'd ever met. What had he been thinking? He'd been drunk when he met her the first time around, and then there'd been the whole sneaking-around drama of it, which in Tucker's experience always added another level of intensity; but it wasn't just that. He had wanted to live in her world. He wanted to know the people she knew; it was his *right* to go over to Faye Dunaway's house for dinner. He was owed that. He had the talent, but he didn't have the lifestyle that he felt should accompany that talent. In other words, he'd behaved like an asshole, and *Juliet* was going to serve as some kind of permanent reminder of his embarrassment and shame.

June the twelfth was a day like most of the others. They'd driven from St. Louis to Minneapolis, and he'd slept in the van, read a little, listened to The Smiths on his Walkman, inhaled the repulsive Cheez Doodles farts of the rhythm section. They'd done the sound check, eaten, and Tucker had nearly finished off the bottle of red wine he'd promised himself he wouldn't touch until after the show. He'd abused his band—mocked his drummer's ignorance of current events, questioned his bass player's personal hygiene—and hit obnoxiously on the promoter's wife. And then, after the show, someone had suggested checking out some band in some club, and Tucker was drunk by then and didn't want to stop drinking and he thought he'd heard something good about the band anyway.

He was standing by the bar on his own, squinting at

the stage and trying to remember the name of the person who'd told him that these losers were worth walking nine blocks to see. And then he wasn't on his own anymore. He'd been joined by a big, long-haired guy in a cap-sleeved T-shirt, exposing upper arms that looked like a wrestler's thighs. I'm not going to get into a fight with this guy, Tucker told himself for no reason at all, although over the last year or so, since he'd become thirstier, no reason at all had often been reason enough for a fight. The guy leaned against the wall next to him, mimicking Tucker's stance, and Tucker ignored him.

The guy leaned into him and shouted into his ear, above the noise. "Can I talk to you?"

Tucker shrugged.

"I'm a friend of Lisa's. Jerry. I'm the road manager for the Napoleon Solos."

Tucker shrugged again, although he felt a tiny surge of panic. Lisa was the girl he'd been seeing when he met Julie. Lisa had been badly treated. He'd go so far as to use the active voice, in fact: he'd treated Lisa badly. He hadn't even stopped sleeping with her when he was chasing Julie Beatty, mostly because that would have required a conversation that he wasn't prepared to have. In the end, he'd just . . . not returned. He didn't want to speak to any friends of Lisa's.

"You don't want to know how she's doing?"

He shrugged for a third time.

"I have a feeling you're going to tell me anyway, whatever I want."

"Fuck you," said the guy.

"Fuck you, too," said Tucker. He suddenly remembered that it was Lisa who liked the band they were watching, and he felt regretful. He probably wouldn't have grown old with her, but at least their relationship wasn't a permanent and public embarrassment to him. (Oh, but it was hard, thinking about this stuff. What would have happened to his music, if he'd never met Julie? He'd never thought he had an album like *Juliet* in him, and Lisa would never have drawn it out. So if he'd stayed with her, he'd probably like himself more, but he still wouldn't have gotten any attention. And because he wouldn't be getting attention, he'd be hating himself. Argh.)

The guy had pushed himself away from the wall and was about to leave.

"I'm sorry," said Tucker. "How's she doing?"

"She's doing okay," said the guy, which seemed like a somewhat anticlimactic reply. All those "fuck yous" for this?

"Good. Say hi from me."

The band was building, with great opacity of purpose, a pretty terrifying Berlin Wall of sound, consisting entirely of feedback and cymbal clashes. Jerry said something that Tucker didn't catch. Tucker shook his head and pointed at his ear. Jerry tried again, and this time Tucker caught the word "mom." Tucker had met Lisa's mother. She was a nice lady.

"That's too bad," said Tucker.

Jerry looked at him as though he wanted to hit him. Tucker suspected that there might have been a misunderstanding. He shouldn't get hit for expressing sympathy, surely?

"Her mother died, right?"

"No," said Jerry. "I said . . ." He leaned right into Tucker and bellowed in his ear. *"Did you know she was a mom?"*

"No," said Tucker. "I did not know that."

"I didn't think so."

She didn't waste much time, thought Tucker. They only split a year ago, which meant that she'd had to have . . .

"How old is the kid?"

"Six months."

Tucker calculated in his head, and then on his fingers, behind his back and then in his head again.

"Six months. That's . . . interesting."

"I think so," said Jerry.

"Interesting in two possible ways."

"I'm sorry?"

"I SAID, THERE ARE TWO WAYS THAT MIGHT BE INTERESTING TO ME."

Jerry held two fingers up, apparently to confirm the numbers, and mouthed the word "two." They were, Tucker thought, quite a long way from being able to access the meat of this conversation. They had only just confirmed the exact number of ways it might be interesting.

"Two what?" said Jerry.

Later, Tucker wondered why it had occurred to neither of them to take it outside. Force of habit, he guessed. Both of them were used to conversing in noisy rock clubs, and both of them were long used to the idea that, if you didn't catch much, or even any, of the conversation, you weren't missing anything. Now Tucker was being circumlocutory in order to find out something that might be very important to him. It wasn't working.

"TWO WAYS . . ." Oh, fuck this. "Are you telling me this kid is mine?"

"Your kid," said Jerry, nodding vigorously.

"I'm a dad."

"You," said Jerry, poking him in the chest. "Grace."

"Grace?"

"GRACE IS YOUR DAUGHTER."

"HER NAME'S GRACE?"

"GRACE. YOU. THE. DAD."

And that was how he found out.

Suddenly, the feedback stopped. It was replaced by a

bemused and muted applause. Now that he could talk, though, he didn't know what to say. He certainly didn't want to say what he was thinking: he was thinking about his work, his music, about *Juliet* and the tour. He was thinking that the combination of a child and *Juliet* would be a permanent and unbearable humiliation. It must already be so for Lisa. (And maybe that last thought redeemed him, he was hoping. It seemed to have an ethical dimension to it. Certainly it was a thought about somebody else. He hoped God caught that one, even though it had been kind of tacked on to the end of a lot of other stuff, all about himself.)

"What are you going to do about it?" said Jerry.

"I'm not sure there's much I can do, is there? In most states, they don't allow abortions after the kid has actually been born."

"Nice," said Jerry. "Classy. You going to see her?"

"Good to meet you, Jerry."

Tucker drained his drink and put it down on the bar. He didn't want to talk to this guy about his responsibilities. He needed to be on his own, outside.

"I wasn't going to say this part," said Jerry. "But you seem like kind of a jerk, so what the hell?"

Tucker made a be-my-guest gesture.

"That record. *Juliet*. It's really full of shit, isn't it? I mean,

I can see you wanted to fuck her. She's a good-looking girl, from the pictures I've seen. But all that drama? I don't buy it."

"Very wise," said Tucker. He gave Jerry an ironic salute and left. He was intending to walk straight out the door, but he needed to take a piss first. So that was kind of bathetic, because he ended up giving Jerry the same ironic salute on the way back from the restroom.

Years later, little knots of bedraggled fans started meeting together on the Internet, and that visit to the toilet started getting some serious analysis. Tucker was always amazed by their literal-mindedness. If Martin Luther King had needed to take a leak right before the "I Have a Dream" speech, would these people have come to the conclusion that he'd come up with the whole thing midflow? While Tucker was walking out of the restroom, his drummer, Billy, was on the way in; Billy's mind had been completely fucked by weed, so it was almost certainly Billy who'd decided that a mystical event had taken place in there. Tucker's conversation with Jerry had remained private, to Jerry's enormous and eternal credit.

On the way home he puked against a wall somewhere between the club and the motel. He was puking up cold cuts and red wine and Irish whiskey, but it felt like something else was coming out, too. And the next morning he called his manager. It wasn't such a big deal, really, that night, no matter what the people on the Internet said. He found out he was a father. He canceled a tour. That night, there were probably musicians all over America finding out and canceling—it's what musicians do. It wasn't as if the day after was a big deal, or the day after that, either, ad nauseam, six thousand times. It was a cumulative thing.

twelve

At first, Annie was glad Tucker and Jackson were late. It gave her time to compose herself, think about the version of herself she wanted to present. Yes, there was some kind of connection between her and Tucker, maybe, but it was a gossamer cyberthread: blow on it and it would break. And yet, if he'd arrived right on the dot of three, she would probably have been unable to resist running up to him and throwing her arms around his neck, which was presuming a reciprocal depth of feeling for which she had no evidence whatsoever. By ten past, she had resolved to give him a friendly peck on the cheek, and ten minutes after that she was wondering whether the peck shouldn't be downgraded to a handshake, although she'd do that two-handed-clasp thing to convey warmth. By quarter to four, she didn't really like him very much anyway.

And, of course, if she'd known there was any chance of outrageous rudeness on this scale, she'd have suggested meeting somewhere other than Dickens's house in Doughty Street. There weren't any shops or cafés around, nowhere she could sit inside and watch the entrance to the museum while sipping on a cappuccino that would cost roughly the same as a terraced house back in Gooleness. She just had to stand there in the street, feeling stupid. And though she had known, somewhere inside her, that a feeling of foolishness would be an inevitable and unavoidable consequence of this silly flirtation (could a flirtation be as one-sided as this one, without becoming merely a crush?), she'd rather hoped that it would come later on, when he didn't reply to her e-mails afterward. It hadn't occurred to her that he simply wouldn't show up. But what did she expect? He was a reclusive recovering alcoholic former rock star. None of that suggested a person who'd trot up to a museum at three o'clock on the dot on a Thursday afternoon. What to do? After an hour, and after considering and then rejecting a tour of the house on her own (because she suddenly didn't love Dickens as much as she'd made out), she walked toward Russell Square. She'd given him her cell number, but he'd offered nothing in return—cunningly, she could see now. All she knew was that he was staying in his daughter's apartment, but even if she were detective enough to obtain the relevant details, she wouldn't call, and she certainly wouldn't knock on the door. She had some pride.

Somewhere in her she hadn't given up on him, otherwise she'd have gone back to her cheap and musty hotel room near the British Museum, collected her overnight bag and gone back to Gooleness on the train. She didn't want to, though. When she got to Russell Square, she saw a poster outside an arts theater advertising a French movie, and she sat on her own in the dark for a couple of hours, squinting at the subtitles. She set the phone to vibrate, and checked it every few minutes just in case she'd somehow failed to feel the vibrations, but there was no message, no missed call, no evidence that she'd ever arranged to meet anyone.

She only knew a couple of people who still lived in London, Linda in Stoke Newington and Anthony in Ealing; one by one her friends had paired off and moved out. Many of them were teachers that she'd met at college, and they'd decided that they might as well earn their measly salaries in towns that were cheaper to live in than London, at schools where the pupils were exposed to knife crime only through rap songs.

Annie tried Linda first, on the grounds that she worked at home and therefore might be in to answer the phone, and that, as far as she could tell, Stoke Newington was closer than Ealing. As luck would have it, Linda was in, and bored, and offered to drop what she was doing and come and take her out for cheap Indian food in Bloomsbury. Less fortunately, however, Linda was almost unbearably annoying, a quality Annie had completely forgotten until halfway through the three-minute phone call.

"Oh, my God! What are you doing down here?"

"I came down . . . Well, it was an Internet date, actually."

"There is so much in that last sentence which needs unpacking. First, what happened to the dreaded Duncan?"

To her surprise, Annie found herself stinging a little.

"He wasn't so dreaded. Not by me, anyway."

She had to defend him in order to defend herself. That was why people were so prickly about their partners, even their ex-partners. To admit that Duncan wasn't up to much was to own up publicly to the terrible waste of time, and terrible lapses in judgment and taste. She had stuck up for Spandau Ballet in just the same way at school, even after she had stopped liking them.

"And second—what? It's over already? At six o'clock? Was it a speed date?" And she laughed maniacally at her own witticism.

"Oh, well. You win some and you lose some."

"And this one was a loser?"

Yes, Annie wanted to say. That's what the expression means, you dimwit. Nobody comes down from the Olympic rostrum with a gold medal around their neck and says "You win some, you lose some."

"I'm afraid so."

"Hold that thought. I'm comin' to getcha. See you in half an hour or so."

Annie squeezed her eyes shut and swore.

After Linda had crawled under the fence surrounding her north London high school, she'd set about making a living as a freelance journalist, writing about liposuction and cellulite and leather boots and cats and sex aids and cakes and just about anything else the more down-market women's magazines thought their readers might want to know about. Last time Annie had talked to her, she was just about getting by, although she gave the impression that the work was disappearing quickly down the Internet drain. Linda had hennaed hair and a loud voice, and whenever she and Annie met up, she always wanted Annie's "take" on something or other, Barack Obama, or a reality TV show she never watched, or a band she'd never heard of. Annie didn't really have a "take" on very much, really, unless a "take" was the same thing as an opinion, but she always had the feeling that it wasn't, that it was something altogether more aggressive, definitive and unusual. Even if Annie had any of these qualities, she wouldn't waste them on a "take." Linda lived with a man who was every bit as hopeless as Duncan, although for some reason everyone had to pretend that he wasn't, that his novel would get finished, and published, and recognized as a work of rare genius, and he could stop teaching English to Japanese businessmen.

"So?" said Linda, as they sat down in the restaurant, even before Annie had taken her coat off. "Pray tell all."

Maybe Linda and Duncan should get together, Annie thought. Then they could "pray tell" and "aghast" each other to death.

"I left Mike at home so we could have a proper girly chat."

"Oh, goody," said Annie. Were there two words in the English language that combined more dispiritingly than "girly" and "chat"?

"What did you do? Where did you go? What did you talk about?"

Annie wondered for a moment whether Linda was parodying interest. Nobody could be as fascinated by a damp Internet date as the width of her eyes suggested.

"Well." What would they have done? "We went for a cup of coffee, and then we went to see a French film at the cinema in Russell Square, and then . . . That was it, really."

"What happened at the end?"

"The woman found out her husband had been sleeping with a poet and she moved out."

"No, at the end of the date, stupid."

Typical Linda: she'd missed the admittedly mild witticism, but she made Annie seem like the idiot.

"Yes, I . . ."

Oh, what did it matter? It was all ridiculous. She had invented an Internet date, and the Internet date had been invented to replace another date that she was beginning to feel might have been half fantasy anyway. Why not continue on the same path and give Linda something to goggle at?

"We just said good-bye. It was . . . It was all slightly awkward, actually. He brought his girlfriend with him, and I think he was hoping . . ."

"Oh, my God!"

"I know."

If the story she was telling were ever to be published, she'd have to thank Ros in the acknowledgments, maybe even offer her coauthorship. According to Ros, that sort of thing would almost certainly have happened, if she had really met somebody over the Internet.

"It happens more than you think," said Annie. "The stories I could tell."

She was beginning to feel like a real novelist, suddenly. Her first fiction was semiautobiographical, but now that she had some confidence she was pushing off into deeper imaginative territory.

"Have you been doing a lot of Internet dating, then?"

"Not really." It was harder than it looked, storytelling. It involved chucking the truth out altogether, something that Annie clearly wasn't prepared to do just yet. "But the couple of dates I've been on were so weird that I could probably tell you five or six stories about each one."

Linda shook her head sympathetically. "I'm so glad I'm not out there."

"You're lucky."

This last sentiment wasn't a reflection of Annie's true feelings. The time she'd spent with Mike had led her to believe that Linda was one of the unluckiest people she had ever met.

"And Duncan?"

"He met somebody else."

"You're kidding me. I don't believe it. My God."

"He wasn't so bad."

"Oh, Annie! He was ghastly."

"Well, he was no Mike, true, but . . ."

Was that overdoing it? Surely even Linda could see that she was being satirical. But no. Linda just allowed a faint, smug smile to scud across her face. "Anyway. He met somebody else."

"Who on earth did he meet? If that's any of my beeswax."

"A woman called Gina who teaches with him at the college."

"She must be desperate."

"Lots of lonely people are."

It was a gentle rebuke, but it did the trick. Linda seemed to recognize loneliness. Possibly she could see it sitting opposite her, sipping lager and trying not to lose its temper. It was an illness, loneliness—it made you weak, gullible, feebleminded. She'd never have stood for an hour outside the Dickens Museum like that if she hadn't just been coming down with it.

Annie's cell phone rang just as the papadums were being served. She didn't recognize the number, which was why she took the call.

"Hello?"

The voice was deeper than she had imagined, but weaker, too—tremulous, almost.

"Is this Annie?"

"Yes."

"Hello. This is Tucker Crowe."

"Hello." The first word she had ever said to him, and it came encrusted with ice. "I hope you have a good excuse."

"Moderately good. Mildly good. I had a mild heart attack, pretty much as soon as I got off the plane. I wish I could tell you that it was more serious than that, but there we are. It was enough."

"Oh, my God. Are you okay?"

"I'm not so bad. Most of the damage seems to be psychic. Apparently I'm not going to live forever, as I previously thought."

"What can I do?"

"I'd welcome a visit from somebody outside my own family."

"Done. And what can I bring you? Do you need anything?"

"I could probably use some books. Something English and foggy. But not as foggy as *Barnaby Rudge*."

Annie laughed a little more than Tucker would have understood, got the name of the hospital, ended the call and blushed. She was always blushing these days. Perhaps she was literally getting younger, shooting all the way backward to prepubescence. And the whole terrible business could start all over again.

"And was that one of your stories?" Linda asked her. "It looks like it, from the color you've turned."

"Well. Yes. I suppose he is."

He was a story at least, even if he never became anything else.

Nobody, she discovered the next morning, ever waited impatiently outside a bookstore for it to open. She was on her own in the cold. She'd got to Charing Cross Road at eight-fifty, only to discover that none of them opened their doors before nine-thirty; she went for a coffee, came back, and at nine-thirty-one she was watching through the plate-glass door as the staff fiddled around with the displays in the front of the store. What were they doing? Surely they must have worked out that she wasn't hopping up and down because she needed a celebrity cookbook. It was just as well that nobody could die of a thirst for literature: these people would just leave you gasping on the sidewalk. Finally, finally, a young man with stubble and long, greasy hair unlocked the door and slid it back, and Annie wriggled through the gap.

She'd had a few ideas overnight. Tucker would never find out, but the truth was that she'd been unable to sleep, because she'd been constructing a reading list in her head. At two in the morning she'd decided that ten books would be enough to cover his wants and her enthusiasms, but when she woke up she could see that turning up with a teetering tower of paperbacks would provide Tucker with all the evidence he needed to prove that she was unbalanced and obsessed. Two would be plenty, three if she really couldn't decide. She ended up buying four, with the intention of ruling out two of them on the way to the hospital. She had no idea whether he'd like them, mainly because she knew nothing about him, other than that he liked Dickens. The hospital was somewhere near Marble Arch, so she walked up to Oxford Street and got a bus in what she hoped was a westerly direction.

Except . . . surely everyone who liked nineteenth-century fiction had read *Vanity Fair*? And was a book titled *Hangover Square* an appropriate gift for a recovering alcoholic? And then there was the sex in *Fingersmith* . . . Would he think that was some kind of come-on? And wasn't the sex mostly of the lesbian variety? Would he think she was trying to warn him that she wasn't interested in him in that way? When in fact the whole idea was that she was trying to indicate the opposite? Plus, he'd had a heart attack, so maybe no book containing sex of any variety was tactful. Oh, shit. She looked out the window of the bus, saw a chain bookstore and got off at the next stop.

At the entrance to the hospital, Annie found herself stuffing four brand-new paperbacks that she couldn't afford into a trash can and feeling sick with guilt. She was throwing the books away because she'd bought too many and didn't know where to hide the ones she didn't need; also because he might decide that some of her choices were overobvious and patronizing; also because she hadn't read one or two of them, and she should have, and if he asked her what they were about she would stutter and blush. She was in a panic, of course, she could see that. She was nervous, and when she was nervous she overthought everything. She caught sight of herself in the mirrored door of the elevator on the way up to his room: she looked awful, tired and old. Maybe instead of worrying about Victorian novels she should have worried more about her makeup. And she wished she'd slept better; she never looked good when she'd had less than seven hours' sleep. He probably wasn't looking so great, though, which was some consolation. Maybe that was the Annie Paradox: she could only appeal to men too sick to do much about anything. She flicked uselessly at her hair and walked out of the elevator and down the hall.

On the way to Tucker's room, she saw Jackson walking toward her, hand in hand with an impossibly glamorous but intimidatingly sulky woman in her late forties. Annie tried to smile at her, but she could feel the smile bounce off the woman's face: Natalie, if that's who the woman was, clearly didn't dish out smiles for no reason, thus devaluing their currency. Annie was glad she had resisted the temptation to introduce herself; she'd have been like one of those crazy women who shout at soap-opera stars on the street because they think they know them. Just because Jackson spent his life stuck to her fridge didn't mean that she could run up to him and frighten him half to death. As they walked past, she could see that he looked frightened enough as it was, and Annie hoped that didn't mean she was walking into a room containing a very sick man. Supposing Tucker died when she was in there? And his last words were "Oh, I've read all those." She'd have to make something up. *And* she'd never had to deal with a dying person. *And* it would be grotesquely inappropriate, hers being the last face he saw. Perhaps she should just go home. Or wait until she was sure there was somebody else in there, somebody he actually knew.

But then she was knocking on the door and he was saying, "Come in," and before she knew it she was sitting on his bed, and they were beaming at each other.

"I bought you some books," she said, much too soon. The books should have been an afterthought, not an introduction.

"I'm sorry," he said. "I meant to say I'd pay you back. I don't know you well enough to ask you to spend money on me."

She'd asked for that by coming in and yelling about her kindness. Idiot.

"Good grief, I don't need paying back. I just didn't want you to think I'd forgotten. Terrible, being in hospital with nothing to read."

He nodded at his bedside table. "I still have old Barnaby. But he's not as much fun as I'd hoped. You read that one?"

"Ummm . . ." Oh, come on, woman, she told herself. You know the answer to the question. You've read about four Dickens novels, and that's not one of them. *Barnaby Rudge* isn't going to be a deal breaker. On the other hand, why take the risk?

"I'm like you," she said brightly. "I got about a third of the way through and put it down. Anyway. You've had a heart attack, and we're talking about me not finishing a book. How are you?"

"Not so bad."

"Really?"

"Yeah. Tired. A little anxious about Jackson."

"I think I saw him walking down the corridor."

"Yeah. Natalie's taken him to a toy store. It's all too weird."

"They'd never met before this trip?"

"Shit, no." She laughed at his eyes widening in alarm. "Why would I do that to him? And I want him to look up to me. I don't want him judging me on the basis of my past mistakes."

"But she's being nice to him."

"Yeah. I guess. And me. Her old man paid for us to fly over here. And then I keel over in the reception of the fanciest hospital in London, so he gets to pay for that, too."

He laughed wheezily.

"So she's not all that bad."

"Apparently not. Now I find out."

"How did you end up married to an Englishwoman?"

"Ohhhh . . ." And he waved a hand, as if a wife from another continent were inevitable at some stage in the career of a serial husband, and the details were therefore wearyingly inconsequential.

She told herself not to ask too many questions, even though there was so much she wanted to know about him. She liked to think she was curious about people, but her hunger for information went beyond curiosity: she wanted to piece the entirety of his adult life together and she seemed to be lacking even the straight edges that would get her started. Why did she care so much? Part of it was because of Duncan, of course: she was thinking with his fan's head and she felt obliged to collect as much information as she could, because nobody else was in a position to do so. But it wasn't just that. She'd never been given the opportunity to meet someone this exotic, and she feared she'd never be given it again, unless some other vanished bohemian contacted her out of the blue.

"Ah," she said. "One of those."

"Did that seem as if I'm being mysterious?" he said.

"It seemed as though you weren't feeling up to talking about the marriage before last to someone you've only just met."

"Perfect. Amazing what you can do with the limp flap of a wrist."

"How's your daughter doing?"

"Not so great. Okay physically, but angry. Angry with me, too."

"With you?"

"I've gone and fucked it all up for her again. For once, she was supposed to be the center of attention."

"I'm sure that's not what she means."

In the first five minutes, she had defended both Lizzie and Natalie, and she vowed not to say anything nice about anybody related to Tucker for the remainder of the visit. It made her sound bland and boring and good and exactly the sort of person that a reclusive cult musician in recovery wouldn't like, if she knew anything about reclusive cult musicians in recovery, which she didn't. And in any case, there was every chance that these people were horrible. She'd only seen Natalie for two seconds in the hallway, but those two seconds had been salutary: they suggested to her that the rich and beautiful really were different. "I'm sure that's not what she means . . ." How would she know what the daughter of a model meant?

"Do you know many people in London?"

"Nope. Lizzie and Nat. And you, now that you're in London."

"So you haven't been bombarded with visitors?"

"Not yet. But I understand there are a fair few on the way."

"Really?"

"Really. Nat and Lizzie decided in their wisdom that my children should all come here to see me before I croak. So I've got three more kids and another ex-wife on the way."

"Oh. And how do you feel . . . ?"

"I don't care for the idea much."

"No. Well. I can see that."

"The truth is, Annie, I'm not going to be able to go through with it. I'm going to need you to get me out of here. If you live in a small seaside town a ways away from this hospital, then that sounds like exactly the sort of place I need to rest up in. Might be fun for Jackson, too."

For a moment, Annie forgot to breathe. She had written that last sentence for him several times since he'd called to tell her what had happened, although it sounded better in his voice, of course, and there were some linguistic details that she'd never have come up with: "a ways away," "rest up." And then, after she had started inhaling and exhaling again, with a little more noise than she might have wished, she started thinking about train times. She'd been intending to get the two-twelve, unless she'd been given a compelling or even a mildly plausible reason to stay in London; if Jackson came back from the toy store in time, they could jump in a cab to King's Cross and be back in Gooleness by four-thirty.

"What do you think?" She'd not only forgotten to breathe; she'd forgotten that she was supposed to be taking part in a conversation with a real person.

"I don't think Jackson would have much fun. It's not such a fun place, especially this time of year."

"You still got that shark's eye?"

"I have loads of pieces of shark."

"Well, that's a happy afternoon right there."

The trouble was, she couldn't help but be boring and bland and sensible and good. There was nothing she wanted more than to nurse Tucker back to health in Gooleness, yet the desire was untrustworthy, and dangerously, self-indulgently whimsical: it was the crush talking. For a start, he'd had a heart attack, not a bout of flu. He probably didn't need blankets and hot-water bottles and homemade soup; for all she knew, any of those things might kill him. And stealing him away from his family, it seemed to her, would be wrong and bad and none of her business; she tried not to think conventionally, but she probably did believe that families were important, that fathers had a duty to their children, that Tucker couldn't just run away from them out of fear or embarrassment or both. All of these doubts, when she examined them, started to lead to the unwelcome conclusion that Tucker was a real person, with actual problems, and neither he nor the problems could comfortably be accommodated in her life, or in her house, or in Gooleness. If that was where doubts led, then she didn't especially want to follow them.

"I don't know if I'm capable of looking after you. I mean, what have they done to you? And what still needs doing?"

"They gave me an angioplasty."

"Ah. Well I don't even know what that is. I couldn't give you another one."

"Jesus, I wouldn't ask you to."

Was it all in her imagination, or was this part of the conversation vaguely smutty? Smutty and prudish all at the same time, seeing as she was refusing to do things and he was saying he wouldn't ask for them in the first place? Almost certainly, it was her imagination. Maybe if she'd taken Barnesy up on his offer the other night, she'd be less preoccupied now.

"What is it?"

"Basically, they put little balloons into you and blow them up to clear your arteries."

"So you've had an operation? In the last thirty-six hours?"

"It wasn't such a big deal. They stick the balloons in with a catheter."

"And do you really want to run away from your kids, when they're flying halfway across the world to see you?"

"Yes."

She laughed. It was the kind of yes that knew its own mind.

"Your boys? They fly across the Atlantic, aged . . . What . . . ?"

"Twelve. Give or take."

". . . And their dad has checked out of the hospital and can't be found?"

"Precisely. It's not any one child I don't want to see. It's all of them. Because you know what? I've never seen them all in the same room, together. Never have, never wanted to. So I need to get out while the going's good."

"Seriously? You've never been with all your children at the same time?"

"God, no. The mechanics of that . . ." He shuddered theatrically.

"How long have you got? Before they all get here?"

"The boys arrive this afternoon. Lizzie's downstairs,

Jackson you know about . . . So that just leaves Grace. Nobody seems to know where she is."

"Where does she live?"

"Ah," he said. "Well. Now this isn't going to sound good."

"You're not sure?"

"'Not sure' is a kind way of putting it. It suggests I might be able to offer you some kind of idea."

"But someone knows?"

"Oh, someone always knows. The most recent partner always has a way of getting in touch with the one before. So they just work the chain all the way back."

"How come they know how to get in touch?"

"Because I let the women make the arrangements involving children, I guess. I wasn't very good at it, and the current partner always wanted to show the previous one she was a decent and caring human being, so . . . I know, I know. It kind of reflects badly on me, doesn't it?"

Annie tried to get her face to register the disapproval he seemed to be expecting, and then gave up. To disapprove would be to diminish him, turn him into the sort of person she already knew; she wanted and needed to hear about his complicated domestic life, and to suggest that she didn't much like it might mean that he stopped telling her stories that she would remember forever.

"No," she said.

He looked at her.

"Really? Why not?"

She didn't know why not, really. Losing touch with daughters through indolence and carelessness was, on the face of it, an unattractive habit.

"I think . . . people end up doing things they're good at. If your partners were better at making arrangements, then what's the point of leaving it to you to mess up?"

For a moment she allowed herself to imagine that Duncan had a daughter from a previous relationship, and she was the one who had ended up speaking to the child's mother while he scratched his balls and listened to his Tucker Crowe bootlegs. Is that the view she would have taken in those circumstances? Almost certainly not.

"I don't think you really believe that. Or if you do, you're the first woman I've ever met who does. But I thank you for your tolerance. Anyway. This isn't getting me out of here."

"I'll get you out when you've seen them all."

"No, see, it'll be too late by then. The whole point of going is so I don't see them."

"I know, but . . . I'd feel guilty. And you don't want that."

"Listen . . . Will you be able to come again? Tomorrow? Or do you have to go back?"

Incredibly, there was more blushing. Would it never stop? Was she going to blush forever, at anything anyone said? This time it was more of a flush than a blush, a response to the pleasurable sense of being needed by somebody she found attractive, and it occurred to her that the physiological response might have happened at any time in the last fifteen years; it was simply that there'd been no pleasure, of this kind at least, to be taken.

"No," she said. "I don't have to go back. I can, you know . . ." And she could. She could take vacation days and get one of the Friends to open up the museum; she could stay with Linda; she could do whatever it took.

"Great. Hey! Here she is!"

Tucker was referring to the dramatically pale young woman who was walking slowly toward them in her bathrobe.

"Lizzie, meet Annie."

Lizzie evidently didn't want to meet Annie, because she ignored her. Annie found herself hoping Tucker would tell her off, but that was unrealistic. These two had to share a hospital, and in any case, Lizzie was scary.

"Grace was in Paris," she said. "She'll be here tomorrow."

"Did you tell her she doesn't need to come, now that we know I'm not on the way out?"

"No. Of course she needs to come."

"Why?"

"Because this has gone on long enough."

"What?"

"You keeping us apart."

"I don't keep you all apart. I just don't get you all together."

Annie stood up. "I should, you know . . ."

"So you'll be in tomorrow?"

Annie looked at Lizzie, who didn't look back.

"Maybe tomorrow isn't . . ."

"It is. Really."

Annie took his hand and shook it. She wanted to squeeze it, too, but she didn't.

"Hey, thanks for the books," he said. "They're perfect."

"Good-bye, Lizzie," said Annie, provocatively.

"Okay. So you can call Grace and tell her she's not welcome," said Lizzie.

Annie was getting the hang of it now, and she was quite enjoying it. Even the rudeness was exotic and precious and enviable.

thirteen

S o none of this is really for my benefit," said Tucker.

He said it, he thought, mildly. "Mild" was the word of the week. He was determined to be mild forever, or at least until he had a serious heart attack, at which point he would become serious, or frivolous, depending on the directional advice he received from specialists.

"I'd . . . I'd sort of hoped it was," said Lizzie. "I'd sort of hoped that you might want to see us all together."

There was something weird about Lizzie's voice. It was deeper than it had been a couple of minutes earlier, before Annie had left. It was as if she were trying out for one of those Shakespeare plays where a young woman disguises herself as a young man. She was speaking more quietly than she usually did, too. And on top of that, her tone was disconcertingly pacific. Tucker didn't like it. It made him feel as though he were much sicker than he'd been told.

"Why are you talking like that?"

"Like what?"

"Like you're about to have a sex-change operation."

"Fuck off, Tucker."

"That's better."

"Why should everything be for your benefit, anyway? Can you really not imagine a small pocket of human activity that isn't?"

"I just thought that you were all gathering because I was dangerously sick. And now that I'm not, we can forget all about it."

"We don't want to forget all about it."

"You're speaking for who, here? Everyone? The majority? The senior members? 'Cause I don't think Jackson gives too much of a shit one way or the other."

"Oh, Jackson. Jackson thinks what you tell him to think."

"That often happens with six-year-olds. Maybe the withering contempt is inappropriate."

"I'm sure I am speaking for the majority when I say that I wish we'd all had the protection that Jackson has been offered."

"Oh, right. Because you've all had such fucking miserable lives, haven't you?"

If this conversation were a prophet, it would be one of those scary Old Testament guys, rather than gentle Jesus, meek and mild. Mildness was clearly an elusive quality; you couldn't just turn it on and off when you felt like it. But then, that was the trouble with relationships generally. They had their own temperature, and there was no thermostat.

"And that gets you off the hook?"

"I'd say that on the whole it does, yes. If I'd left you all in the shit then I'd feel worse than I do."

"It was nothing to do with you, us surviving."

"Not strictly true."

"Oh, is that right?"

He knew it was, but he didn't know how to explain it without causing more trouble. His paternal talent, before Jackson anyway, came down to this: he only impregnated charismatic and beautiful women. And after he had made a mess of them, they were pursued by successful men. They were pursued by unsuccessful men, too, of course, but by then they were all done with fuckups of any kind, so they sought out decent, solvent partners who could offer stability and material comfort. It was all pretty basic Darwin, really, although he wondered what Darwin would have to say about the coupling with Tucker that resulted in the women becoming mothers in the first place. There wasn't much evidence of an instinct for survival there.

So that was it, his aftercare service; it was better than a trust fund, if you thought about it. Trust funds ruined kids; fond, well-heeled, but clear-eyed stepfathers didn't. It wouldn't work for everyone, he could see that, but it had worked for him. There was even a little blowback, too, seeing as how Lizzie's stepfather was footing his hospital bill. He wouldn't go so far as to say the guy—and he'd forgotten his name again—*owed* him. But it was quite the charming family he'd inherited, so long as he was prepared to overlook the charmlessness.

"Probably not." It was too sophisticated an idea to explain from a prone position.

Lizzie took a deep breath.

"I was thinking," she said. "This was the only way it was ever going to happen, wasn't it?"

She was trying to sound like a boy again. He wished she'd just choose a voice and stick to it.

"What?"

"Your life gathering around you. You've always been so good at hiding from it. And running from it. And now you're stuck in bed, and it's heading toward you."

"And you think that's what a sick man needs?"

He could try, couldn't he? It wasn't as if a heart attack were a pretend illness. Even a mild coronary was serious, relatively speaking. He was entitled to a little R&R.

"It's what a grieving woman needs. I've lost a child, Tucker."

Her voice had changed key for the third or fourth time. He was glad he didn't have to provide guitar accompaniment; he'd be retuning every couple of minutes.

"So like I said, it's not really for my benefit."

"Exactly. It's for ours. But who knows? It might do you some good."

Maybe she was right. Kill or cure. If Tucker had any money, he knew which of those outcomes he would bet on.

When Lizzie had gone, he picked up the books Annie had left him and read the blurbs on the covers. They looked pretty good. She was the only person he knew in this whole country, maybe in any country, who could have done that for him, and he suddenly felt the lack—both of her and of the sort of friends who might have provided the service. Annie was much prettier than he'd imagined her to be, although she was the sort of woman who'd be amazed to hear that she could hold her own against somebody like Natalie, who knew, still, the effect she had on men. And, of course, because she didn't know she was pretty, she worked hard to be attractive in other ways. As far as Tucker was concerned, it was work that paid off. He really could imagine resting up in some bleak but beautiful seaside town, taking walks along the cliffs with Jackson and a dog they'd maybe have to rent for the occasion. What was that English period movie where Meryl Streep stared out to sea a lot? Maybe Gooleness would be like that.

Jackson came back from a visit to the toy store with Natalie holding an oversized plastic bag.

"You look like you did well," said Tucker.

"Yeah."

"What did you choose?"

"A kite and a soccer ball."

"Oh. Okay. I thought you were going to buy something that made it less boring for you in here."

"Natalie said she'd take me outside to play with them. Maybe before we go to the zoo this afternoon."

"Natalie's taking you to the zoo?"

"Well, who else is there to go with?"

"Are you angry with me, Jack?"

"No."

They hadn't really had any kind of conversation since the unfortunate medical event. Tucker hadn't known what to say, or how to say it, or even whether it was worth saying.

"So why don't you want to talk to me?"

"I don't know."

"I'm sorry about what happened," said Tucker.

"This soccer ball is what the pros use. In England, and other countries."

"Cool. You can teach me some tricks when we're out of here."

"Will you be able to play soccer?"

"Even better than I could before."

Jackson bounced the ball on the floor.

"Maybe not in here, Jack. Somebody somewhere will be trying to get some rest."

Bounce.

"You are mad at me."

"I'm just bouncing a ball."

"I understand. I promised you I wouldn't get sick."

"You promised me you couldn't die if you were well the day before."

"Do I look dead to you?"

Bounce.

"Because I'm not. And the truth is, I didn't feel well the day before."

Bounce.

"Okay, Jack. Give me the ball."

"No."

Bounce, bounce, bounce.

"Okay, I'm coming to get it."

Tucker made a show of pulling the sheets back from the bed.

Jackson let out a wail, threw the ball over to his father and collapsed onto the floor with his hands over his ears.

"Come on, Jack," said Tucker. "It's not such a big deal. I asked you to stop bouncing the ball and you wouldn't. And now you have. I wasn't going to give you a beating."

"I'm not scared of that," said Jackson. "Lizzie said that if you strain your heart, you'll die. I don't want you to get out of bed."

Well, thank you, Lizzie.

"Okay," Tucker said. "So don't make me."

Whatever works, he thought wearily. But it was going to be hard to pretend from now on that he was just your regular elementary-school dad.

Jesse and Cooper turned up later that afternoon, looking disheveled and bewildered and resentful. They were both wearing iPods; they were both listening to hip-hop with one ear. The other white buds, the ones they'd removed in the clearly unexpected event that their father might say something they'd want to hear, hung loose by their sides.

"Hey, boys."

Mumbled greetings were formed in his sons' throats and emitted with not quite enough force to reach him; they

dropped somewhere on the floor at the end of his bed, left
for the cleaning staff to sweep up.

"Where's your mother?"

"Huh?" said Jesse.

"Yeah, she's okay," said Cooper.

"Hey, fellas. You don't want to turn those things off for
a little while?"

"Huh?" said Jesse.

"No thanks," said Cooper. He said it politely enough,
so Tucker understood that he was turning down something
else entirely—the offer of a drink, maybe, or an invitation
to the ballet. Tucker performed a little mime restating
his desire to converse without the hearing impediments.
The boys looked at each other, shrugged and stuffed the
iPods into their pockets. They had acceded to his request
not because he was their father, but because he was older
than them, and possibly because he was in a hospital bed;
they'd have done the same if he were a paraplegic stranger
on a bus. In other words, they were decent enough kids,
but they weren't *his* kids.

"I was asking where your mother was."

"Oh. Okay. She's outside in the hall." Cooper did most
of the talking, but always managed to give the impression
that he was channeling his twin brother somehow. Maybe
it was the way they stood side by side, staring straight
ahead, arms dangling from their sockets.

"She doesn't want to come in?"

"I guess."

"You don't want to get her?"

"No."

"That was my way of saying 'Would you get her?' "

"Oh. Okay."

They both walked to the door, peered right and then left, and beckoned their mother toward them.

"He wants you to, though." And then, after a pause long enough to accommodate dissent, "I don't know why."

"She doesn't really want to come in," said Cooper.

"But she's coming in," said Jesse.

"Okay."

She didn't come in.

"So where is she?"

They had readopted their previous positions, standing stiffly side by side, staring straight ahead. Maybe when they'd turned their iPods off they'd somehow turned themselves off, too. They were in standby mode.

"Maybe the restroom?" said Cooper.

"Yeah, I think so," said Jesse. "The restroom. And maybe there was someone in there already?"

"Oh," said Tucker. "Sure."

Tucker suddenly became wearied by the pointlessness of the exercise that Lizzie had planned. These kids had flown thousands of miles to stand in a hospital room and stare at a man they no longer knew very well at all; this debate about whether their mother had gone to the bathroom or not was the most animated conversation the three of them had managed so far. (Tucker would miss it when it was over, but to extend it any further would probably entail scatological detail that he wouldn't feel comfortable with, although the boys might enjoy it.) And then, in a moment, the ambient room temperature would become further chilled by the arrival of an ex-wife—not one he was particularly afraid of, nor one that bore him a great deal of ill will, as far as he knew, but not a person he'd had any real desire to see again during the time remaining to him on the planet. And then, sometime in the next hour or two, this ex-wife would bump into another one, when Nat came back with Jackson. And these two boys would stare at a half sister they'd never seen before and mumble at her, and . . . Jesus. There had been a part of him that was half joking when he'd asked English Annie to get him out of here, but that part was gone now. There was nothing funny about this.

The door opened, and Carrie peered around it cautiously.

"This is us," said Tucker cheerily. "Come on in."

Carrie took a few steps into the room, stopped and stared at him.

"Jesus," she said.

"Thanks," said Tucker.

"Sorry. I just meant . . ."

"It's okay," said Tucker. "I got a lot older, plus the light in here isn't so flattering, plus I had a heart attack. I accept all of these things with equanimity."

"No, no," said Carrie. "I just meant, I guess, Jesus, it's been a while since I saw you."

"Okay," said Tucker. "Let's leave it at that."

Carrie, of course, looked good, healthy and sleek. She'd put on weight, but she'd been too skinny when he'd left her anyway, due to the misery he'd inflicted on her, so the few extra pounds indicated only psychic health.

"How've you been?" she said.

"Today and yesterday, not so bad. The day before, not great. The last few years, mostly not so bad."

"I heard you and Cat split."

"Yeah. I managed to mess up another one."

"I'm sorry."

"I'll bet."

"No, really. I don't suppose we have a whole lot in common, but we all worry about you. It's better for us if you're in a relationship."

"You're all in some sort of recovery group together?"

"No, but . . . You're the father of our children. We need you to be okay."

Carrie's choice of words allowed him to imagine that he was some kind of polygamist in an isolated religious community, that Carrie was here as the elected representative of the wives. It was certainly hard to think of himself as a single man. He tried, for a moment. Hey! I'm single! I have no ties to anyone! I can do what I want! Nope. Wasn't working, for some reason. Maybe when he was off the drip attached to his arm he'd feel a little more footloose.

"Thank you. How have you been, anyway?"

"I'm fabulous, darling, thank you. Work's good, Jesse and Cooper are good, as you can see . . ." Tucker felt obliged to look, although there wasn't too much to look at, apart from a brief flicker of animation at the sound of their own names.

"My marriage is good."

"Great."

"I have a fantastic social life, Doug's business is solid . . ."

"Excellent." He was working on the basis that if he threw enough approving adjectives in her direction she'd stop, but this policy showed no signs of working.

"Last year I ran a half marathon."

He was reduced to shaking his head in speechless admiration.

"My sex life is better than it's ever been."

Finally the boys came out of standby. Jesse's face creased into a mask of distaste, and Cooper crumpled as if he'd been punched in the stomach.

"Gross," he said. "Please. Mom. Stop."

"I'm a healthy woman in her thirties. I'm not gonna hide."

"Good for you," said Tucker. "I'll bet your bowels work better than mine, too."

"You'd better believe it," said Carrie.

Tucker was beginning to wonder whether she had actually gone crazy at some point in the last decade. The woman he was talking to bore no resemblance to the one he used to live with: the Carrie he knew was a shy young woman who had wanted to combine her interest in sculpting with her interest in disabled children. She loved Jeff Buckley and REM and the poetry of Billy Collins. The woman in front of him wouldn't know who Billy Collins was.

"There's a lot to be said for being a suburban soccer mom," Carrie said. "No matter what people like you think."

Oh, okay. Now he got it. They were fighting some kind of culture war. He was the cool rock 'n' roll singer-songwriter who lived in the Village somewhere and took drugs, and she was the little woman he'd left behind in Nowhere County. The fact was that they lived remarkably similar lives, except Jackson played Little League, not soccer, and Carrie had almost certainly been to NYC more recently than he had. She'd probably even smoked a little pot at some time in the last five years, too. Maybe everyone was going to come in here swinging their insecurities like baseball bats. That would certainly spice things up a little.

They were saved by the return of Jackson, who ran the length of the room in order to punch both Jesse and Cooper in the stomach. They responded with smiles and whoops: finally, somebody was speaking their language. Natalie's entrance was a little more stately. She waved a greeting to the boys, who ignored her, and introduced herself to Carrie. Or maybe she was reintroducing herself, Tucker couldn't remember. Who knew who had already met before? They were definitely checking each other out now. He could tell that Natalie had absorbed Carrie completely and then somehow spat her out again, and that Carrie knew she'd been spat out. Tucker accepted completely that women were the fairer and wiser sex, but they were also irredeemably vicious when the occasion demanded.

The boys were still fighting. Tucker noted gloomily that Jackson was responding to the appearance of his half brothers with enormous relief and enthusiasm; their chief attraction was that they showed no signs of being about to die, unlike their father. Kids could smell these things. The rats who left sinking ships weren't morally culpable. They were just wired that way.

"How was the zoo, Jackson?"

"It was cool. Natalie bought me this." It was a pen with a monkey's head precariously attached to its cap.

"Wow. Did you say thank you?"

"He was impeccably behaved," said Natalie. "A pleasure to be with. And he knows more or less everything there is to know about snakes."

"I don't know how long all of them are," said Jackson modestly.

The boys stopped wrestling, and a silence fell on the assembled company.

"So here we all are," said Tucker. "Now what?"

"I suppose this is where you read your last will and testament," said Natalie. "And we find out which of your kids you love the best."

Jackson looked at her, and then at Tucker.

"It was Natalie's idea of a joke, son," said Tucker.

"Oh. Okay. But I suppose you'd tell us you loved us all the same," said Jackson, and the tone of his voice implied that this state of affairs would be unsatisfactory and possibly mendacious.

He'd be right, too, thought Tucker. How could he love them all the same? Just seeing Jackson and his ill-concealed bundle of neuroses in the same room as those two solid and, let's face it, dull and kind of dumb boys exposed the lie for what it was. He could see that fatherhood was important when you actually were a father—when you sat with kids in the middle of the night and convinced them that their nightmares were as insubstantial as smoke, when you chose their books and their schools, when you loved them however hard they made it for you to feel anything other than irritation and occasionally fury. And he had been around for the twins during the first few years, but ever since he'd left their mother, he'd cared for them less and less. How could it be any other way? He'd tried to pretend to himself that all five of them were equally important, but these two annoyed and bored him, Lizzie was poisonous, and he didn't really know Gracie at all. Oh, sure, most of this was his fault, and he'd like to think that, if he and Carrie had survived, Jesse and Cooper wouldn't be quite so fucking characterless. But the truth was that they were fine. They had a perfectly serviceable dad with his own car-rental company, and they were mystified by everybody's insistence that their relationship with a man who lived far away was somehow important to their well-being. Meanwhile, Jackson tweaked some kind of nerve in his dad's gut simply by turning the TV on when he was still half-asleep in the morning. You couldn't love people you didn't know, unless you were Christ. Tucker knew enough about himself to accept that he wasn't Christ. So who did he love, apart from Jackson? He ran through a quick mental checklist. No, Jackson was pretty much it, nowadays. With five kids and all the women, he never thought for a moment that a shortage of numbers was going to be his particular problem. Weird how things turned out.

"I'm pretty tired," he said. "How about you all go and visit Lizzie?"

"Will Lizzie want to be visited by us, though?" Carrie asked.

"Sure," he said. "That's part of the point of all this. That we get to know each other as a family." And if it all happened in somebody else's hospital room, then so much the better.

They came back a couple of hours later, giggly and apparently melded together into a coherent unit. They had picked up an extra member, too, a young man with a ridiculous bushy beard who was carrying a guitar.

"Have you met Zak?" said Natalie. "He's your something or other. Your common-law son-in-law."

"Big fan," said Zak. "I mean, really big."

"That's nice," said Tucker. "Thank you."

"*Juliet* changed my life."

"Great. I mean, great if your life needed changing, that is. Maybe it didn't."

"It did."

"So, great. Happy to have helped."

"Zak wants to play you a couple of his songs," said Natalie. "But he was too shy to ask, himself."

How bad could death be, really, Tucker wondered. A quick heart attack and out, and he would have avoided hearing songs by bearded common-law sons-in-law for his entire life.

"Be my guest," said Tucker. "You got a captive audience."

"Who's yours?" Gina asked Duncan.

They were listening to *Naked* again. For a week they'd been living off bootleg performances of the *Juliet* songs: Duncan had made nine different playlists that followed the running order of the album, each taken from different nights of the '86 tour. Gina eventually professed a preference for studio albums, though, on the grounds that drunk people didn't shout all the way through her favorite tracks.

"Who's my what?"

"Your . . . What does he call her? 'Princess Impossible'?"

"I don't know. Most of the women I've had relationships with were pretty reasonable, really."

"That's not what he's on about, though, is it?"

Duncan stared at her. Nobody had ever attempted to argue with him about Tucker Crowe's lyrics. Not that Gina was arguing with him, exactly. But she seemed to be on the verge of an interpretation that differed from his own, and it made him feel a little irritable.

"What's he on about, then, O, great Crowologist?"

"Sorry. I didn't mean to . . . I'm not setting myself up as an expert."

"Good," he said, and laughed. "It takes a while."

"I'm sure."

"But isn't she Princess Impossible because she's out of reach? Not because she's an impossible person?"

"Well," he said generously, "that's the great thing about great art, isn't it? It can mean all sorts of things. But by all accounts, she was very difficult."

"In that first song, though . . ."

" 'And You Are?' "

"Yes, that one . . . There's that line in there . . ."

" 'They told me that talking to you / Would be chewing barbed wire with a mouth ulcer / But you never once hurt me like that.' "

"How does that fit in with her being impossible? If she never once hurt him like that?"

"She became impossible later, I suppose."

"I thought it was more, you know, her being out of his reach. 'Your Royal Highness, way up there, and me on the floor below.' Isn't it that he thinks he's out of her league?"

Duncan felt himself panicking a little: a lurch in the stomach, the sort of thing you get when you know you've left your keys on the kitchen table just after you've shut the

front door. He'd invested quite a lot in Juliet's impossibility. If he hadn't got it right, then who was he?

"No," he said, but he offered up nothing more.

"Well, you know more about it than me, as you say.
Anyway, if that *is* what he meant . . ."

"Which he didn't . . ."

"No, but forgetting about Tucker and Juliet, because
I'm interested anyway: have you had one of those? When
you knew you were out of your depth?"

"Oh, I expect so." He flicked through the index file of
his sexual relationships, much of which consisted of blank
cards kept at the back. He looked under I for "Impossible" and D for "Depth, Out of," but there was nothing. He
could think of friends who'd had that sort of experience, but
the truth was that Duncan had never so much as attempted
to form an attachment to someone as glamorous as Juliet,
or indeed to anyone who could be described as glamorous.
He knew his place, and it was two floors below, not one,
thus preventing any kind of contact at all. You couldn't even
see unattainable women from where he usually stood. If you
imagined it all as a department store, he was in the basement, with the lamps and the dishes; the Juliets were all in
Ladies' Intimates, a couple of escalator rides away.

"Go on."

"Oh, you know. The usual thing."

"How did you meet her?"

It struck Duncan that, as they were already in the kingdom of the self-deprecating, he had to come up with something, otherwise it was all too grim. Nobody was so big a loser that he didn't even have a story about losing. He tried to conjure up the kind of exoticism Gina would be expecting; he saw dramatic eye makeup, elaborate hairdos, glittery clothes.

"Do you remember that band the Human League?"

"Yes! Of course! God!"

Duncan smiled enigmatically.

"You went out with one of the girls in the Human League?"

And immediately Duncan lost his nerve. There was probably a website which provided a helpful list of the names of all the men that the girls in the Human League had dated; she'd be able to check.

"Oh, no, no. My . . . ex wasn't actually in the Human League. She was in a sort of second-rate version. At college." This was more like it. "Same deal, synthesizers and funny haircuts. Anyway, we didn't last very long. She went off with a bass player from, from some other eighties band. What about yours?"

"Oh, an actor. He slept with everyone at drama college. I was silly enough to think I was different."

He'd negotiated that pretty well, he thought. They

were well matched in their failures. He was, however, still feeling uneasy about whether he'd spent two decades misreading the tenor of the relationship between Tucker and Juliet.

"Does it make any difference, do you think? Whether Juliet was impossible as in difficult or impossible as in out of reach?"

"Any difference to what? Or who?"

"I don't know. I just . . . I'd feel a bit daft if I'd been wrong all this time."

"How can you be wrong? You know more about this album than anyone on the planet. Anyway. Like you say. There's no such thing as wrong."

Had he ever listened to *Juliet* in the way Gina heard it? He was beginning to wonder. He'd like to think that there wasn't a single allusion he'd missed, in the lyrics or in the music: the steal from Curtis Mayfield here, the nod to Baudelaire there. But maybe he'd spent so long underneath the surface of the album that he'd never come up for air, never heard what a casual listener might hear. Maybe he'd spent too long translating something that had been written in English all along.

"Oh, let's change the subject," he said.

"Sorry," said Gina. "It must be awfully annoying, me chirruping away without knowing the first thing about anything. I can see how this sort of thing gets addictive, though."

. . .

When Annie went to visit Tucker the next morning, he was dressed and ready to go. Jackson was sitting beside him, red-faced and looking swamped in a blue puffy jacket that had clearly not been designed with warm hospitals in mind.

"Okay," said Tucker. "Here she is. Let's go."

The two of them walked past Annie and toward the door. Jackson's showy determination, all jutting jaw and quick, even steps, led Annie to believe that the move had been rehearsed to within an inch of its life.

"Where are we going?" said Annie.

"Your place," said Tucker. He was already halfway down the hall, so she could only catch his words by scurrying after him, and even then she nearly dropped them.

"My hotel? Or Gooleness?"

"Yeah. That one. The seaside-y one. Jackson needs some saltwater taffy. Don't you, Jackson?"

"Yum."

"Some what? I've never heard of it. You won't be able to find it."

The elevator had arrived, and she squeezed in just as the doors were shutting.

"What do you have that he'd like, then?"

"Probably rock candy. But it's pretty bad for your teeth," said Annie.

What, she wondered, was her immediate ambition here? Did she want to become the wanton lover of a rocker, or a home-care nurse? Because she suspected that the two careers were incompatible.

"Thanks," said Tucker. "I'll watch out for that."

She looked at him, to see if there was anything in his expression other than impatience and sarcasm. There wasn't.

The elevator pinged, and the door opened. Tucker and Jackson strode out onto the street, and immediately they started trying to hail cabs.

"How do you know when they're busy? I can't remember," said Tucker.

"The yellow lights."

"Which yellow lights?"

"You can't see it because they're all busy. Tucker, listen . . ."

"Yellow light, Dad!"

"Cool."

The cab pulled over, and Tucker and Jackson got in.

"Which railway station do we need?"

"King's Cross. But . . ."

Tucker gave the cabdriver complicated instructions involving a west London address, which Annie presumed was Lizzie's place, and a long journey back across town to the station. She was pretty sure they'd need to stop at an ATM. He had no money and he'd be shocked by the fare.

"You coming with us?" said Tucker, as he tugged on the door handle of the cab. It was, of course, a rhetorical question, and she was tempted to decline the invitation, just to see what he said. She jumped in.

"We have to get our luggage from Lizzie's place first. Do you know the train schedule?"

"We'll miss the next one. But probably we'll only have to wait half an hour or so for the one after."

"Time for a comic book, a cup of coffee . . . I don't know if I've ever been on an English train."

"Tucker!" said Annie. The word came out shrill and unpleasant, and much louder than she had intended; Jackson looked at her in alarm. If she were him, she would be wondering how much fun this seaside holiday was going to be. But she had to interrupt the constant deflecting flow of chatter somehow.

"Yes," said Tucker mildly. "Annie?"

"Are you okay?"

"I feel fine."

"I mean, are you allowed to just walk out of hospital without telling anybody?"

"How do you know I haven't told anybody?"

"I'm just guessing. From the speed at which we left the hospital."

"I said good-bye to a couple people."

"Who?"

"You know. Friends I've made in there. Hey, is that the Royal Albert Hall?"

She ignored him. He shrugged.

"Have you still got any balloons inside you? Because you won't find anyone to take those out in Gooleness."

This wasn't turning out right. She was talking to him as if she were his mother—if, that is, he'd been born somewhere in Yorkshire or Lancashire in the 1950s, to parents who ran a boardinghouse. She could almost hear the bare linoleum and the boiled liver in her voice.

"No. I told you. I might have some little vent thing left in there. But it won't bother you."

"Well, it will bother me if you keel over and snuff it."

"What does 'keel over and snuff it' mean, Dad?"

"Doesn't mean anything. English crap. We don't have to come and stay, okay? If you're uncomfortable, just drop us off at a hotel somewhere."

"Have you seen all your family?" If she could just get through her list of questions, she would turn herself into a host—a good one, welcoming and worldly and obliging.

"Yep," said Tucker. "We had a jolly old tea party yesterday afternoon. Everyone's fine, everyone got on, all good. My work there is done."

Annie tried to catch Jackson's eye, but the boy was

staring out of the taxi window with a suspicious intensity. She didn't know him, but it seemed to her that he was trying not to look at her.

She sighed. "Okay, then." She had done her part. She had checked on his health, and she had checked on whether he had fulfilled his paternal responsibilities. She couldn't refuse to believe him. And she didn't want to do that anyway.

Jackson was happy enough on the train, mostly because he was taking a crash course in English sweets; he was allowed to go to the café car whenever he felt like it. He came back with "pastilles" and "biscuits" and "crisps," and he rolled the exotic words around his mouth as if they were Italian wines. Tucker, meanwhile, was sipping litigiously hot tea from a Styrofoam cup and watching the little town houses roll out in front of him. It was all very flat out there, and the sky was full of ill-tempered dark gray swirls.

"So what is there to do in your town?"

"Do?" And then she laughed. "Sorry. The combination of Gooleness and an active verb took me by surprise."

"We won't be staying long, anyway."

"Just until your children have given up on you and started traveling the thousands of miles back home."

"Ouch."

"I'm sorry." And she was. Where was this disapproval coming from, all of a sudden? Wasn't his checkered past half the attraction? What was the point of becoming attracted to a rock musician, if she wanted him to behave like a librarian?

"How was Grace, anyway?"

Jackson flashed his father a look, and Annie caught it, before examining it and lobbing it along to its intended recipient.

"Yeah, Gracie's doing good. Living in Paris with some guy. Studying to, to be something."

"I know you didn't see her." Shut *up*. God.

"I did. Didn't I, Jacko?"

"You did, Dad, yeah. I saw you."

"You saw him seeing her?"

"Yeah. I was watching all the time he was looking at her and talking to her."

"You're a little fibber, and you're a big fibber."

Neither of them said anything. Maybe they had no idea what a fibber was.

"Why that one?"

"Which one?"

"Why Grace?"

"Why Grace what?"

"How come you don't mind seeing the others, but she scares you?"

"She doesn't scare me. Why would she scare me?"

Maybe Duncan should be sitting on the train listening to this stuff. She knew already that Duncan would give an eye and several internal organs to be sitting on the train listening to this stuff; she meant that it would do him good to be here, that his obsession with this man would dwindle away, perhaps to nothing. Any relationship, it seemed to her, was reduced by proximity; you couldn't be awestruck by someone sipping British Rail tea while he lied shamelessly about his relationship with his own daughter. In her case, it had taken about three minutes for passionate admiration and dreamy speculation to be replaced by a nervous, naggingly maternal disapproval. And that, it seemed to her, was a pretty good description of how some of her married female friends felt, some of the time. She had married Tucker somewhere between the hospital room and the taxi.

"I don't know why she would scare you," said Annie. "But she does."

There was something about the journey to Gooleness that reminded Tucker uncomfortably of *The Old Curiosity Shop*. He didn't think he was crawling through the English countryside to die, although English trains surely didn't move much faster than Little Nell and her dad, and they'd had to walk to wherever the hell they were going. (The train had stopped three times already, and a man kept apologizing to them all through the loudspeaker, in a blank, unapologetic voice.) But he definitely wasn't at his best, and he was heading north, and he was leaving a whole lot of shit behind. He certainly felt more like a sick young girl from the nineteenth century than he'd ever felt before. Maybe he was coming down with something—a sickness of the soul, or one of those other existential bugs that was going around.

Tucker liked to think that he was reasonably honest with himself; it was only other people he lied to. And he'd ended up lying to people about Grace her whole life, pretty much. He'd lied to her quite a lot, too. The good news was that these lies were not constant, that there were long periods of time when he didn't have to bullshit anybody; the bad news was that this was because Grace was way off his radar most of the time. He'd seen her two or three times since she was born (one of these times was when she made a disastrous trip out to stay with him and Cat and Jackson back in Pennsylvania, a visit that Jackson remembered with unfathomable fondness), and thought about her as little as possible, although this turned out to be much more than he was comfortable with. And here he was, on a train a long way from home with someone he hardly knew, lying about Grace again.

The lies weren't so surprising, really. He couldn't have a third-person existence—"Tucker Crowe, semilegendary recluse, creator of the greatest, most romantic breakup album ever recorded"—and tell the truth about his eldest daughter. And as he didn't really have a first-person existence anymore, hadn't had since that night in Minneapolis, it had been necessary to get rid of her. He'd gone into therapy when he'd given up drinking, but he'd lied to his therapist, too; or rather, he'd never helped guide his therapist toward Grace's importance, and the therapist had never done the math. (Nobody ever did the math. Not Cat, not Natalie, not Lizzie . . .) It had always seemed to Tucker that talking about Grace meant giving up *Juliet*, and he wasn't prepared to do that. When he turned fifty, he began to think about what he'd done, like people do at that age, and *Juliet* was pretty much it. He didn't like it, but other people did, and that was just about enough: surely a man could sacrifice a kid or two to preserve his artistic reputation, especially when there wasn't much else to him? And it wasn't like Grace had suffered, really. Oh, sure, she was probably fucked up about fathers, and men generally. And somebody, her mother or her stepfather, had had to shell out for her therapy sessions, just as Cat had paid for his. But she was a beautiful, smart girl, as far as he could tell, and she'd live, and she already had a boyfriend and a career path, although he couldn't recall what the hell it was. It didn't seem like she was paying such a big price for her old man's vanity. That wouldn't be how they saw it on Maury Povich's show, if Grace ever forced him to go on the show to confront his inadequacies. But the world was more complicated than that. It wasn't just good guys and bad guys, great dads and evil dads. And thank God for that.

Annie was frowning.

"What's up?"

"I was just trying to work something out."

"Can I help?"

"I would hope so. When was Grace born?"

Fuck, Tucker thought. Someone is doing the math. He felt nauseous and relieved, all at the same time.

"Later," said Tucker.

"Later than who or what?"

"I think I might be ahead of you."

"Really? I'd be surprised. Seeing as I don't know why I want you to tell me how old Grace is."

"You're a smart woman, Annie. You'll get there. And I don't want to talk about it until later."

He cocked his head toward Jackson, whose head was deep in a comic book.

"Ah."

And when she looked at him, he could see that she was halfway there already.

. . .

When they arrived in Gooleness, it was already dark. They dragged their bags out to the taxi stand at the front of the station, where one malodorous taxi was waiting. The driver was leaning against his car, smoking, and when Annie told him her address he threw his cigarette down on the ground and swore. Annie shrugged at Tucker helplessly. They had to put their own luggage in the trunk, or rather, Annie and Jackson had to do it. They wouldn't let Tucker lift anything.

They passed overlit kebab shops, and Indian restaurants offering all-you-can-eat specials for three pounds, and bars with one-word names—"Lucky's," "Blondie's," even one called "Boozers."

"It looks better in the light," Annie explained apologetically.

Tucker was finding his bearings now. If he translated some of the ethnic foods into Americans' favorites and swapped a few of the bookies for casinos, he'd be at one of the trashier resorts in New Jersey. Every now and again, one of Jackson's school friends got dragged off to a seaside town like this, either because the kid's parents had misremembered a vacation from their youth, or because they had failed to spot the romanticism and poetic license in Bruce Springsteen's early albums. They always came back appalled by the vulgarity, the malevolence and the drunkenness.

"Do you like fish and chips, Jackson? Shall we get some for supper?"

Jackson looked at his father: did he like fish and chips? Tucker nodded.

"There's a good chippy down the road from us. From me. You'll be okay if you just eat the fish, Tucker. Don't touch the batter. Or the chips."

"Sounds great," said Tucker. "We might never leave."

"We will, Dad, won't we? Because I need to see Mom."

"Just a joke, kiddo. You'll see Mom."

"I hate your jokes."

Tucker was still distracted by the conversation they'd had on the train. He didn't have a clue how he was going to talk to Annie; he didn't know whether he was capable of it. If it were up to him, he'd write it all down, hand her a piece of paper and walk away. That was pretty much how he'd got to know her in the first place, now that he came to think about it, except he'd written everything down on cyberpaper.

"Have you got a computer at home?"

"Yes."

"Can I write you an e-mail?"

He tried to imagine that he was at his computer in the upstairs spare bedroom and he'd never met Annie, and she was thousands of miles away; he didn't want to think about having to talk to her in half an hour's time. He told her how he'd found out he had a first daughter, and how, even then, he hadn't rushed to see her, because of his embarrassment and cowardice, how he'd only seen her three or four times in her life. He'd told her how he didn't even like Julie Beatty much, so he had to stop singing songs about how he'd been crushed by the weight of his sorrow and desire and blah, blah, and when he'd stopped singing those songs he couldn't find any others.

He'd never put it all together like this before; even his ex-wives didn't know as much as Annie would. They'd never done the math either, not that he'd helped them—he'd lied about Grace's age more than once. And when he stared at the sum total of his crimes on the screen, it seemed to him that they didn't amount to a whole lot. He hadn't killed anyone. He looked again: there must be something missing. Nope. He'd done twenty years for crimes he hadn't committed.

He called down the stairs to Annie.

"You want me to print it out? Or you going to read it on the screen?"

"I'll read it on the screen. Do you want to put the kettle on?"

"Is that easy?"

"I think you'll manage."

They passed each other on the stairs.

"You can't throw us out on the streets tonight."

"Ah. So now I see why you wanted to wait until Jackson was asleep. You were playing on my good nature."

He smiled, despite the churning in his stomach, went to the kitchen, found the electric kettle, pressed its switch. While he was waiting for the kettle to boil, he spotted the picture of him and Jackson, the one that Cat had taken outside Citizens Bank Park when they'd gone to see the Phillies. He was touched that she'd taken the trouble to print it out and stick it up there. He didn't look like a bad man, not in that photo. He leaned against the kitchen counter and waited.

fourteen

"Okay," she said, when she'd read what he'd written. "First of all, you call an ex-wife or one of your children or somebody now."

"That's all you have to say? About my whole career?"

"Now. Nonnegotiable. I'm presuming here that one of the things you're owning up to is running away from Grace before she arrived at the hospital."

"Oh. Yeah. Ha. I forgot I hadn't owned up to that already."

"You don't have to speak to Grace, although you probably should. But somebody has to let her know. And you must tell them all you're safe anyway."

He chose Natalie. She'd be angry and cold and withering, but it wasn't as if it mattered so much. He wasn't counting on her to make him soup in his old age. He called her cell, she answered it, and he walked through the hailstorm of arrows to deliver the basic information she needed. He even gave her Annie's phone number, as if he were a regular father.

"Thank you," said Annie. "Second thing: *Juliet* is brilliant. Don't lump the music in with the rest of it."

"Have you been taking any of this in?"

"Yes. You're a very bad man. You've been a useless father to four of your five children, and a useless husband to every single one of your wives, and a rubbish partner to every single one of your girlfriends. And *Juliet* is still brilliant."

"How can you think that? Now that you know what a bunch of crap it all is."

"When did you last listen to it?"

"God. Not since it was released."

"I played it a couple of days ago. How many times have you heard it?"

"You know I, like, made it, don't you?"

"How many times?"

"All the way through? Since it was finished?"

Had he ever? He was trying to remember. There had been a moment in just about every relationship when he'd walked in on somebody listening to his music furtively; he could remember all the startled guilty faces. It had even happened with a couple of his kids, although not Grace, thankfully. But then, he hadn't seen enough of Grace to catch her doing anything furtively. He shook his head.

"Never?"

"I don't think so. Why would I have done that? But I played those songs on stage every night for a while, remember. I'd know if there was anything in them. And there isn't. They're all lies."

"You're telling me that art is *made up*? My God."

"I'm telling you that my . . . art is inauthentic. Sorry. Let me rephrase that. I'm telling you my rock album is a fake bunch of crap."

"And you think that matters to me?"

"I wouldn't like it if I found out John Lee Hooker was a white accountant."

"Is he not?"

"He's dead."

"You see, this is all news to me. Anyway, what you're saying is I'm an idiot."

"Huh? Where did that come from?"

"Well, I've listened to it hundreds of times, and it still doesn't feel to me as though I've emptied it. So I must be daft. It's all just facts, isn't it, as far as you're concerned? It's a rotten album, fact. And if I can't grasp the facts, then that makes me stupid."

"No, no, I'm sorry, I didn't mean that."

"So, go on. Square your feelings about *Juliet* with mine."

He studied her. As far as he could tell, she was really irritated, which had to mean that she really did have something invested in the music. And whatever it was, he was dumping all over it.

He shrugged.

"I can't. Unless I say, you know, everyone's opinion is valid."

"Which you don't believe?"

"Not in this case, no. See . . . It's like I'm a chef, and you're eating in my restaurant, and you're telling me how great my food is. But I know I pissed all over it before I served it up. So, you know, your opinion is valid, but . . ."

Annie wrinkled her nose and laughed. "But it demonstrates a certain lack of taste."

"Exactly."

"So Tucker Crowe thinks his fans can't taste pee when it's served to them."

That was exactly what Tucker Crowe thought during that tour. He hated himself, sure, but he also despised everyone who lapped it all up. That was one of the reasons it had been so easy to quit.

"You know that bad people can make great art, don't you?" said Annie.

"Yes, of course. Some of the people whose art I admire the most are assholes."

"Dickens wasn't nice to his wife."

"Dickens didn't write a memoir called *I'm Nice to My Wife*."

"You didn't make an album called *Julie Beatty Is a Deep and Interesting Human Being and I Didn't Impregnate Anyone Else While I Was with Her*. It doesn't matter how it came about. You think it was all accidental. But like it or not, believe it or not, the music that Julie inspired was wonderful."

He threw up his hands in mock despair and laughed.

"What?" said Annie.

"I can't believe I told you all those things, and we've ended up talking about how great I am."

"But we're not. You've confused the two things again. You're not great. You're a, a shallow, feckless, self-indulgent . . . *wanker*."

"Thanks."

"Well, you were, anyway. We're talking about how great your *album* is."

He smiled.

"Okay. Compliment accepted, if not believed. And abuse accepted, too. I can honestly say that nobody has ever called me a wanker before. I quite enjoyed it."

"You can only honestly say that you've never *heard*

anybody call you a wanker before. I'll bet it's happened. Don't you ever read the Internet? Actually, I know you do. That's how we met."

She paused. He could see that she wanted to say something and she was stopping herself.

"Go on," he said.

"I have a confession to make, too. And it's almost as bad as yours."

"Good."

"You know the guy who wrote the first review on that website? The one where you found mine?"

"Duncan somebody. Talking about wankers."

Annie stared at him, then clapped her hands to her mouth. He'd have worried that he'd said something out of turn, except that her eyes were bright with a kind of astonished mischief.

"What?"

"Tucker Crowe knows who Duncan is and he called him a wanker. I cannot tell you how weird that is."

"You know that guy?"

"He's . . . This was his house, up until a few weeks ago." Tucker stared at her.

"So he's the one? The man you wasted all those years with?"

"He's the one. That's why I've heard your music so

much. That's why I got to hear *Juliet, Naked*. That's why I posted a review on his website."

"And . . . Oh, shit. He lives in this town still?"

"A few minutes' walk away."

"Jesus Christ."

"Does that worry you?"

"It's like . . . Of all the gin joints, in all the towns, in all the world, I have to walk into his. That's incredible."

"Except not. As I said. Because without him, we wouldn't know each other. I'd like you to meet him."

"No."

"Why not?"

"Because (a) he's a fucking fruitcake, and (b) I might kill him, and (c) if I didn't kill him, he'd drop dead from the excitement anyway."

"Well, 'c' is a definite possibility."

"Why do you want me to meet him?"

"Because no matter what you think, he's not stupid. Not about art, anyway. And you're the only artist alive who's made any sense to him, just about."

"The only artist alive? Jesus Christ. I could write you a list of a hundred people better than me off the top of my head."

"It's not about better, Tucker. You speak to him. For him. He connects. You plug right into a very complicated-looking socket in his back. I don't know why, but you do."

"So I don't need to meet him, then. We've already talked."

"Oh, it's up to you. It's weird. He was unfaithful, and that relationship cost me a lot. But you staying here and me not telling him . . . That seems like a betrayal beyond all comprehension."

"So tell him after I've gone."

They finished their tea, and Annie found a spare duvet and pillows for the sofa. Jackson was fast asleep in the spare room; Tucker had already lost an argument about who was going to sleep in her bed.

"Thank you, Annie," he said. "Really." And he kissed her on the cheek.

"It's nice, having people to stay," she said. "Hasn't happened since Duncan left."

"Oh. Yeah. Thanks for that, too." He kissed her on the other cheek and went upstairs.

Saturday morning was, despite Annie's warnings, clear and bright and cold, but in Tucker's considered opinion the town didn't look a whole lot better: without the cheap nighttime neon it just looked tired, like a middle-aged hooker wearing no makeup. They walked down to the sea after breakfast; they took a detour so that Annie could show her visitors where the museum was, and they stopped at a store where the candy was kept in jars, and you had to ask for a quarter-pound of what you wanted. Jackson bought some lurid-looking pink candy shrimp.

And then, while they were down on the beach trying to teach Jackson how to skip stones on the waves, Annie said, "Uh-oh."

A pudgy middle-aged man was jogging toward them, red-faced and sweaty, despite the temperature. He stopped when he spotted Annie.

"Hello," he said.

"Hi, Duncan. I didn't have you down as a jogger."

"No, me neither. It's a, a new thing. New regime."

Tucker knew enough about the relationships between ex-partners to realize that this exchange was bursting with meaning, but there was nothing on Annie's face he could read. The four of them stood there for a moment. Annie was clearly trying to work out the best way of breaking the news, but Duncan made a big deal of sticking his hand out, as if he were being magnanimous in some way.

"Hello," said Duncan. "Duncan Thomson."

"Hello," said Tucker. "Tucker Crowe." He had never been more conscious of the weight of his own name.

Duncan dropped Tucker's hand as if it were red-hot and looked at Annie with real contempt.

"That's just pathetic," he said to Annie. And he jogged away.

The three of them watched as he plodded off along the beach.

"Why did that man call you pathetic?" said Jackson.

"It's complicated," said Annie.

"I want to know. He was mad at us."

"Well," said Tucker. "I think that man thought I wasn't who I said I was. He thought Annie had told me to say that my name was, was my name because she thought it would be funny."

There was a beat, while Jackson examined every side of this misunderstanding for any possible trace of humor.

"That's way not funny," said Jackson.

"No," said Tucker.

"So why did you think it would be?" Jackson addressed this question to Annie, as the originator of the incomprehensible joke.

"I didn't, sweetheart," said Annie.

"Dad just said you did."

"No, he said . . . You see, I know who your dad is. But that man doesn't. That man knows who Tucker Crowe is, but he doesn't think that's who your dad is."

"Who does he think Dad is? Fucker?"

Annie presumably knew better than to laugh at the sound of an obscenity emerging from the mouth of a six-year-old, but she laughed anyway. Tucker understood the impulse. It was the combination of the curse with the boy's earnestness, his attempt to understand what had just happened.

"Yes!" said Tucker. "That's exactly who he thinks I am."

"There's actually a further complication," said Annie. "I know the confessional window has closed, but . . ." She took a deep breath. "He also thinks you're somebody I'm . . . seeing."

"Why would he think that?"

"He asked about the photo on the fridge, and I didn't want to tell him the truth, and . . ."

At least Tucker now understood the implied generosity of the handshake.

"So there we are," said Tucker. "That man thinks I'm Annie's boyfriend. And he thinks Fucker is Tucker."

"I was right," said Jackson. "It's so, so not funny."

"No."

"Cool," said Jackson. "Because I don't like it when jokes are funny for everybody else."

"Anyway," said Tucker. "All in all, I'm a long way from being me at the moment."

"Exactly."

"Do I have to go to all the trouble of proving it?"

"The trouble is, he knows more about Tucker Crowe than you do."

"Yeah, but I have the documentation."

About fifteen minutes later, Duncan called her on her cell phone. She was outside the museum with Tucker and Jackson, fishing around in her bag for her work keys: the charms of Gooleness had been exhausted already, so, much earlier than anticipated, she was about to show her guests pieces of long-dead shark.

"I can't believe you did that," said Duncan.

"I haven't actually done anything," said Annie.

"If you want to make a sad spectacle of yourself around town with someone old enough to be your dad, then that's up to you. But the Tucker business . . . What's the point? Why would you do that?"

"I'm actually with him now," said Annie. "So this is slightly embarrassing."

Tucker waved at the mouthpiece.

"You should have thought about that before you made him take part in your juvenile games."

"It's not a game," said Annie. "That was Tucker Crowe. Still is. You can ask him any question about himself, if you want."

"Why are you doing this?" said Duncan.

"I'm not doing anything."

"I sent you a picture of Tucker Crowe a few weeks ago. You know what he looks like. He doesn't look like a retired accountant."

"That wasn't him. That was his neighbor John. Also known as Fake Tucker, or Fucker, because of a misunderstanding that people like you have spread all over the Internet."

"Oh, for God's sake. So how did you meet 'Tucker Crowe,' actually?"

"He e-mailed me about that review of *Juliet, Naked* I wrote."

"E-mailed you."

"Yes."

"You post up one piece and you get an e-mail from Tucker Crowe."

"Listen, Duncan, Tucker and Jackson are standing here and it's cold and . . ."

"Jackson."

"Tucker's son."

"Oh, he's got a son now, has he? And where did he appear from?"

"You know how babies are made, Duncan. Anyway. You saw a picture of Jackson on my fridge."

"I saw a picture of your retired accountant and his grandson on your fridge. This is a circuitous argument."

"It's not an argument. Listen, I'll call you later. You can come round for tea if you want. Bye."

And she hung up on him.

Ros had worked hard over the couple of days Annie had spent in London. The day before she left, the two of them had gone over to Terry Jackson's house to rummage through his collection of Gooleness memorabilia and had ended up taking most of it, in the absence of anything else to show; Terry's wife, denied the use of a spare bedroom for the whole of her married life because of all the old bus tickets and newspapers, was insisting that it was a gift, not a loan. Terry had been unable to provide any kind of budget for the exhibition, so they were using anything they had on hand—old photo frames, unused dusty cases—to display his stuff. A lot of it was still in garbage bags, a conservation decision that would get them thrown out of the Museums Association if anyone ever found out.

"Gross," said Jackson, when Annie showed him the eye.

Annie admired his determination to say the right things, but the eye didn't really stare at you, in the way that Annie and Ros had hoped it might, mostly because it didn't really look like an eye any longer, unfortunately. They had decided to keep it in the exhibition because of what it said about the people of Gooleness, rather than what it said about sharks, although they would not be explaining their decision to the people of Gooleness.

Tucker liked Terry's Stones poster, though, and he loved the photograph of the four pals on their day out at the seaside.

"Why does it make me feel sad?" he said. "Even though they're happy? I mean, sure, they're all old or dead now. But it's more than that, I think."

"I have exactly the same reaction. It's because their leisure time was so precious, I think. We have so much, by comparison, and we get to do so much more with it. When I first saw it, I'd just had this three-week holiday trekking around the U.S., and . . ." She stopped.

"What?"

"Oh," she said. "You don't know about that, either."

"What?"

"My American holiday."

"No," said Tucker. "But then, we only met recently. There are probably a few holidays I need to catch up on."

"But this one should have come up in the full disclosure section of our conversation."

"Why?"

"We went to Bozeman, Montana. And the site of some studio that isn't there anymore in Memphis. And Berkeley. And the toilet in the Pits Club in Minneapolis . . ."

"Shit, Annie."

"I'm sorry."

"Why did you go with him?"

"It seemed like as good a way of seeing America as any. I enjoyed it."

"You went to San Francisco to stand outside Julie Beatty's house?"

"Ah. No. Not guilty. I let him get on with it. I went to San Francisco to walk across the Golden Gate Bridge and to do some shopping."

"So this guy Duncan . . . he's like a real stalker."

"I suppose he is."

For a moment, Annie felt a little pang of envy. It wasn't that she'd ever wanted Duncan to stalk her, exactly. She didn't want to see him hiding behind her hedge, or ducking behind a supermarket aisle when she was doing her shopping. But she wouldn't have minded if he'd had the same appetite for her that he'd shown for Tucker. She had only just realized that the man talking to her now was much more of a rival than another woman could ever be.

Duncan poured himself an orange juice and sat down at the kitchen table.

"Gina."

"Yes, my sweet."

She was sitting at the kitchen table, drinking coffee and reading the *Guardian* magazine.

"What do you think are the chances of Tucker Crowe being in Gooleness?"

She looked at him.

"*The* Tucker Crowe?"

"Yes."

"*This* Gooleness?"

"Yes."

"I'd say the chances were very slim indeed. Why? Do you think you just saw him?"

"Annie says I did."

"Annie says you did."

"Yes."

"Well, without knowing why she said it, I'd have to say that she's winding you up."

"That's what I think."

"Why did she tell you that? It seems quite a peculiar thing to say. And quite cruel, given your . . . interests."

"I was jogging along the beach, and she was there with a, a respectable-looking middle-aged man and a young boy. And I stopped, and introduced myself to the man, and he said he was Tucker Crowe."

"That must have been a bit of a shock to you."

"I just couldn't understand why she made him say it. I

mean, it's not very clever. Or funny. And then I just called her from the bedroom before my shower and she's sticking to her story."

"Did he look like Tucker Crowe?"

"No. Not at all."

They found their eyes straying over to the mantel-piece, and the photograph he'd brought with him when he'd moved in: Tucker onstage, maybe at the Bottom Line, sometime in the late seventies. Duncan could feel the beginnings of another little panic, rather like the panic he'd felt the other night when he was talking to Gina about *Juliet*. The man he saw on the beach this morning wasn't the man who'd sung "Farmer John" in a club a few weeks ago, that was for sure. And the man he saw on the beach this afternoon definitely wasn't the man in the famous Neil Ritchie shot, the wild man lunging for the camera. What was troubling Duncan now was that, for the first time, he'd begun to wonder whether the young man on the mantel-piece could possibly be the crazy person with the matted hair who'd tried to attack Ritchie. They looked nothing like each other, really. Their eyes were different, their noses were different, their coloring was different. He'd never for a second doubted the wisdom of the Crowologists until now; he'd accepted the Neil Ritchie story as a piece of his-tory, fact. Except—and these panics were coming thick and fast now—Neil Ritchie was an idiot. Duncan had never met him, but his ignorance, his rudeness and his self-importance were common knowledge, and Duncan had had an e-mail from him a few years back that had been offensive and a little deranged. Neil Ritchie was a man who'd traveled God knows how many miles in order to invade the privacy of a long-retired singer-songwriter who didn't want to be disturbed. This, let's face it, was not normal behavior. And yet this was the man Duncan was prepared to trust more than Annie and the pleasant-looking chap on the beach? If one took the two Farmer John pictures out of the equation and put glasses on the singer in the Bottom Line picture, changed his hair color to silver, trimmed it . . .

"Oh, God," said Duncan.

"What?"

"I can't think of any good reason why that man would introduce himself as Tucker Crowe unless he actually was."

"Really?"

"Annie's not really a cruel person. And the person on the beach looked a little bit like the person in that picture. Except older."

"And did she explain how she knew him?"

"She said he wrote to her. Out of the blue. After she posted that review of *Naked* on our website."

"If that's true," said Gina, thoughtfully, "then you must want to hang yourself."

. . .

Unfortunately, Duncan was not physically capable of jogging through the streets of Gooleness for the second time
in less than an hour, so he had to settle for a brisk walk,
with occasional pauses. He needed the time to think, anyway; there was a lot to think about.

Duncan had not been a regretful man, not until
recently. However, over the last few weeks, he had found
himself wishing that he had done a lot of things differently.
He had been impulsive, and overeager, and lacking in judgment. He'd got a lot of things wrong, and he hated himself
for it. And the thing he'd got most wrong, he'd come to
realize, was *Juliet, Naked*. What had he been thinking of?
Why had he responded like that? After about five more
plays, the songs in their acoustic form had started to pall;
after ten, he'd decided he didn't want to hear the album
again. Not only was it a weak, malnourished, puny thing,
but it had started to diminish the magnificence of *Juliet*:
who wanted to see the rusty old innards of a work of art,
really? It was of interest to scholars, and he was a scholar.
But how had he come to the conclusion that it was better than the original? He knew part of the answer to that
question: he'd had access to *Naked* before any of his peers,
and to post a review saying that it was dull and pointless
would have thrown away his advantage. But then that's

what art is, sometimes, he always felt: something that confers advantages. His had come at a cost, though. He'd had currency, but the exchange rate turned out to be dismally low. Why hadn't he just taken the wretched review down? He turned back—to run home to his computer—and then spun around again. He'd do it later.

All that, and now this. If it was true that Tucker Crowe was in Gooleness—*staying in his old house*—then he had many other reasons to mourn the temporary desertion of his critical faculties. If he hadn't been so irritated by Annie's indifference, they might not have split up, and they might have met Tucker together. If he'd posted the same kind of review that Annie had written, Tucker might have e-mailed him. It was all too much, really. He'd lived his whole life cautiously, and on the one occasion when he'd screwed his caution up into a ball and thrown it to the wind it had ended like this. (And there was Gina, too, of course, which was another narrative strand in the same story. Gina was, metaphorically, *Naked*, and her literal nakedness, or the offer of it, had only served to underline the aptness of the metaphor. He'd jumped too quickly there, too.)

Most of his adult life he'd wanted to meet Tucker Crowe, or at least to be in the same room, and here he was, possibly on the verge of realizing that ambition, and he was scared. If Tucker had read Annie's piece, then the chances were he'd have read Duncan's, too. Presumably he'd hated it, and hated its author. Tucker Crowe knows who I am, thought Duncan, and he hates me! Is that possible? Surely he'd recognize and appreciate the passion for the work, at least. Wouldn't he? Or would he hate that, too? It would be better for everyone if, after all, Annie were playing some kind of cruel and juvenile trick. He turned toward Gina's place for a second time, thought better of it again.

And in the middle of all these doubts and anxieties, all this self-loathing, Duncan found himself trying to think of test questions that would either prove Tucker was who he said he was or expose him as a fraud. It was difficult, though. Duncan had to concede that Tucker Crowe was an even greater authority on the subject of Tucker Crowe than Duncan Thomson. If he were to ask him, say, who played that pedal steel on "And You Are?" and Tucker insisted that it wasn't Sneaky Pete Kleinow, that the album sleeve was wrong, then who was he to argue? Tucker would know, surely. He could win those arguments every time. No, he needed something different, something that only the two of them could possibly know about. And he thought he had it.

When Annie saw Duncan skulking on the other side of her front hedge, obviously trying to summon up the courage necessary to knock on what was, until comparatively recently, his own front door, and trying to peek through the window without anybody noticing, she almost hooted at the irony. Less than two hours before, she'd been quietly lamenting his lack of passion for her, her inability to provoke in him the desire to hide behind her hedge trying to catch a glimpse of her; and now here he was, doing exactly that. And then very quickly she realized that there was no irony here at all. Duncan was hiding behind her hedge because Tucker Crowe was in her kitchen. She was still not enough, in exactly the same way she hadn't been enough before.

She opened the front door.

"Duncan! Don't be an idiot. Come in."

"I'm sorry. I was just . . ." And then, unable to come up with any plausible explanation for his behavior, he shrugged and walked down the path into the house. Jackson was at the kitchen table, drawing, and Tucker was frying bacon for their brunch.

"Hello again," said Duncan.

"Hello there," said Tucker.

"There is a possibility that I might perhaps owe you an apology," said Duncan.

"Okay," said Tucker. "And when will you know for sure?"

"Well, it's all very difficult, isn't it?"

"Is it?"

"I'm beginning to think that there's no real reason for you to tell me you're Tucker Crowe if you're not."

"That's a good start."

"But as I'm sure Annie has explained . . . I'm a, a long-term admirer of your work, and for some years now I've been under the impression that you don't look like that."

"That's Fucker," said Jackson, without looking up from his drawing. "Fucker is our friend Farmer John. A man took a photo of him and told everyone it was Daddy."

"Right," said Duncan. "Well. I can see how . . . It's plausible, I grant you."

"Thanks," said Tucker, genially. "If it helps, I have a passport."

Duncan looked stunned

"Oh," said Duncan. "I hadn't thought about that."

"Sorry to disappoint you," said Tucker. "You were probably thinking more along the lines of some exhaustive trivia questions. But there's your world, which is full of, you know, rumor and conspiracy theories and scary photos of people who aren't me. And there's my world, which is all passports and PTA meetings and insurance claims. It's pretty banal in my world. There's plenty of paperwork."

Tucker went to a jacket hanging over the arm of a chair, and pulled his passport out from the inside pocket.

"There." He handed it to Duncan.

Duncan flicked through it.

"Yes. Well. That all seems to be in order."

Annie and Tucker burst out laughing. Duncan looked startled, and then forced a smile.

"Sorry. That probably sounded a little officious."

"You want to see Jackson's? I can see you might think that I've forged this one. But would I go to all the trouble of forging a passport for a kid just so he has the same last name as me?"

"Can I use your loo, Annie?" said Duncan. And he left the room, without receiving permission.

"I think he's a little overcome," said Annie. "He needs to recover his composure. Try and be nice to him. Just remember: this is the most amazing moment of his life."

When Duncan came back in, Tucker gave him a big bear hug.

"It's okay," Tucker said. "Everything's okay."

Annie laughed, but Duncan held on a little too long, and she could see that he had his eyes closed.

"Duncan!" she said. And then, to make it sound as though she wasn't telling him off, "Do you want to eat with us?"

They chatted, as best they could, while toast was buttered and eggs were scrambled. Annie could have kissed Tucker:

he could see how nervous Duncan was, and he was asking him questions—about the town, his work, the kids at the college—that he seemed reasonably sure Duncan could answer without crying. There was a tremble in Duncan's voice whenever he spoke, and he was adopting a slightly over-formal register for the occasion, and sometimes he'd giggle for no apparent reason, but most of the time it was possible to imagine that the four of them were participating in a casual weekend social occasion, the sort of thing they'd all done before and might do again.

Annie could have kissed Tucker for lots of other reasons, too. It struck her that everybody in her kitchen loved him with some degree of intensity. (Everybody else, anyway—she knew him well enough to understand that he wasn't too keen on himself.) Jackson's love was the most neurotic and needy, but well within the realms of the normal, as far as she could remember from her child psychology classes; Duncan's was weird and obsessive; and hers . . . She could characterize it as a crush, or the beginnings of something deeper, or the pathetic fantasy of an increasingly lonely woman, or the recognition that she needed to sleep with someone before the decade was out, and sometimes she thought of it as all of these things at once, and she always wished that she hadn't told him off so often over the previous twenty-four hours. And yes, he'd needed it, sort of, but only if he were to stay in the world he'd stepped into. There'd been a subtext to the scoldings: if you're going to live with me in Gooleness, then you have to do right by your family. That's how we do things around here. But seeing as he wasn't going to live with her in Gooleness, what business was it of hers? It was like telling Spider-Man not to climb up buildings while he was here, because of health and safety. She was missing the point of him.

The social occasion soon fell, inevitably, into something else, mostly because every single thing that either Jackson or Tucker said either confirmed or disproved theses that Duncan had been constructing for years.

"Well," said Duncan, as they sat down. "This looks nice."

"My sister doesn't eat bacon," said Jackson, and Annie could see Duncan wrestling with himself: What was he allowed to ask?

"Have you got other brothers and sisters, Jackson?" he asked eventually, presumably on the grounds that to ask nothing at all would be rude.

"Yeah. Four. But they don't live with me. They have different moms."

Duncan choked on a piece of toast.

"Oh. Well. That's . . ."

"And none of the moms is named Julie," said Tucker.

"Ha!" said Duncan. "We'd rather given up on that theory anyway."

Jackson looked at the men, uncomprehending.

"Don't worry about it, Jack," said Tucker.

"Okay."

"I took Tucker and Jackson into the museum this morning," said Annie. There was very little neutral ground for them to clamber on, in this conversation, seeing as every little detail about Tucker's personal life would offer a life-threatening level of excitement. "Showed them the shark's eye. Do you remember me telling you about that?"

"Yes," said Duncan. "Indeed. Your exhibition must be opening soon."

"Wednesday."

"I must try and get along to see it."

"We're having a little drinks reception for it on Tuesday night. Nothing much. Just a few councillors, and the Friends."

"You should get Tucker to sing," said Duncan. It was going to be impossible, Annie could see that now. Duncan might only ever get one shot at this and he wasn't going to waste it.

"Yes," said Annie. "I'm sure that, if Tucker wanted to break his twenty-year silence, then the Gooleness Seaside Museum would be the most appropriate venue."

Tucker laughed. Duncan looked down at his plate.

"I'd enjoy it, anyway. I . . . I don't know what Annie's told you, but I really am a very big admirer of your work.

I'm . . . Well, I don't think it would be overstating the case were I to describe myself as a world expert."

"I've read your stuff," said Tucker.

"Oh," said Duncan. "Gosh. I . . . Well, you can tell me where I've gone wrong."

"I wouldn't know where to start," said Tucker.

"Would you maybe like to do an interview? To set the record straight? You've possibly seen the website, so you know you'd get a fair hearing."

"Duncan," said Annie. "Don't start."

"Sorry," said Duncan.

"There isn't a record," said Tucker. "There's me and my life, and fifteen people like you who have for reasons best known to yourselves spent too much time guessing what that life is."

"I suppose that's what it must look like. From your perspective."

"I'm not sure there's another one."

"We could limit the questions to the songs."

"Don't push it, Duncan," said Annie. "I don't think Tucker's keen on the idea."

"Was I right, by the way?" said Tucker. "Did you have some questions that you thought would prove that I am who I said I was?"

"I . . . Well, yes. I did have one."

"Hit me. I want to see if I know my own life."

"It's possibly . . . I'm wondering whether it's possibly too invasive."

"Is it something I'd have to send Jackson out of the room for?"

"Oh, no. It's just . . . Well, it's silly really. I was going to ask you who else you've drawn, apart from Julie Beatty."

Annie could feel the drop in temperature. Duncan had said something he shouldn't have said, although she didn't understand why he shouldn't have said it.

"What makes you so sure I drew her?"

"I can't divulge my sources."

"Your sources are no good."

"I respectfully beg to differ."

Tucker put down his knife and fork.

"What is it with you guys? Why do you think you know stuff, when you know nothing at all about anything?"

"Sometimes we know more than you think."

"Doesn't sound like it to me."

Duncan was suddenly unable to make eye contact with anyone at the table, which in Annie's experience was the first sign that he was losing his temper. His anger was so carefully and closely managed that it only came out through the wrong holes.

"It's a lovely drawing, the one of Julie. You're good. I'll bet she doesn't smoke anymore, though."

That last detail was triumphantly delivered, but the triumph was diminished by Tucker standing up, reaching across the table and lifting Duncan up by the neck of his Graceland T-shirt. Duncan looked terrified.

"You went into her house?"

Annie remembered the day Duncan had gone out to Berkeley. He'd come back to the hotel in a peculiar mood, flustered and a little evasive; that night he'd even told her that he felt his Tucker Crowe obsession was waning.

"Only to use the toilet."

"She invited you in to use her toilet?"

"Tucker, please put him down," said Annie. "You're frightening Jackson."

"He's not," said Jackson. "It's cool. I don't like that guy anyway. Punch him, Dad."

The request was enough to loosen Tucker's grip on Duncan.

"That's not nice, Jackson," said his father.

"No, it isn't," said Duncan.

Tucker shot him a warning look, and Duncan held both hands up in immediate apology.

"So come on, Duncan. Explain to me how you ended up using Julie's toilet."

"I shouldn't have done it," said Duncan. "When I got to her house, I was bursting. And there was this kid there who knew where she kept her front-door key. And she was out, so we let ourselves in, and I went for a pee, and he showed me the picture. We were in there for five minutes maximum."

"Oh, that makes it okay," said Tucker. "Seven would have constituted a violation of her privacy."

"I know it was stupid," said Duncan. "I felt terrible about it. Still do. I tried to forget it ever happened."

"And now you're boasting about it."

"I just wanted to prove that I'm . . . a serious person. A serious scholar, anyway."

"It doesn't look as though those two identities are compatible, does it? A serious person doesn't break into somebody's house."

Duncan took a deep breath. For a moment, Annie was frightened that he was going to confess to something else.

"All I can say in my defense is that . . . well, you asked us to listen. And some of us listened a little too hard. I mean, if someone had had a chance to break into Shakespeare's house, he should have taken it, shouldn't he? Because then we'd know more. It would have been perfectly legitimate to . . . to rummage around in Shakespeare's sock drawer. In the interests of history and literature."

"So according to your logic Julie Beatty is Shakespeare."

"Anne Hathaway."

"Jesus Christ." Tucker shook his head bitterly. "You people. And for the record: I'm not even Leonard Cohen, let alone Shakespeare."

. . .

You asked us to listen . . . That much at least was true. It had
to be. He'd always said the right things, back in the days
when he still spoke to local radio DJs and rock writers: he'd
told anyone who wanted to know that there wasn't anything
he could do about being a musician, he just *was* one, and
he'd be one whether people wanted to listen to him or not.
But he'd also told Lisa, Grace's mother, that he wanted to
be rich and famous, that he wouldn't be happy until his talent got recognized in all the ways that talent could be recognized. The money never really happened—even *Juliet* only
provided a decent living wage for a year or two—but other
stuff did. He got the respect and the reviews and the fans
and the model who used to hang out with Jackson Browne
and Jack Nicholson. And he got Duncan and his buddies.
If you wanted to get into people's living rooms, could you
then object if they wanted to get into yours?

"This will probably sound silly," said Duncan, "and
not what you want to hear. But I'm not the only person
who thinks you're a genius. And while you might think
we're . . . we're inadequate as people, we're not necessarily
the worst judges in the world. We read, and watch movies,
and think, and . . . I probably blew it as far as you're concerned with my silly *Naked* review, which was written at
the wrong time, and for the wrong reasons. But the origi-

nal album . . . Do even you know how dense that was? I still haven't peeled it all away, I don't think, even after all this time. I don't pretend to understand what those songs meant to you, but it's the forms of expression you chose, the allusions, the musical references. That's what makes it art. To my mind. And . . . sorry, sorry, one last thing. I don't think people with talent necessarily value it, because it all comes so easy to them, and we never value things that come easy to us. But I value what you did on that album more highly than, I think, anything else I've heard. So thank you. And now I think I should leave. But I couldn't meet you without telling you all that."

And as he stood up, Annie's phone rang. She answered it and held the receiver out to Tucker. Tucker didn't notice it for a moment. He was still staring at Duncan, as if the words he'd just said were suspended somewhere near his mouth in a speech bubble and could be reread. Tucker wanted to reread them.

"Tucker."

"Yeah."

"Grace," she said.

"Yay," said Jackson. "Gracie."

For most of the last twenty years, Tucker had Grace down as the key to a lot of things. She was why he'd stopped working; every time he'd taken the lid off himself and taken a peek inside, he'd had to close it quick. She was the spare room that never got tidied, the e-mail that never got answered, the loan that never got repaid, the symptom that never got described to a doctor. Except worse than any of that, obviously, what with her being a daughter, rather than an e-mail or a rash.

"Grace? Hold on a minute."

As he took the handset from the kitchen to the living room, he suddenly saw that this strange little seaside town was perfect for the sort of reconciliation that could bring that whole sorry story to an end. He didn't think he could ask Annie to accommodate yet another member of his family, but Grace could stay in a B&B or somewhere for a couple of days. The bleak pier they'd seen that morning . . . He could see them sitting on the boards, dangling their feet under the railings, talking and listening and talking.

"Tucker?"

"Dad" was an appellation you had to earn, he guessed, mostly by being one. Maybe that's how their conversation on the pier would end: she'd call him "Dad," and he'd weep a little.

"Yeah. Sorry. I was just taking the phone somewhere more private."

"Where are you?"

"I'm in this weird little seaside town on the east coast of

England called Gooleness. It's great. You'd dig it. Grungy, but kind of cool."

"Ha. Okay. You know I came from France to see you in the hospital?"

She had her mother's voice. Or rather—and this was worse, really—she had her mother's temperament: he could hear the same determination to think the best of him and of everybody else, the same puzzled smile. Neither Grace nor Lisa had ever made it easy for him: they'd both been heartbreakingly tolerant and sympathetic and forgiving. How was one supposed to deal with people like that? He preferred the chilly sarcasm that was his usual lot. He could ignore that.

"Yeah, Grace, I heard you were coming."

"So, you know. Why did you run away?"

"I wasn't running from you."

He couldn't afford too many lies, if he was really aiming at truth and reconciliation, but one or two little ones, judiciously positioned right at the beginning of the road in order to ease access, might be necessary. "I didn't want to see you with all those other people."

"Ummm . . . Is it unreasonable to point out that most of those other people are your children?"

"Most, sure. But not all. There were a couple of ex-wives in there. They were making me feel uncomfortable. And since I wasn't feeling so great . . ."

"Well, I guess only you know how much you could cope with."

"What I was thinking was, you could come up here," said Tucker. "That way, you and I could . . ."

Some terrible words and phrases were coming into his mind: "quality time," "heal," "bond," "closure." He didn't want to use any of them.

"What could we do, Tucker?"

"We could eat stuff."

"Eat stuff?"

"Yeah. And I guess talk."

"Hmmm."

"What do you think? Should I get you the train schedule?"

"I think . . . I think I don't want to do that."

"Oh."

He couldn't quite believe it. Where was the accommodation in that?

"I didn't really want to come to London to see you. I couldn't . . . I couldn't quite see the point."

"That was Lizzie's idea."

"I mean, the point of any sort of visit, anywhere. I don't wish to be difficult, Tucker. I think you're an interesting and talented guy, and I used to love reading stuff about you. Mom kept a whole heap of things. But we don't have much going on, do we?"

"Not . . . recently."

Grace laughed, not unpleasantly.

"Not in the last twenty-two years, anyway."

She was twenty-two already?

"And I'm pretty sure that my very existence is sort of awkward. I mean, I've listened to that album. You can't hear me in there. Or Lisa."

"It was a long time ago now."

"I agree. A long time ago, you chose art over . . . Well, over me."

"No, Gracie, I . . ."

"And I understand. Really. I didn't use to. But, you know. I like artists. I get it. So what would you do with me now? I can see that there's room for some painful conversation in a godforsaken town miles from anywhere. But there's no room for anything after that, is there? Not unless you want to own up to being a phony. And I wouldn't want you to do that. I'm not sure you've got enough going on to let go of *Juliet*."

She hadn't got that degree of perspicacity from Lisa. He could be proud of that.

He went back into the kitchen and handed Annie the handset.

"How did it go?"

He shook his head.

"I'm sorry."

"It's okay. I blew that one a long time ago. I've been watching too much daytime TV."

Duncan was making a big deal of putting his coat on, desperate to glean anything he could from what might be his last couple of minutes with Tucker.

"You don't have to leave," Tucker said, wearily. Duncan looked at him disbelievingly, a sixteen-year-old who'd just been told that the prettiest girl in class wasn't going to finish with him just yet.

"Really?"

"Really. I . . . What you said before—it meant a lot. Thank you. Sincerely."

And now the prettiest girl in class was taking off her panties and . . . Actually, this whole analogy was too weird. Weird and disturbingly self-serving, if anyone cared to examine it properly.

"If you would like to talk to me about my work, I'd be happy to do so. I can see you're serious about it."

What was the big deal? Why had he spent half his life trying to hide from people like Duncan? How many of them were there? A handful, scattered all over the globe. Fuck the Internet for collecting them all in one place and making them look threatening. And fuck the Internet for putting him right at the center of his own little paranoid universe.

"I really am sorry about taking a pee in Julie Beatty's toilet," said Duncan.

"I'm not sure I care as much as I pretended. Off the record? Among certain people, Julie Beatty has enjoyed a long and unsullied reputation as a fiery muse. In retrospect, she was kind of a pretty airhead. If someone pees in her toilet every now and again, it's a fair price to pay."

The two biggest parts of a man's life were his family and his work, and Tucker had spent a long time feeling wretched about both of them. There was nothing much he could do about big chunks of his family now. Things would never be right with Grace, and he could see that his relationship with Lizzie would always wobble between something they could both tolerate and something that would hurt his ears. He wasn't so interested in the older boys. That left Jackson, which gave him a 20 percent success rate as a father. There was no examination worth taking where you could pass with a mark like that.

It had never occurred to him that his work was redeemable, or that he was redeemable through his work. But as he listened that afternoon to an articulate, nerdy man tell him over and over again why he was a genius, he could feel himself hoping that it might actually be true.

fifteen

Councillor Terry Jackson had come to the museum for a private view and seemed pleased with what he'd seen. Indeed, he was so pleased that he now had ambitions for the launch.

"We should try and get a celebrity to come along and open it."

"Do you know any celebrities?" said Annie.

"No. You?"

"No."

"Oh, well."

"Who would you invite if you could?"

"I'm not very good at celebrities. I don't watch enough TV."

"Anyone in world history. Fantasy guest."

"Hmmm," she said. "And what function would this

person be serving? I mean, would we be inviting him or her to say a few words?"

"I would have thought so," said Terry. "Something to get the local press interested. Maybe even the nationals."

"I'd have thought that if a dead person from world history opened an exhibition at the Gooleness Seaside Museum, we'd be fighting the media off."

"So who would you have?"

"Jane Austen," said Annie. "Or Emily Brontë, I suppose, seeing as we're not that far from Brontë country."

"You think the national press would come up here for Emily Brontë? I know they would for Jane Austen. Bollywood and all that."

Annie had no idea what this meant and as a consequence chose to ignore it.

"Even for Emily Brontë."

"Well," said Terry. He was clearly dubious. "If you say so. Anyway. Let's keep it within the realms of the possible."

"So you're asking me to name a famous person who might actually come to the Gooleness Seaside Museum to open an exhibition? Because that's different."

"No it isn't. Aim as high as you like."

"Nelson Mandela."

"Lower."

"Simon Cowell."

Terry thought for a moment.

"Lower."

"The mayor."

"The mayor's got another do on. If you'd sorted this out quicker, we could have asked her first."

"I've got an American singer-songwriter from the eighties staying with me at the moment. Would he be any good?"

She hadn't planned to mention him, but Terry Jackson's unfair attack on her organizational skills had stung. And in any case, she couldn't quite believe that he'd chosen to stay: Tucker and Jackson had been with her for three nights already and showed no desire to leave.

"Depends who he is," said Terry.

"Tucker Crowe."

"Tucker who?"

"Tucker Crowe."

"No. No good whatsoever. Nobody's heard of him."

"Well, which American singer-songwriter from the eighties would have done the trick?"

He was beginning to annoy her now. Where had this sudden need for celebrity come from? It was always the way, with councillors. At the beginning of a project, it was all about the needs of the town; by the end it was all about the *Gooleness Echo*.

"I thought you were going to say Billy Joel or someone.

Is he a singer-songwriter? He'd have got us out of a hole. Anyway, thanks but no thanks, Tucker Crowe."

He made air quotes around the name and he chuckled, apparently at the depths of Tucker's obscurity.

"I've an idea," said Terry.

"Go on."

"Three words."

"Right."

"Have a guess."

"Three words?"

"Three words."

"John Logie Baird. Harriet Beecher Stowe."

"No. Neither of them. Oh. And I should probably say that one of the words is 'and.' "

" 'And'? Like Simon and Garfunkel?"

"Yes. But not them. I think you should give up."

"I give up."

"Gav and Barnesy."

Annie burst out laughing. Terry Jackson looked hurt.

"I'm sorry," said Annie. "I wasn't being . . . That wasn't the direction I was looking in."

"What do you think? They're local legends, and a lot of people around here recognize them . . ."

"I like it," said Annie, decisively.

"Really?"

"Really."

Terry Jackson smiled.

"Bit of a brainwave, really. Even if I do say so myself."

"There'd probably be no national press interest," said Annie.

"That's all right. That was always going to be a long shot."

Annie had once heard someone say that in the future everyone would be famous to fifteen people. In Gooleness, where Tucker Crowe slept in her bedroom, and Gav and Barnesy were invited to open exhibitions, the future had arrived.

On Wednesday, the day of the launch party, Tucker and Jackson were still with her; their departure was postponed one day at a time. Annie didn't want to press them on their plans, because she couldn't bear the thought of them leaving; every morning she was fearful that they would come into the kitchen for breakfast with their bags packed, but instead they announced plans to fish, or walk, or take a bus along the coast. She had no idea whether Jackson was supposed to be at school but again she didn't want to ask, in case Tucker suddenly slapped his forehead and dragged his son off to the station.

She couldn't have explained to anybody what she was hoping for—or at least, she wouldn't have wanted to, because the explanation would have sounded pathetic, even to her. She was hoping, she supposed, that they would stay forever, in any formation that they chose. If Tucker didn't want to share a bed with her, well, fine, although she firmly intended to sleep with someone at some stage, and if he didn't like it, he could shove it. (These scenarios had been imagined quite fully, hence the confrontational tone; she had scripted this particular conversation on Sunday night, when she was trying to get to sleep, and she had found herself getting irritated by Tucker's predicted indifference.) She would, of course, have to replace Cat, at least for most of the year—she fully anticipated trips back to the U.S. during the longer holidays, although Jackson would be attending school in Gooleness, maybe at Rose Hill, which had an excellent reputation and an impressive website, which she happened to have stumbled across the previous evening. How hard would that be for Jackson? He hadn't talked about his mother that much, which gave her hope—his primary relationship was clearly with Tucker, and she was pretty sure that, if Tucker was unambiguous about what he wanted, his boy would fall into line. She would offer to e-mail Cat weekly or daily or whatever she wanted, and she could attach pictures, and they could talk on the phone, and she could download the thing that allowed you to see someone in Australia on the computer, and Cat could stay whenever she wanted . . . If everyone was determined to make it work, then it would. After all, what was the alternative? That they just went home and resumed their lives, as if nothing had happened?

The trouble was that nothing had happened, of course. If Tucker and Jackson were able to hear the inside of her head, they'd have backed slowly out of the house, with Tucker brandishing whatever weapon he could lay his hands on in order to protect his son. Did her mother entertain similar fantasies when Christmas was coming to an end, and she knew that she was going to be left with and by herself for another eleven and three-quarter months? Probably. Everything had come too soon, that was the problem. Annie would have been happy enough looking forward to Tucker's e-mails, with the remote and tantalizing possibility of an actual meeting to be dreamed about only slowly, over months and then years. Because of the various medical misfortunes, she'd ended up scoffing the whole lot within weeks, and now she was left with an empty chocolate box and a vague feeling of nausea.

She had to concede, reluctantly, that there was another interpretation of recent events: the problem wasn't the empty box, but the metaphor. The short visit of a middle-aged man and his young son shouldn't be a gourmet pastry; it should be a store-bought egg-salad sandwich, a distracted bowl of cereal, an apple snatched from a fruit bowl when you didn't have time to eat. She had somehow constructed a life so empty that she was in the middle of the defining narrative incident of the last ten years, and what did it consist of, really? If Tucker and Jackson did after all decide that their lives should be lived elsewhere—and so far, anyway, they had given very little indication to the contrary—she had to make sure that, if they did ever come back, their stay would be an irritation, something she could have done without, something she wouldn't even remember a couple of weeks after they'd gone. That was how it was supposed to be with houseguests, wasn't it?

When she came downstairs she was wearing a skirt and some makeup, and Tucker looked at her.

"Oh, shoot," he said.

It wasn't what she might have hoped for, but at least it was a reaction. He'd noticed, anyway.

"What?"

"I'm going to have to go like this. I guess I might have a clean T-shirt, but I think it might have the name of a lap-dancing club on it. It's not like I'm a customer, or anything. It was a thoughtful present from somebody. What about you, Jack? Got anything clean left?"

"I put a couple of things in the wash," said Annie. "There's a new Something-Man T-shirt on your bed."

A lot of women had to say a version of that sentence every single day of the week, probably, without feeling particularly emotional about it. Or rather, the emotion they were most likely to feel was a very deep self-pity, rather than an ache of love and loss and longing. That seemed like an ambition, of sorts: to get to a stage where she wanted to hang herself because putting a T-shirt on a child's bed seemed indicative of the slow and painful death of the spirit. At the moment, she wanted to hang herself because it seemed like the first tiny glimmers of a rebirth.

"Spider. Is Spider-Man okay for your party?"

"I'm the only one who has to go dressed up," she said. "You're the exotic special guests."

"Only because we'll be wearing T-shirts," said Tucker.

"And you come from the U.S. When we first started thinking about a Gooleness in 1964 exhibition, we really weren't banking on American visitors."

"The exchange rate was bad back then," said Tucker. "You watch, there'll be hordes of us."

Annie laughed with inappropriate volume and vigor, and at preposterous length, and Tucker stared at her.

"You nervous?"

"No."

"Oh. Okay."

"I was just thinking about you leaving. I don't want you to. And that made me laugh too loudly at your joke. For some reason. Maybe just in case it was the last joke you made in this house."

She regretted the explanation immediately, but that

was because she always regretted everything. And then, after the regret had flared and burned out, she didn't care. He should know, she thought. She wanted him to know. She felt something for somebody, and she'd told him.

"Okay. Who said we're leaving, anyway? We like it here, don't we, Jacko?"

"Yeah. A bit. But I wouldn't want to live here or anything."

"I could live here," said Tucker. "I could live here in a heartbeat."

"Really?" said Annie.

"Sure. I like the sea. I like the . . . the lack of pretension."

"Oh, it's not pretentious."

"What does that word even *mean*?" said Jackson.

"It means, the town doesn't pretend to be something it isn't."

"And some towns do that? What do they pretend to be?"

"Paris. Giraffes. Whatever."

"I'd like to go somewhere that pretends to be somewhere else. That sounds fun."

He was right: it sounded fun. Who wanted to be in a place that prided itself on its lack of ambition, its pig-headed delight in its own plainness?

"Anyway," said Jackson. "I have to see Mom, and my friends, and . . ."

And even then Annie hoped for some clinching argument from Tucker, as if she were watching a courtroom
drama, and Jackson was the slow-witted and obstructive
juror. But he just put his arm on his son's shoulder and
told him not to worry, and Annie gave another inappropriate laugh, just to show that nothing was serious and everything was funny and it didn't matter that Christmas was
nearly over. She was nervous now.

Tucker was worried for Annie when they walked into the
cold and ominously empty museum, but then he remembered that she was the host, and she had to be there first.
And they didn't have to wait very long before people
started turning up; late wasn't a fashion option in Gooleness, apparently. Before long, the room was full of town
councillors and Friends of the Museum and proud owners
of shark pieces, all of whom seemed to have taken the view
that the later you turned up, the narrower the choice of
sandwiches and potato chips.

Once upon a time, Tucker hated going to parties
because he couldn't introduce himself without people
making some kind of a fuss when he told them his name. It
turned out to be the same at this party, except the people
who made the fuss were people who'd apparently never
heard of him.

"Tucker Crowe?" said Terry Jackson, the councillor who owned half the exhibition. "*The* Tucker Crowe?"

Terry Jackson was probably in his sixties, and he had a weird gray hairdo, and Tucker was surprised that his name had any currency in weird-gray-hairdo circles. But then Terry gave Annie a big wink, and Annie rolled her eyes and looked embarrassed, and Tucker understood that something else was going on.

"Annie wanted you to be the special guest tonight. But then I pointed out that nobody knew who the bloody hell you were. What was your big hit, then? Just kidding." He patted Tucker on the back mirthfully. "But you really are from America?"

"I really am."

"Well, then," said Terry, consolingly. "We don't get many American visitors to Gooleness. You might be the first one ever. That's special enough for us. It doesn't matter about the rest of it."

"He really is famous," said Annie. "I mean, if you know who he is."

"Well, we're all famous in our own living rooms, aren't we? What are you drinking there, Tucker? I'm going to get myself another one."

"Just a water, thanks."

"I don't think so," said Terry. "I'm not getting Gooleness's only American visitor a glass of bloody water. Red or white?"

"I'm actually . . . I'm in recovery," said Tucker.

"All the more reason to have a drink, then. Always helps me, when I'm under the weather."

"He's not under the weather," said Annie. "He's a recovering alcoholic."

"Oh, you'd just be normal here. When in Rome and all that."

"I'm fine, thanks."

"Oh, well. Suit yourself. Here they are, the real stars of the evening."

They had been joined by two men in their forties, obviously uncomfortable in jackets and ties.

"Let me introduce you to two Gooleness legends. Gav, Barnesy, this is Tucker Crowe, from America. And this is Jackson."

"Hello," said Jackson, and they shook his hand with exaggerated formality.

"I've heard that name before," one of the men said.

"There's a singer named Jackson Browne," said Jackson. "Also there's a place called Jackson. I've never been there. Which is kind of weird, if you think about it."

"No, not your name, sonny Jim. His. Tucker Wotsit."

"I doubt it," said Tucker.

"No, you're right, Barnesy," said the other one. "It's come up recently."

"Did you get here okay?" said Annie.

"*You* were going on about him," said the man who had to be Gav, triumphantly. "That night we met you. In the pub."

"Was I?" said Annie.

"Oh, she's always going on about him," said Terry Jackson. "In her head, he's famous."

"You're country and western, is that right?"

"I never said that," said Annie. "I said I'd been listening to you recently. Because of *Naked*, I suppose."

"No, you said he was your favorite singer," said Barnesy. "But . . . is he the person you said you were seeing? In America?"

"No," said Annie. "That was someone else."

"Bloody hell," said Barnesy. "You know more Americans than an American."

"I'm sorry," said Annie, when they'd gone. "We seem to keep bumping into people who think we're together."

"You just told him you were seeing some other American."

"Well, I'm not."

"I guessed."

Tucker had known for some time that Annie had some sort of crush on him, and he was too old to feel anything other than a childish sense of delight. She was an attractive woman, good company, kind, younger than him. Ten or fifteen years or so ago, he would have felt obliged to enumerate all the individual items on his baggage carousel and point out that their relationship was doomed, that he always made a mess of everything, that they lived on separate continents and so on; but he was almost certain that she'd been paying enough attention to what he'd been saying, so caveat emptor. But then what? He didn't even know if he was capable of having sex, or whether having sex would kill him if the capability was there. And if sex was going to kill him, then would he be happy to die here, in this town, in Annie's bed? Jackson wouldn't be happy, that was for sure. But was Tucker prepared not to have sex until Jackson was capable of looking after himself? He was six now . . . Twelve years? In twelve years, Tucker would be almost seventy, and that would raise a whole lot of other questions. For example: who'd want to have sex with him when he was seventy? If he was even capable of having sex?

The worst thing about his little medical event was the questions, which had started to come in an apparently unstoppable flood. Not all of them were about whether anyone would want to have sex with him when he was almost seventy; there had been a few really tricky ones related to the empty decades since *Juliet*, and the decades—he liked to think of a plural—to come. There weren't going to be any answers to these tricky questions, either, which made them seem tauntingly rhetorical.

If he were a character in a movie, a few days in a strange town with a kind woman would renew his faith in something or other, and he'd go straight home and make a great album, but that wasn't going to happen: the tank was as empty as it had always been. And then, just as Tucker was about to give in to his gloom, Terry Jackson pressed a button on a boom box, and the room filled with the sound of a soul singer Tucker recognized—Major Lance? Dobie Gray?—and Gav and Barnesy started doing backflips and headspins on the museum carpet.

"I'll bet you could do that, Dad, couldn't you?" said Jackson.

"Sure," said Tucker.

Annie was stuck with the most faithful Friend the museum had ever had, but out of the corner of her eye she saw an elderly lady having her picture taken beside the photograph of the four workmates on their day off. Annie made her excuses and went over to introduce herself.

"Hello, Annie the Museum Director," said the elderly lady. "I'm Kathleen. Kath."

"Do you know any of those people?"

"That's me," said Kath. "I knew my teeth were bad, but I didn't know they were that bad. No wonder I lost them."

Annie looked at the photo, then back at the old woman. As far as Annie could tell, she was seventy-five now, and she'd been sixty in 1964.

"You've hardly aged a bit," Annie said. "Really."

"I know what you're saying. I was old then and I'm old now."

"Not a bit of it," said Annie. "Do you keep in touch with the others?"

"That's my sister. She's passed on. The lads . . . They'd come up for the day. From Nottingham, I think. I never saw them again."

"You look like you were having fun."

"I suppose so. I wish we'd had a bit more though. If you know what I mean."

Annie made an appropriately scandalized face.

"He wanted to. His hands were everywhere. I fought him off."

"Well," said Annie, "you can never go wrong not doing something. It's only when you do things that you get into trouble."

"I suppose so," said Kath. "But now what?"

"What do you mean?"

"I mean, I'm seventy-seven and I never got into any trouble. So now what? Have you got a medal for me?

You're a museum director. Write to the queen and tell her. Otherwise it was all a bloody waste of time, wasn't it?"

"No," said Annie. "Don't say that."

"What should I say instead, then?"

Annie smiled blankly.

"Would you excuse me for a moment?" she said.

She went to find Ros, who seemed to be giving an impromptu lecture on the typography of Terry Jackson's Rolling Stones poster, and told her to take Jackson away from his father and stuff him full of Twiglets. Then Annie pulled Tucker into the corner where they had displayed Terry Jackson's old bus tickets, which weren't attracting as much traffic as they'd hoped.

"You okay?" said Tucker. "Seems to be going pretty well."

"Tucker, I was wondering whether, whether . . . If you'd be interested."

"In . . ."

"Oh. Sorry. Me."

"I'm already interested in you. The conditional is unnecessary."

"Thank you. But I suppose I mean sexually."

The blush, which she had more or less kept in check over the last few days, was returning with a pent-up force; the blood had clearly been pooling, frustrated, somewhere in the region of her ears. She really needed her face to do something different when she asked a man to sleep with her. It seemed to her that the very act of asking made the request irritatingly unlikely.

"What about the party?"

"I meant later."

"I was kidding."

"Oh. I see. Anyway, I told myself I'd . . . I'd broach the subject. I've done it now. Thank you for listening." And she turned to go.

"Pleasure. And, of course, I'm interested, by the way. If the answer to your question isn't beside the point."

"Oh. No. It isn't. Good."

"I would have jumped on you by now if it hadn't been for my little scare the other day. And it still worries me."

"I did actually look that . . . side of things up on the Internet."

Tucker laughed.

"This is what constitutes foreplay, when you get older—a woman who's prepared to look your medical condition up before she sleeps with you. I like it. It's kind of sexy. What did the Internet have to say?"

Annie could see Ros leading Jackson toward them.

"You don't get breathless going up stairs?"

"Nope."

"Well, you should be okay, then. As long as, as I, well, do the work."

She was, she felt, the color of an eggplant now, a kind of purply black. Maybe he'd like that.

"That's the way I've always done it! We'll be fine!"

"Right. Well. Good, then. I'll see you later."

And she went to give her little welcome speech to the great and the good of Gooleness.

Later, home and drunk, she felt a kind of precoital *tristesse*. Most of her *tristesses* were precoital, she thought gloomily. How could they not be, seeing as most of life was precoital? But this one was sharper than most, possibly because the coitus was a more real prospect than most. It began with an attack of nerves, a sudden lack of self-confidence: she'd seen pictures of Julie Beatty, and Julie Beatty had been breathtakingly beautiful. True, she'd been twenty-five or so when Tucker was with her, but Annie hadn't looked anything like that when she was twenty-five; Natalie was still beautiful, and she was older than Annie. They all must have been, she realized, the ones she knew about and the scores—hundreds?—she didn't. And then she tried to console herself with the knowledge that Tucker must have lowered the bar by now, and, of course, that was no consolation at all. She didn't want to be the dying embers of his sex life, and she certainly didn't want to be a low bar. While Tucker was putting Jackson to bed she made tea and looked for something else to drink; when he came downstairs she was pouring some very old banana liqueur into a tumbler and trying not to cry. She really hadn't thought the museum thing through, when she first took the job. She hadn't worked out that it would make absolutely everything, even a one-night stand, feel as though it were already over, behind glass, a poignant relic of an earlier, happier time.

"Listen," said Tucker, "I've been thinking," and Annie was convinced that he had come to the same conclusion himself, that he was about to tell her that, yes, though his bar was no longer at Olympic height, it hadn't dropped that far just yet, and he'd come back to her in a decade or so. "I should look at this stuff myself."

"Which stuff?"

"The stuff on the Internet that told you whether sex will kill me."

"Oh. Of course. No problem."

"It's just . . . If I did drop dead, you'd probably feel bad."

"Almost certainly."

"You'd feel responsible. And I'd rather it was me who had the post-death guilt."

"Why would you feel guilt?"

"Ah, you're not a parent, are you? Guilt is pretty much all I feel."

Annie found the website she'd been looking at and showed him the section titled "Recovery."

"Can I trust this one?" said Tucker.

"It's the National Health Service. They usually want to keep you out of the hospital. The government can't afford you, and anyway the hospitals kill you."

"Okay. Hey, there's a whole sex section. 'Having sex will not put you at further risk of another heart attack.' We're good to go."

"It also says that most people will feel comfortable about resuming sexual activity about four weeks after a heart attack."

"I'm not most people. I feel comfortable now."

"And then there's that bit."

She pointed at the screen, and Tucker read from it.

"A thirty-percent chance of erectile dysfunction. That's good."

"Why?"

"Because if there's nothing going on, you needn't blame yourself. Even though it would probably be your fault."

"There won't be any erectile dysfunction," said Annie, mock confidently.

She was blushing, of course, but they were looking at a screen in the dark of the office, and Tucker didn't notice, so for a moment she wanted to undercut the moment out loud—clap a hand over her mouth, or make a joke at her own expense—but she resisted the urge, and . . . well, there was an atmosphere, she thought. She wasn't sure she'd ever created an atmosphere before, and she would never have thought it could be achieved by talking to a man with health problems about erectile dysfunction. It was just as well, really. For the best part of forty years she had genuinely believed that not doing things would somehow prevent regret, when, of course, the exact opposite was true. Her youth was over, but there might be some life left in life yet.

They kissed for the first time then, while the NHS website glared at them; they kissed for so long that the computer went to sleep. Annie wasn't blushing anymore, but she was feeling embarrassingly emotional and she was worried that she'd start to cry, and he'd think she had too much invested in him, and he'd change his mind about the sex. If he asked her what the problem was, she'd tell him she always got weepy after exhibition openings.

They went upstairs, took their clothes off with their backs to each other, got into her cold bed and started to touch.

"You were right," said Tucker.

"So far, anyway," said Annie. "But there was that bit about maintenance."

"And I'll tell you," said Tucker, "you're not making maintenance much easier."

"I'm sorry."

"Have you . . . I didn't come prepared. For under-standable reasons. You don't keep anything lying around, do you?"

"Oh," said Annie. "Yes. Of course. But I don't have any condoms. You'll have to excuse me for a moment."

She'd already thought about this moment; she'd been thinking about it since her conversation with Kath. She went to the bathroom, stayed in there for a couple of min-utes and then went back to make love to him. She didn't kill him, even though it felt like parts of her had been asleep for as long as Tucker's career.

The following day, Jackson talked to his mother on the phone and became upset, and Tucker booked their flights home. On the last night, Tucker and Annie shared a bed, but they didn't have sex again.

"I'll come back," said Tucker. "I like it here."

"Nobody comes back."

Annie didn't know whether she meant the town or the bed, but either way there was some bitterness in there, and she didn't want that.

"Or you could come over."

"I've used up a lot of my holidays."

"There are other jobs."

"I'm not taking lectures on alternative careers from you."

"Okay. So. I'm never coming back here, you're never going over there . . . It's difficult to find the place where we can at least pretend that there's some sort of future."

"Is that what you normally do after a one-night stand?" said Annie. "Pretend there's a future?" She couldn't seem to change the tone in her voice, no matter what she did. She didn't want to scoff and taunt; she wanted to find a way to hope, but she only seemed to be able to speak one language. Typical bloody British, she thought.

"I'm just going to ignore you," said Tucker.

She put her arms around him. "I'll miss you. And Jackson."

There. It wasn't much, and it was entirely unrepresentative of the grief and panic that were already probing for promising-looking ways of escape, but she hoped at least he heard uncomplicated affection.

"You'll e-mail, right? A lot?"

"Oh, I've got nothing to say."

"I'll tell you when I'm bored."

"Oh, God," she said. "Now I'll be scared to write anything."

"Jesus Christ," said Tucker. "You don't make it easy."

"No," said Annie. "That's because it isn't. That's why mostly it goes wrong. That's why you've been divorced a thousand times. Because it isn't easy."

She was trying to say something else; she was trying to say that the inability to articulate what one feels in any satisfactory way is one of our enduring tragedies. It wouldn't have been much, and it wouldn't have been useful, but it would have been something that reflected the gravity and the sadness inside her. Instead, she had snapped at him for being a loser. It was as if she were trying to find a handhold on the boulder of her feelings, and had merely ended up with grit under her nails.

Tucker sat up in bed and looked at her.

"You should make up with Duncan," he said. "He'd take you back. Especially now. You've got about nine years' worth of material for him."

"Why? What good would that do me?"

"None at all," said Tucker. "That would be the point."

She tried one last time.

"I'm sorry. I don't know what to say. I know that . . . that love is supposed to be transformative." Now that she'd used the word she felt her tongue loosen. "And that's how I'm trying to look at it. There. Bang. I've been transformed, and however it happened it doesn't matter. You can go or stay, and it will still have happened. So I've been trying to look at you as a metaphor or something. But it doesn't work. The terribly inconvenient fact is that, without you around, everything slides back to how it was before. It can't do otherwise. And I have to say, books haven't helped much with all this. Because whenever you read anything about love, whenever anyone tries to define it, there's always a state or an abstract noun, and I try to think of it like that. But actually, love is . . . Well, it's just you. And when you go, it's gone. Nothing abstract about it."

"Dad."

Annie was confused, but Tucker seemed to know who it was immediately. Jackson was standing by the bed, damp and malodorous.

"What's up, son?"

"I just threw up in my bed."

"Okay."

"I don't think I like Twiglets anymore."

"You've maybe been hitting them a little hard. We'll get you cleaned up. Do you have any spare sheets, Annie?"

As they washed him and changed the bedding, Annie was trying not to feel unlucky, doomed, born under a bad sign. Feeling unlucky, she had noticed, was her default mood, and yet she could see that there were alternative interpretations of her current predicament. For example: if you choose to fall in love with an American—an American with a young son and a home in America—who comes to stay for a couple of days, how much ill fortune is involved in his leaving you? Or could someone brighter have seen that coming? Or here's another way of looking at it: you write a review on an obscure website of an album by an artist who has chosen to remain a recluse for over twenty years. Said artist reads the review, gets in touch, comes to stay. He's very attractive and seems to be attracted to you, and you sleep with him. Is there any bad luck in that? Or could someone with a sunnier disposition come to the conclusion that the last few weeks contained something like seventeen separate miracles? Yes, well. She didn't have a sunny disposition, so tough. She was going to stick with the notion that she was the unluckiest woman alive.

How did that fit in with the previous night, when she had pretended to put in a contraceptive device in an attempt to secretly get pregnant? How lucky would she have to be, at her age, at his age, in his state of health? But maybe there was no contradiction. She could already feel the disappointment that would arrive along with her period, and maybe that was the point: final, incontrovertible proof that there was no point in trying anything that might make her happier, because she'd fail regardless.

"Can I get into your bed?" said Jackson.

"Sure," said Tucker.

"Can it be just you?"

"Sure."

Tucker looked at Annie and shrugged.

"Thanks," he said. Over the next few weeks, that one word was subjected to more analysis than it could probably stand.

. . .

"What should I tell Mom about the trip?" said Jackson, when they were waiting for the plane to take off.

"Tell her anything you want."

"She knows you got sick, right?"

"I think so."

"And she knows you didn't die?"

"Yep."

"Cool. And how do you spell Gooleness?"

Tucker told him.

"It's funny," said Jackson. "It seems like I haven't seen Mom for ever. But when I think about what we did . . . It wasn't that exciting, was it?"

"I'm sorry."

"That's okay."

"Maybe if I watched a lot of *SpongeBob* on the way home it would seem more exciting."

Tucker didn't know whether he'd been listening to an elaborate ruse intended to obtain parental indulgence or a simply expressed but complicated idea about the relationship between time and narrative. Jackson had put his finger on something, though. Not enough had happened, somehow. In the space of a few days, he'd had a heart attack, spoken to all of his children and two of his ex-wives, gone to a new town and slept with a new woman, spent some time with a man who had made him think differently about his work, and none of it had changed a thing. He had neither learned nor grown.

He must have missed something. In the old days, he maybe could have squeezed a few songs out of this trip: there had to be a good lyric about a far-death experience, say. And Annie . . . he could have turned her into a pretty and redemptive girl from the north country who had helped him to feel, and heal. Maybe steal, and kneel, if he pushed it. She'd certainly cooked him a meal. And maybe without her he'd congeal. But if he couldn't write, what was he left with?

The truth about autobiographical songs, he realized, was that you had to make the present become the past, somehow: you had to take a feeling or a friend or a woman and turn whatever it was into something that was over, so that you could be definitive about it. You had to put it in a glass case and look at it and think about it until it gave up its meaning, and he'd managed to do that with just about everybody he'd ever met or married or fathered. The truth about life was that nothing ever ended until you died, and even then you just left a whole bunch of unresolved narratives behind you. He'd somehow managed to retain the mental habits of a songwriter long after he'd stopped writing songs, and perhaps it was time to give them up.

· · ·

"Well," said Malcolm, and then there was nothing, and it was all Annie could do not to laugh. She had spoken quickly and unhaltingly and without swearing (she had remembered to refer to Fake Tucker, rather than its contraction) for fifteen minutes, and however much silence he was going to inflict on them now, she wasn't going to break it. It was his turn.

"And can you still buy his CDs?"

"I just explained, Malcolm. This last one has only been out for a few weeks. That's how we met, sort of."

"Oh. Yes. Sorry. Should I buy it?"

"No. I just explained that, too, Malcolm. It's not his best one. Anyway, I'm not sure that you listening to Tucker's music would help us much."

"We'll see. You'd be surprised."

"This sort of situation has come up before, has it?"

Malcolm looked hurt, and Annie felt sorry for him. She didn't need to be unkind. She was feeling rather fond of him, actually; her fifteen-minute splurge had justified her entire painful relationship with him. For months she'd been coming in here and telling him about Duncan's failure to buy milk when he'd been explicitly asked to do so, and they'd poked about in the ashes of her inner life in an effort to find some tiny spark of feeling. This morning she'd told him about recluses and heart attacks and failed marriages and one-night stands and duplicitous attempts to get pregnant, and she thought he might explode with the effort of trying to act as if he'd been expecting a story like this all along.

"Can I ask a couple of other questions? Just to make sure I've got things straight?"

"Of course."

"What did this man think you were doing in the bathroom?"

"Inserting a contraceptive device."

Malcolm made a note of some kind—from Annie's position, it looked like *inserting cont. device*—and underlined it emphatically.

"I see. And . . . When did his last relationship end?"

"A few weeks ago."

"And this woman is the mother of his youngest child?"

"Yes."

"What's her name, actually?"

"Do you really need to know that?"

"Saying her name makes you feel uncomfortable, perhaps?"

"Not really. Cat."

"Is that short for something?"

"Malcolm!"

"I'm sorry. You're right. There was quite a lot in there.

I'm struggling to know where to start. Where do you want to start? How are you feeling?"

"Bereft mostly. A bit exhilarated. How are you feeling?" She knew she wasn't supposed to ask that, but she was aware that Malcolm had been through a lot in the previous twenty minutes.

"Concerned."

"Really?"

"It's not my position to judge. As you know. Actually, scrap that last remark. Strike it from the record. And the concerned bit."

"Why?"

"Because I want to ask you a question and I don't want you to think it's judgmental."

"I have wiped my memory clean."

"I'm just concerned about the part you might have played in ending this man's relationship. And also you bringing a child into the world with no father."

"I thought we'd scrapped 'concerned.' "

"Oh. Yes. Anyway. How do you feel about that?"

"Malcolm, this is hopeless."

"What have I said now?"

"I'm really not worried about the morality of it all."

"I can see that."

"So can't we talk about what I am worried about?"

"If we must. What are you worried about?"

"I want to throw everything in and move to America. Tomorrow. Sell the house and go."

"Has he asked you?"

"No."

"Well, then. I think we're better off talking about how to make the best of a bad job here."

" 'The best of a bad job'?"

"I know you think I'm a square, or whatever you call it. But I don't see how we can call it a, a *good* job. You're unhappy, and you might be an unwed mother, and . . . Anyway. Now you're thinking about Cloud Cuckoo Land."

"Which is where, exactly?"

"America. I mean, it's not Cloud Cuckoo Land for Americans. But it is for you."

"Why?"

"Because you live here."

"And that's it. So there isn't really any possibility of change, then, is there?"

" 'Course there is. That's why you're here."

"But not much."

"Not with the way house prices have gone recently, anyway. I don't know what you paid for yours, but you won't get it back in the current climate. Even rentals aren't very good. I've got a friend who's been trying to rent her house for next summer. Never had any trouble before, until now."

Annie had always heard the town speaking through Malcolm, ever since her first session, but now she heard the voice of the country she had grown up in: she heard teachers and parents and teaching colleagues and friends. This was how England spoke, and she couldn't listen to her anymore.

She stood up, walked over to Malcolm, kissed him on the top of his head.

"Thank you," she said. "I'm all better now." And she left.

Topic: *So Where Was I?*

Duncan

Member

Posts: 1019   Gentlemen, so. I have it. I've had it
for a couple of days, in fact, but after the debacle
of *Naked* (mea culpa, mea culpa, mea maxima
culpa), I have allowed it to stew for a couple of
days before committing myself. But there's no
putting it off. To quote another critic, writing in
another time and another place, but about a similar artistic disaster: *"What is this shit?"* We have
a song about the pleasures of reading in the afternoon sunshine. We have a song about homegrown
green beans. We have a cover of the Don Williams
"classic" "You're My Best Friend." We have a
major tragedy.

Re: *So Where Was I?*

BetterthanBob
Member

Posts: 789   Thank God. I thought I was going crazy. I got home from work, downloaded the album, transferred it onto my iPod and shut myself away for the night in my study—told the Boss that she couldn't come in before ten p.m. I was out by 8:45! Couldn't take it anymore! Ran screaming to the pub! I spent most of the night trying to think of a more disappointing "comeback": drew a blank. There's nothing I would willingly play for a second time. Oh, Tucker, Where Art Thou?

Re: *So Where Was I?*

Julietlover
Member

Posts: 881   This album should be called *Happiness Is Poison*. Who gives a toss if Tucker Crowe has found inner peace? Talk about "be careful what you wish for." I have thought about a new Tucker Crowe album just about every day for twenty years, and now I wish he'd stayed a recluse. I heard it got turned down by every major label in America. Do you think he cares that he's let himself and everyone else down? It doesn't sound like it. Won't get fooled again. RIP Tucker Crowe.

Re: *So Where Was I?*

MrMozza7
Newbie

Posts: 2   Hahahahahahahahaha. I told you he was overrated. Now go and listen to everything MORRISSEY has ever sung, you muppets.

Re: *So Where Was I?*

Uptown Girl
Junior Member

Posts: 1   Hi, everyone! First-time caller, or whatever you are on the Internet! My husband and I recently came across the album *So Where Was I?* by Tucker Crow and we both absolutely love it!

We found another one called *Juliet* but it's a bit gloomy for our liking! Can you recommend any others of his we might enjoy?

Re: *So Where Was I?*

BetterthanBob
Member

Posts: 790   **Dear God.**

ACKNOWLEDGMENTS

Thanks to: Tony Lacey, Geoff Kloske, Joanna Prior, Tom Weldon, Helen Fraser, Caroline Dawnay, Greil Marcus, DV DeVincentis and Eli Horowitz. Special thanks to Helen Bones and Sarah Geismar, without whom this book really wouldn't have been written.